DESERT OF DEATH

It looked like the lunar surface—huge boulders scattered across rocky terrain. Now that they were so close to the enemy, it was vital that Camellion and his four accomplices not make the slightest sound—almost an impossibility on this loose ground rock. Each time a man put his foot down, he had to be absolutely certain rock would not snap under his weight.

Their H&K and TAC-1 carbines ready to fire, the Death Merchant and West entered a natural passageway between two immense boulders. The last scream had come from not too far ahead.

Camellion moved up the passage, came to the edge of the boulder and looked around the edge. To the left was an open area. Three bodies lay spread grotesquely on the rocks, two of the corpses on their backs, the third face down, all three as broken and as bloody as mannequins slugged with sledgehammers and splattered with red paint.

There was a fourth man. His right side was a mass of blood and he was crawling, his left leg dragging. Cammelion tensed. Ahead several men stepped out from the side of a boulder. They wore dark glasses, walking shorts, were naked to the waist and deeply suntanned. Each carried a Vz61 Skorpion machine pistol.

"We have company," Camellion whispered. "Hold it. Three more have stepped out."

Camellion and West opened fire . . .

THE DEATH MERCHANT SERIES:

#43 in the incredible adventures of the

DEATH MERCHANT

THE DEVIL'S TRASHCAN

by Joseph Rosenberger

PINNACLE BOOKS   LOS ANGELES

This is a work of fiction. All the characters and events portrayed in this book are fictional, and any resemblance to real people or incidents is purely coincidental.

DEATH MERCHANT #43:
THE DEVIL'S TRASHCAN

Copyright © 1981 by Joseph Rosenberger

An original Pinnacle Books edition, published for the first time anywhere.

First printing, February 1981

ISBN: 0-523-41021-2

Cover illustration by Dean Cate

Printed in the United States of America

PINNACLE BOOKS, INC.
2029 Century Park East
Los Angeles, California 90067

This book is dedicated
to
Mark Roberts
and
William Fieldhouse

and a
special dedication
to
James D. Flikkema,
chemical engineer and
master diver—

and sincere thanks
for his technical advice
(any mistakes are mine,
not his).

Joseph R. Rosenberger
Patchoque, Long Island,
New York.

Those who kill for pleasure are sadists.
Those who kill for money are professionals.
Those who kill for both are mercenaries
Those who kill because they want to keep
America free are patriots.

There is an overbundance of sadists; the
streets are full of such low trash.
There are a couple of hundred expert professionals,
and a handful of true mercenaries.

To the everlasting shame of this nation,
genuine patriots are becoming as rare as
penguins on roller skates. . . .

Richard J. Camellion
Votaw, Texas.

Chapter One

It's like a chess game, mused Richard Camellion, watching the alarm board in the darkened room. A tiny light cast a faint blue sheen over the foot-square panel. *A chess game that requires concentration and, above all, patience.*

Convinced that agents of ODESSA[1] would make an attempt to stop the motorized expedition, the Death Merchant had planned meticulously for any eventuality. The distance from Köln (Cologne), West Germany to Bad Aussee, Austria, was slightly more than a thousand kilometers. It was almost a certainty that ODESSA would make it's move before the expedition reached Lake Toplitz in the *Totes Gebirge,* the gloomy "dead mountains." There were too many stab-in-the-back opportunities between Cologne and Bad Aussee. Here at the *Gasthof,* or inn, in Ottobrunn, the conditions for an ambush were excellent. Like the town, the *Gasthof* was ancient and retained its medieval Gothic grimness. Only four stories high, the small inn was not on the regular tourist route, and was on the edge of the town. ODESSA gunmen could do their best, then lose themselves in München (Munich), which was only fourteen kilometers to the northwest.

The parking lot east of the *Gasthof* was an assassin's dream. The south side entrance was open, the stone wall on each side of the opening so low that a man could easily jump over it. Back on the narrow alley, thirty meters east of the inn, was a long brick building that was used as a garage. Modern cyclone fencing fronted the alley between the east side of the inn and the west end of the garage, as

---

[1]From the initials of *Organization der ehemaligen SS Angehörigen,* or, in English, 'Association of ex-SS Members'. This organization still exists. It is very powerful, very wealthy, very deadly, and world-wide. German Nazism is far from dead.

well as between the east end of the garage and the west side of the bakery next door on Dachauer Strasse; but wire snips could easily make an opening in the fence.

In anticipation of a silent attack by ODESSA, the Death Merchant and the men with him had outfitted the ten vehicles of the caravan with Model TX-27TWS warning transmitters activated by motion of any kind, by movement within three feet of the devices. Measuring 115-mm X 60-mm X 24-mm, each M-TX had a carrier frequency range from 26.970 to 27.270 MHz and operated on a 12-volt battery. The six cars had two transmitters each: one toward the rear of the driver's seat and one underneath, fastened to the top center of the muffler. The two motor homes had four M-TXs each: two inside, two underneath the vehicles. The tractor and trailer, containing the diving equipment, was equipped with eight of the little dandies, four above and four below. The van had two on the inside and two on the outside. In addition, the doors of the van could only be opened by proper sequence of the combination locks built into the sliding steel panels. Any attempt to force the doors would set off a very high 114-db sound-level siren, and the interior of the van would be flooded with tear gas.

"I think we're waiting for only shadows," commented Vallie West. "In another hour it will be dawn."

"Let's wait another twenty minutes," Camellion said. "Then we'll have Kaush and Helldorf and Dueselbeck take over and stand watch."

The tip of Franz Ritter's cigarette flared briefly as the head *Bundesnachrichtendienst* agent in the room took a drag. In the opinion of the Death Merchant, of the four BND West German intelligence agents, the cold-eyed Ritter was the most efficient.

"We're trying to swim in a pool without water," Ritter said in slightly accented English. "ODESSA isn't going to be obvious about what it might try to do to stop us. Don't kid yourself, Herr Camellion. O-agents will expect us to be using electronic surveillance of some kind. But I agree with you. They won't expect any of the devices to be outside the vehicles."

"If they're really smart, they won't show up at all," West said earnestly. "I'm inclined to think ODESSA will do the unexpected—wait to try something after we've set up shop at Lake Toplitz."

2

Ritter didn't reply; neither did the Death Merchant who, privately, felt that ODESSA would never hedge its bets. The sinister organization of ex-SS officers and men would hit the expedition not only while it was on route, but after it had set up camp at Lake Toplitz, the "Devil's Trashcan."

Bored with the whole business, Camellion stared at the signal board which contained eleven rows of tiny bulbs, each the size of a bulb in a penlight, twelve bulbs to a row. However, only 32 of the circuits were activated, one for each M-TX transmitter in use on the vehicles.

Although expecting many of the bulbs to light up, Camellion felt a tingle of excitement when one of the bulbs began to flash red—on/off—on/off—the fragile red glow briefly tingeing the faces of the three men with crimson.

"By God!" growled West. "They've walked into it."

"Wir sind angekommen!" hissed Ritter. So excited that he had spoken in German, he leaned sideways in his chair and looked at the board. From the marking above the light, he saw that the transmitter that had turned on the light was one underneath one of the motor homes.

"Nein, mein Freund," Camellion said. "It isn't we who have arrived. It's the O-agents who have."

Another light came on and began to flash—one of the transmitters under the van. Then another light, then still another, then another. Within ten seconds, the board resembled a Christmas tree of flashing red lights.

"Damn it, there's a mob of those kraut bastards out there!" West said angrily. Remembering that Ritter was German, he cleared his throat and added apologetically. "Sorry, Ritter. No insult intended."

"None taken," Ritter said drily. "Only we Germans call agents of ODESSA *'schwarze Deutscher,'* or 'black Germans'. Another term we use is *'Schweine schaum'*—swine scum. Such trash who keep Hitler's memory alive are not only a disgrace to honest Germans, but to the human race."

"Then suppose we get rid of some of the *Schweine schaum,* at least the ones outside." The Death Merchant got to his feet and walked toward a table on the other side of the hotel room. West and Ritter got up from their chairs and, in the semi-darkness, followed him, West saying, "Just the three of us? What about waking the others?"

"Shucks, Val, there can't be more than fifteen of them,"

drawled Camellion. "That's only five apiece. And listen, try to take several of them alive, if possible."

Opening one of the Jensen two-pallet aluminum cases, he took out two Browning BDA-380 D/A auto pistols, both of which were equipped with noise suppressors, or "silencers."

Franz Ritter, taking two silenced P-38 Walther auto-pistols from a Jensen case, smiled cryptically. A pragmatist, he had never been intimidated by danger and was not especially in love with life. Neither was West, who was Ritter's senior by ten years. One of Camellion's closest friends, West had a personal insight into Richard Camellion that no other man possessed, not even Courtland Grojean, the paranoid chief of the CIA's covert and dirty-tricks section. Grojean was positive that Camellion had a death wish and was impelled by a desire for self-annihilation. West knew otherwise. Like Camellion, he knew that while death and existence may exclude each other in rational philosophy, they are not psychologically contrary, for death can be experienced as a state of being, as an existential condition. Richard Camellion's constant flirtation with the Cosmic Lord of Death was not based on any urge for total nothingness, but was a demand for absolute reality, a demand for a fuller life through the death experience.

The Death Merchant walked to the door. "Both of you know what to do," he said.

Weapons in hand, they raced down the hall of the third floor to the steps. Down the steps they rushed to the second floor, then on to the first floor. The lobby—hardly more than a large foyer—was empty. No one was behind the high counter. At this hour of the morning Herr Huelsmann, the owner of the *Gasthof*, and the employees of the inn were tight in the arms of Morpheus.

Without a word, the three men split up, the Death Merchant slipping quietly out of the large front door, Ritter and West going across the lobby to a hall that extended to the northwest corner of the building where a door opened to the outside.

The early morning air was comfortable, a cool 75 degrees, the moonless sky dirty with a few scattered clouds and dotted with a billion blue-white stars. The stone sidewalk and cobbled street of Dachauer Strasse were empty.

Next to the southwest corner of the inn was a flower

stall, now closed, shutters drawn across the front opening. As expertly as a 12th century Ninja—knees bent and moving in a slight crouch—the Death Merchant crept toward the northwest corner of the flower stall, looked out toward the garage and waited. There were three cars—two Opels and a Honda—facing the west end of the garage. The three vehicles did not belong to the expedition. He studied the tractor and trailer, that did belong to the expedition, parked in front of the garage, letting his line of vision drift to one side of the huge vehicle. Night visual awareness demands that one should not look directly at an object in order to see it in the dark. One should look alongside of the object. The best method is to glance from side to side. Staring at one side of the object, in the dark, will cause it to disappear. As far as he could detect in the darkness, all was normal. The six cars were in the garage. Ahead of the cab and trailer were the two motor homes and the van, all three vehicles parked in a row, their fronts facing the bakery.

Presently, Vallie West came around the southwest corner of the building. As a precautionary tactic, West had come up the west side of the inn, in the narrow passageway between the *Gasthof* and the *Bierhaus* next door, to the west.

"All we have to do is move in," West said in a husky whisper. He glanced at the streetlight, thirty feet away on the high curb. "It won't be easy with that light. Have you seen any of them by the trailer or the motor homes?"

"Negative," Camellion said. "The street light only hits the side of the first vehicle and the backs of all three. You're sure that Ritter is at the door by the northeast corner?"

"Yeah. He took the rear hall and said he'd wait for a few minutes by the door. Then he said he would sneak up to the three cars parked at the end of the garage. They're not ours, so there shouldn't be any O-agents around them."

"Good enough. You handle things here at the corner of the flower stand. I'm going to sneak along the front wall and try to get across the entrance. They have got to be by the homes on wheels and by the van. If I can get directly across from them, it will increase our chances for success."

"Watch yourself, Richard."

"You, too."

The Death Merchant left the corner of the flower stall,

5

moved to the sidewalk, got down on his haunches and, hunched over as far as possible, began to duckwalk along the outside of the stone wall which was only 0.9 meters (3 ft.) high. He came to the entrance, stopped, and measured the opening in the wall—*At least six meters or twenty feet; and I sure can't make myself invisible.*

A decision had to be made. If he duckwalked and was spotted, he'd lose four or five seconds getting to his feet and making a run for it. Better to run now and hope for the best. He took a deep breath, got to his feet and sprinted across the open space. He was getting down by the end of the opposite wall when a loud shot shattered the early morning stillness and a bullet thudded into one of the stones toward the top of the wall. ODESSA gunmen had spotted him.

Damn it! I've burned the fudge! Not the least bit angered nor rattled, the Death Merchant crawled another ten feet along the outside of the wall, stopping when he heard two loud cracks from the northwest corner of the flower stand. Camellion knew at once what had happened. West was armed with two Safari Arms .45 Enforcer auto-pistols,[2] each equipped with a noise suppressor; yet he was using his Colt Diamondback revolver in order to sight in better. And why bother to be quiet since the enemy had fired the first shot, the echo of which was still dying in the distance.

Almost immediately, hand guns began firing from the van and the two motor homes, but none of the slugs struck the wall. The O-agents were firing at West. Moving once more along the stone wall, the Death Merchant heard Val's Diamondback roar two more times, the last shot followed by a high pitched scream of agony. West had scored a hit on one of the dirt-bags, and Camellion knew that whoever had received the projectile was either dead or poised on the brink of eternity. Val was using .38 Special Norma Magnum cartridges, 110 grain jacketed hollow points whose performance approached that of a true magnum, a .357 magnum slug; yet the .38 Special Norma Magnum ammo did not develop high gas pressures and could be

[2]Safari Arms of Phoenix, Arizona. It's the only company in the U.S.A. that utilizes steel slides on an aluminum frame. The SA pistols are designed primarily as combat and survival weapons.

6

used in handguns that handled regular .38 special loads, small frame revolvers included.

Reaching the outside end of the wall, where the end was flush against the side of the bakery, Camellion heard another yell, this one far to the north, in the direction of the tractor and trailer parked in front of the garage.

Either Val got one or else Ritter has opened fire!

By now, Camellion knew that he was in a position to take out the gunmen who were firing from the front of the van and the two motor homes. His eyes had adjusted to the darkness, and his one hope was that he could do the job without putting holes in any of the vehicles. For a moment he listened to pistols firing only thirty feet in front of him, and judged that the men who had pulled the triggers were in front of one of the motor homes.

But why do it the risky way? He placed one of the Browning BDAs on the sidewalk, searched for and found several small stones, each about twice the size of a marble. Mentally measuring the distance, he tossed one of the rocks over the short wall and heard it hit the roof of one of the vehicles.

Another shot from the west, from Val.

Four more shots from the O-agents who were using the van and the two motor homes as shields.

Then, three loud reports from the north . . .

The Death Merchant tossed the second rock and heard it hit the side of a vehicle. Quickly then, he picked up the BDA, reared up and, catching sight of shadowy figures ahead of him, began firing both auto-loaders, 99 percent of his aim being pure instinct. *Bazzitt bazzitt bazzitt!* Projectiles hissed through the silencers attached to the twin Brownings. One .380 ACP bullet caught Rudolf Hartlaub in the rib and knocked him against Leopold Jagow who had been trying to aim in at Vallie West. The trouble was that the flashes of fire from the muzzle of Val's Diamondback were never in the same place twice. Another .380 bullet poked Wolfgang Kapp in the left shoulder, broke the bone and spun him around. Kapp's misery ended a moment later. A .380 bullet bored into the back of his head and killed him. A fourth bullet broke the lower teeth of the terrified Jagow, who was turning around to get off a shot at Camellion. The slug cut his tongue in half down the middle, tore through his throat and went bye-bye through the back of his neck. Blood pouring out of his mouth, the

7

dying Jagow pitched against the front of the van, the blood crawling down the painted bright blue metal.

Three other O-gunmen were in front of the vehicles—Hans Stuckenschmidt to the left of one motor home, Otto Kiaulehn and Egon Wellesz in front, and on either side of, the second motor home. Stuckenschmidt, momentarily forgetting about West and his deadly Diamondback, tried to escape Camellion's fire by running to the tractor and trailer and joining up with the rest of the ODESSA gunsels.

Only Vallie was no longer using the Colt Diamondback; instead he was using the two SA Enforcers. Stuckenschmidt never heard the two shots, and only for a brief moment did he feel the two .45 Silvertip hollowpoint slugs that tore through his left side, ripped apart his lungs and turned him into a corpse.

Egon Wellesz groaned loudly and went down with two of Camellion's slugs in his chest. Otto Kiaulehn did manage to get off a shot at Camellion with his Mauser HSc automatic. The .32 bullet narrowly missed the Death Merchant who had fired both BDAs as he vaulted the low stone wall. Kiaulehn, who considered himself one of the best triggermen in West Berlin, didn't even have time to know deep fear. A .380 slug struck him in the right side of his wedge-shaped face. A second bullet hit him in the left side of the neck. Bleeding with all the force of a broken water fountain, the West German thug twisted around, dropped the Mauser and wilted to the ground.

The Death Merchant cleared the wall, raced to the front of the big van, fired three quick shots, counted to three, then triggered off three more shots—a prearranged signal to let West and Ritter know that it was he who was behind the van. He shoved the SA Matchmaster auto pistol back into its shoulder holster, listened and waited. Not even five minutes had passed since Wolfgang Kapp had fired the first shot at Camellion.

The shots had served as the loudest alarm clock ever to go off around Herr Emil Eichhorn's *Gasthof*, and lights were being turned on in various rooms. On the east side of the inn, two rooms remained cloaked in darkness. Alfred Dusselbeck and Gunther Helldorf, two other West German intelligence agents had opened the window and were waiting. In the other darkened room, Gerhart Kausch waited to one side of an open window. The BND agent—he was second-in-command, next to Ritter—peered through a night-sight scope attached to a Heckler und Koch G3 SG1 sniper rifle.

Camellion, as quiet as a cat about to pounce, heard a loud cry of pain and surprise ahead of him, far to his right. Yeah, behind the trailer, not far from the outside corner of the garage. The Death Merchant was right. Felix Boess had caught one of Franz Heinz Ritter's 9-mm Parabellum slugs. With the full metal jacketed bullet in his stomach, his brain stunned with shock and disbelief, Boess went down, unconsciousness sliding over him.

The cool-as-a-clam Ritter, crouched behind the right rear of an Opel sedan, sent another silent slug at the second man who had tried to charge the Opel. But Herman Gunche was too fast, his speed increased by the panic of seeing Boess gunned down before his eyes. The heavyset Gunche jumped to the southwest corner of the garage and Ritter's projectile missed him, speeding on its way a foot to his left.

Gasping for breath, Gunche didn't know what to do. He could join the other seven in the garage, but what would that solve? Or he could try to get to the other end of the garage and slip through the hole that Schnabel and Hueberdieck had cut in the fence. He thought of all the shooting he had heard by the van and the two motor homes. Who in hell had shot whom?

He started running toward the east end of the garage at the same time the Death Merchant stormed from around the front of the second motor home and the remaining seven ODESSA gunmen threw open one of the garage doors, charged out, and started running toward the fence.

All hell broke loose in the next few seconds.

The Death Merchant, who had reached the front of the tractor connected to the long trailer, didn't have much of a choice, not while facing eight men with guns in their hands. The hell with trying to take any of them alive. He cut loose with both Brownings the same moment that Gerhart Kausch, in a third floor window of the inn, opened fire with his HK sniper rifle. The round-nose solid steel 7.62-mm bullet speared Manfred Schnabel between the shoulder blades and forced him to do a fast two-step forward before he threw up his arms, then pitched face down to the ground. Wieland Herzfelde—one of Camellion's .380 slugs in his torso—yelled and staggered heavily

9

against Ernst Neudock, who cried out pitifully and dropped his HK 9-mm PSP pistol. With a look of horror on his broad face, Neudock acted for an instant as if he might try to claw out with his two bare hands the two .380 slugs that the Death Merchant had put into his stomach and abdomen. He couldn't, anymore then Kurt Scheller could extract the .380 bullet from his groin.

With dying men falling all over each other, the last three confused ODESSA gunmen didn't get a chance to swing around and fire at the Death Merchant who was darting and weaving and charging them like a whirlwind. With Death grinning over his shoulder, he rused in low, from the corner of his eye seeing that Ritter was darting in from around the southwest corner of the garage.

In the window, Gerhart Kausch muttered, *"Donnerwetter!"* and lowered the HK sniper rifle. *Ya, ein Schaum.* If Ritter and the *Amerikaner* had not rushed in, he could have killed everyone of the ODESSA pigs.

Herman Gunche, who had been knocked to one side by the mortally wounded Neudeck, snorted and lifted his Czech M-50 pistol—for all the good it did him! Camellion slammed one of the Brownings down on his wrist, brought the rounded side of the silencer on the other BDA against the side of Gunche's head, and used a right-legged *Yop Chagi* side-thrust kick that made Gustav Hueberdieck think that a hand grenade had exploded in his stomach. The pain was intolerable, an agony that sent a billion needles of pure hurt stabbing into his brain. Hueberdieck didn't notice the Benelli 9-mm B76 automatic as it slid from his hand. He didn't notice anything. His mind exploded in blackness and he dropped into oblivion.

The last gunman in the employ of ODESSA was Walter Pieck, an underworld character from Munich. A professional killer, smuggler and thief, the burly Pieck snarled in rage and snapped off a shot with his Luger. The Death Merchant, however, having turned his attention toward Pieck, saw the man's hand coming up and ducked to one side as the German pulled the trigger. The 9-mm projectile skimmed close to Camellion's left side and narrowly missed Franz Ritter, who was only 25-ft. away and rushing in fast.

Pieck never knew what hit him! Before he could turn the Luger and get off a second round, the Death Merchant used a hard-attack[3] flying Tae Kwon Do[3] side kick against him. Camellion's left heel crashed into the biceps of Pieck's right arm, the big slam forcing the hand with the luger down, the weapon slipping from the half-paralyzed fingers. The sole and heel of the Death Merchant's right foot made a wreck of Pieck's face. Broken teeth flew. Blood spurted from Pieck's mouth and nose, the latter of which had been mashed like an apple. With his maxilla and mandible—the upper and the lower jawbones—broken, and pain and shock strangling his consciousness, Pieck went down.

The Death Merchant, managing to land on his feet, turned and glanced at Franz Ritter, who was looking at the fallen bodies.

"How many are still alive?" Ritter asked. "Any idea?"

"This one." Camellion indicated the unconscious Walter Pieck whose face and shirt-front were covered with blood. "I don't think he's dead. If he's not, it will be a while before he'll be able to say even 'mamma', not with his jaws wired together."

"He'll be able to nod 'yes' and 'no' and use his hands to write," Ritter said. He pushed with a foot against the body of Gustav Hueberdieck. "This joker's had it. Shock must have killed him."

"Yeah. I guess my foot stab tied his stomach in knots around his spine," commented Camellion. He bent over Herman Gunche and felt for the man's throat pulse. The pulse was weak but steady. "This one is alive. He probably has a concussion."

Vallie West, who had by then reached Ritter and Camellion, said, "so we'll lose a day or two waiting for these two worthies to get in shape to talk. The delay will be worth it. Maybe, if we learn anything of importance. I doubt if we do."

"We won't." Ritter cocked his head slightly, listening to the sirens in the distance getting closer. "It's very seldom that we ever grab anyone who's a member of ODESSA or connected directly with a member. In fact, we almost never grab anyone who's even connected indirectly with those Nazi *schäume*." His gray-green eyes jumped to the Death Merchant. "You had the chance of a century a few weeks ago, back in France. Too bad you had to kill them all."[4]

[3]Tae Kwon Do is among the more difficult in the hard-attack classification, being 80 percent kicks and 20 percent defense. At the soft end is *Aikido*, a defensive technique meant to ward off attacks by means of wristlocks, armlocks, throws.

[4]Death Merchant # 42: High Command Murder

11

Camellion didn't bother to answer Ritter. What had taken place in Brittany was none of the kraut's business.

"We'll wait until daylight to inspect the vehicles," he said, changing the subject. "We'll not have any trouble finding the packages. The Acousti-Sensor can amplify a circuit 5,000 times if required to do so."

"We can be sure that they boobytrapped the machines," Ritter said gently. "If they had only wanted to bug our expedition, one or two transmitters would have done the job. They wouldn't have needed so many men."

"It's all conjectural at this point," said Camellion, "like trying to make a choice whether to die young or old and sloppy. We'll know soon enough, as soon as daylight comes and the police clear the area."

"Ya, we can start with the full light," Ritter said.

"Yeah, after they haul the corpses away and the other two to the hospital," added West. "But we won't like the publicity we'll get out of this. This little fracus will be in every paper in Europe; and if ODESSA had any doubts about the 'expedition' from the Historical Society of Cologne University, they won't have them any longer."

One of the loud sirens suddenly stopped and the first police car, blue lights flashing, pulled into the parking lot. To the east, the three other BND agents and two of the drivers were running toward the garage from the *Gasthof*.

09.30 hours. The task of checking the ten vehicles had been completed. Earlier, with an efficiency so typical of the German race, the police of Ottobrunn cleared the area and stationed men at strategic positions, to make sure that no one entered the dangerous area.

Vallie West carried the Acousti-Sensor case, which resembled an oversized attache case. Camellion wore the headphones and carried the two-foot-long metal probe.

Franz Ritter carried the explosives detector, an S201 unit consisting of a hand-held probe, line operation module, backpack and headphones. Assisting Ritter with the probe was Gunther Helldorf, a large man with blond hair and a quiet kind of reassuring solidity. If any man had reason to hate ODESSA, it was Helldorf, who was half-Jewish. His mother—it was she who had been Jewish—and his father, along with two sisters and a brother, had gone up in smoke in Treblinka. Only nine years old when World War II ended, Helldorf had survived by being kept hidden by a compassionate German family in Leipzig. His luck had held, and so had the fortune of Herr and Frau Borskuehler, the couple who had protected him. Before the tight security and the erection of The Wall, the Borskuehlers had moved to West Germany, taking Gunther with them.

Neither the Death Merchant nor the other men believed that the ODESSA agents had penetrated the inside of any of the vehicles. Obviously the O-agents had not. Not a single alarm had gone off. But they had to be absolutely certain. One single mistake would be the final and last mistake.

They started with the van, Ritter and Helldorf first using the explosives detector. In operation, the device continuously sampled the ambient air and analyzed the vapors of explosives, ignoring interfering substances and any kind of odor that might fool the detector. The detector gave visible indications of ready, caution, alert and an audible tone to indicate vapor concentration.

The Death Merchant and Vallie West followed with the Acousti-Sensor, pinpointing within a foot where each package of explosives was attached underneath each vehicle. When the sweep was completed, Alfred Dueselbeck had removed a half-pound package of *Nitroglyzerin-Blättchenpulver* (nitroglycerine, flaked powder) from underneath each of the six cars. To each package was attached a battery-powered timer and detonator, each set to "ring" at ten hundred hours—at 10:00 in the morning. Two packages of *Ngl Bl P*[5] were taken from underneath the van, two each from the two motor homes, and three from underneath the tractor and trailer—seven and a half pounds of nitro. What a big bang that seven and a half pounds would have made on the highway!

After the police had taken possession of the packages of *Ngl. Bl. P*, Camellion and West checked each vehicle for hidden transmitters, using an Impedance Analyzer that was extra-sensitive because of the very high-gain solid-state circuits. The unit would even find high impedance A/C or D/C coupled devices.

"It's a waste of time," said Franz Ritter. "Those ex-Nazis wouldn't bug vehicles they intended to blow up."

Wouldn't they? Camellion and West found six 5-watt to

[5]German army abbreviation for *Nitroglyzerin-Blättchenpulver*

13

50-ohm load DC nominal transmitters in the six cars, one per car. Two were found underneath the tractor and trailer, and one under the van. ODESSA had planned with total pragmatism: should the explosives be discovered, there was always the possibility that the transmitters would go unnoticed and that ODESSA would have an open line to conversations among the members of the expedition.

Camellion and West, Helldorf and Ritter looked thoughtfully at the nominal transmitters which they had taken into the van and placed on a swing-down table.

"They have a range of eight kilometers at maximum," Camellion said. He gave a sly, knowing grin. "Do I have to tell you that there has to be an ODESSA mobile listening station within five miles of us?"

Helldorf sighed loudly. "They'll try again. There's something positively evil about ODESSA, damned evil!" He picked up one of the transmitters which had been mounted underneath the car by a means of a magnet. The device was about half the size of a pack of cigarettes, the antenna only a quarter of an inch long—a miracle of miniaturization.

Camellion gestured with his right hand. "We'll repaint the trailer before we take the road. The Cologne Historical Society of Cologne University stands out like a red neon sign on a pitch dark night."

"A paint job won't fool ODESSA watchers," Ritter said bitterly.

"Of course not, but there's no use advertising to every country bumpkin between here and Bad Aussee. Once the news of this shootout reaches the press, people in every town will watch for us the way kids watch for a circus."

"In a sense, rubberneckers will be to our advantage," West said. "With spectators around, it will be more difficult for ODESSA gunmen to strike. They don't want publicity anymore than we do."

"Want it or not, we've got it!" Ritter said scornfully. "All we can tell the press is that we were attacked by thieves. The reporters won't believe us. They can't. We did too good a job on the O-swine."

Helldorf switched from English to high German, "Ya, the reporters will want to know why we are carrying guns. And how do we explain the *elektronische Schutzmassnahmen, sonst den bomben?*"

The Death Merchant replied quickly in German. "We

don't. Only we and the police know what we found. We don't tell the press anything about the electronic counter-measures or the bombs. Why the guns? To protect our valuable diving equipment. What else can we say?"

Vallie West glanced at his wristwatch. "What's our next move—the hospital?"

Camellion did not answer right away. He was thinking of what Helldorf had said about ODESSA—positively evil!

I wonder if he's ever heard of the sinister Ahnernerbe, the Nazi occult bureau?

Chapter Two

It was not a guilty conscience that made Señor Alfredo Pinheiro and Señor del Rosa nervous and uncomfortable, although neither ex-SS officer revealed the slightest concern. They had very valid reasons for being uneasy. Not only were the two wanted Nazi war criminals in Europe, but they were in Wien (Vienna), Austria, and Vienna was crawling with Israeli Mossad agents. Added to the danger of Israeli *Schweinerei*, there was the distinct possibility that the *Amerikaner* CIA and the *Westen Deutsch* BND might be on their trail.

There were other reasons for the discomfort of the two officials of the Association of ex-SS Members. Only a few weeks earlier, ODESSA had suffered a total defeat in French Brittany[1] and had failed to grab more than half a billion dollars in gold that American officers had stolen from the *Schutzstaffel*, better known as the SS, during the last days of World War II.

Now the Amerikaner CIA and the *Westen Deutsch* BND were going to search Lake Toplitz in the *Totes Gebirge*, the "Dead Mountains" in Austria. Suppose they found the case that contained the lists and other top secret information. Damn that idiot Kaltenbrunner![2] Much worse was the news that Kohne had just brought Pinheiro, who was actually ex-SS *Gruppenführer* Ernst Rudolf Muller, and del Rosa, who, during the days of Nazi glory, had been SS *Standartenführer* Karl Victor Scherhorn. The *toten Operation* had been a total failure! Only five of the attackers were still alive. Three had escaped in two automobiles when they saw how their comrades were being gunned down. Two others were in the hospital. An in-

[1]Death Merchant Number 42: High Command Murder
[2]Ernst Kaltenbrunner became chief of the Security Police and SD and head of the RSHA on January 30, 1943.

former within the Ottobrunn police department had reported that the members of the so-called "expedition" had discovered not only the packages of *NGL Bl P,* but had found the surveillance transmitters. *Du lieber Gott*! The Devil himself must be on the side of those *verdammen Schweine!*

"What are we going to do?" Herman Kohne burst out furiously, addressing his question to ex-Lieutenant General Muller, who, with his wavy silver hair and sharp features, could have been a statesman.

Muller leaned back in the padded armchair and carefully adjusted the pant legs of his trousers. "We try again. The situation demands that we hit them again when they least expect it. How else can we stop their damned snooping in *die Abfallkanne des Teufels?*"

"Ya, The Devil's Trashcan," Doctor Gunther said slowly, nodding his head slowly. "It's a sinister lake in a sinister area."

Jose del Rosa—ex-SS Colonel Karl Scherhorn—a mild looking man in his sixties, remained silent, his impassibility reminding Herr and Frau Gunther of a sentry in a concentration camp watching the miserable inmates. The gaze of the Gunthers remained fixed on Muller, whom they feared more than Colonel Scherhorn.

Herman Kohne intervened. "Let them poke around the Devil's Trashcan, I say. I did some checking the other day and found that Lake Toplitz has a surface area of over six million four-hundred thousand sq. meters. Let them dive all they want. They won't find anything but a lot of outdated hardware." A young man in his thirties and the son of a *Totenkopfverbände*[3] officer, Kohne seemed annoyed. "Why should we lose more good men in trying to stop those madmen?"

"Madmen? Why do you call them that?" asked ex-Colonel Scherhorn, his tone low but curious.

"Ulrich, one of the men who escaped, reported to Hohehorst that only three men wiped out the gunmen we sent," Kohne said promptly. "Mind you, just three! What else could you call three men who take such chances?"

"I would call them experts," mused Muller with a slight,

[3] The "Death's Head Units," the SS detachments that operated the numerous concentration camps and extermination facilities in Poland.

twisted smile. "Highly experienced kill experts—not mad-men."

"All right, they were experts," Kohne conceded. "But according to Ulrich, they acted as if death couldn't touch them. Such men are extremely dangerous. I feel that there isn't any valid reason why we should risk more men against such devils—just to keep them from diving into that damned lake."

"The two men in the hospital will tell all they know," Ernst Gunther said. "The BND has ways of making *anyone* talk."

Gunther sat on the faded blue sofa, next to his wife. He was 71 years old, and in spite of the palsied trembling that constantly shook his big bony frame, he gave the impression of having a great strength. In the old days, the nurses at the various Lebensborn homes had called him "that handsome Doktor Gunther."

The muscular Herman Kohne, wearing a turtleneck sweater in spite of the summer vacation weather, glanced annoyingly at the old man. "All they can say is that a man named Bernd Steinitz hired them to attack the caravan. They don't know that Steinitz is Hohehorst. To hell with them. Let them talk all they want."

Sitting on a chair, to one side of the couch, Kohne turned again to Muller and Scherhorn. "It's up to you men, but I say leave well enough alone. I don't care if they do have the latest electronic probing equipment. Why in some places, Lake Toplitz is 243 meters deep. There are cross currents, submerged logs and trees, and only God knows what else. These form a kind of treacherous grid and false bottom across the lake's floor and can't be penetrated by divers and probing equipment. There's the mud. Within minutes divers sink in right up to their necks." He slammed his right fist into the palm of his left hand. "*Don-nerwetter nochmal!* Let them dive all they want. Let them make fools of themselves and come up empty-handed. If it were up to me, I——"

"But it isn't!" Ernst Muller interposed, deriving great pleasure from the sudden look of surprise that splashed over Kohne's big face. "Your job is to take orders, to do as you're told, and not to make decisions—*verstand?*"

A nervous, jittery look on his face, Kohn quickly nodded, "Ya, I understand. I was only g-giving my opinion."

"We're not interested in your views," Karl Scherhorn

18

said evenly, his slightly wrinkled face as solemn as a physician's telling a mother that her one and only son has just died. He didn't care for Kohne's beer-hall comradery. He disliked even more Kohne's assumption of equality. The young fool! Only a *dummkopf* could think that Hitler was a great man. But fools like Kohne were needed to do ODESSA's dirty work.

Ach, that damned lake! Scherhorn recalled with bitterness the first time he had seen Lake Toplitz, that dark and sinister body of water set between 8,000 foot cliffs in the rugged Dead Mountains which were a part of the Styrian Alps.

The Third Reich was a smoking ruins, its armies in full retreat on all fronts, when Lake Toplitz had been the center of a 64 sq. kilometer area, a rough, almost inaccessible area that the Nazis had turned into a giant treasure trove during the last days of World War II. It was in this wild and primitive valley that the Nazis had built the famous "Alpine Fortress," the terrible *Alpenfestung*, bragged about by sly Joseph Goebbels.

Another unrealistic fool, thought Scherhorn, but a master liar.

But Herr Doktor Goebbels had not lied about the *Alpenfestung*. The idea for this last-ditch stand redoubt had been conceived in the warped brain of the SS chief Himmler, that dull-witted ex-chicken farmer, who gave the job of fortifying a section of the Austrian Alps—six sq. kilometers—to Ernst Kaltenbrunner, the scar-faced 6'4" head of the Security Police and the SD—the *Sicherheitsdienst*, the intelligence section of the SS.

Memories of the past flooded Scherhorn's mind, bitter memories of what had been. Yes, the idea of a fortress in the Austrian Alps had been practical and did have advantages. By the fall of 1944 entire industries had been moved to the Tyrol from the cities in the north to escape Anglo-American bombers and Russians advancing rapidly in the East. Dr. Meindl, the head of the Steyrer Works, the largest of all Austrian munitions plants, told Kaltenbrunner that he could move his entire plant without loss of production into the area, if Kaltenbrunner could provide the needed caves.

"You'll have them," Kaltenbrunner said. At once he gave orders to move the entire population of Oranienburg concentration camp to a new camp which had been established at Ebensee in the Austrian Alps. These slave laborers were set to work blasting holes in the tough granite. By the end of 1944, Kaltenbrunner reported to Himmler that the *Alpenfestung* was practical.

"We can produce arms and missiles in the caves," Kaltenbrunner said. "The area is the greatest natural fortress in all of Europe . . . almost bombproof."

And it was! Access to the outside world could be maintained only through the numerous trails which linked the area to Italy and Switzerland. Here in the Austrian Alps the *Wehrmacht* might hold out forever.

By this time the Third Reich was a graveyard of ruins, a wilderness of death, a broken giant falling to its death. Hitler killed himself and the war suddenly ground to a halt. The thousand-year-old Reich was gone.

However, the *Alpenfestung* remained. Remembering, Scherhorn felt like laughing. While the Alpine Fortress remained, the SS quickly changed its mind about *Kampf bis zum Letzten*—Fight to the finish! To hell with such nonsense. Instead, they would use the Alpine Fortress to save their lives, as it would be the last place in the Third Reich to be occupied. So while the Allies fanned out all over Germany, the SS headed at full speed for the Austrian Tyrol; and so did the staff of the German Foreign Office.

By May of 1945 this *Auserland* had a population of almost 82,000—about 70,000 above the normal population—most of whom were SS men. There were also a few fascist Hungarian and Romanian contingents. These war criminals included Ante Pavelic of Croatia, who had massacred half a million Serbs; the slimy Monsignor Tiso of Slovakia; and Mihailoff, the leader of the Macedonian fascists. Kaltenbrunner and five of his aides were also there waiting to see what would happen. Scherhorn, and other high SD officials, arrived a day after Kaltenbrunner. With the SS came most of Germany's gold reserves, and the loot of their plunder raids across Europe . . . gold bars by the ton, the wealth of their millions of concentration camp victims, from jewelry and precious stones to melted-down gold teeth, and vast sums of money.

The SS brought more: cases of documents and vital records, the most valuable papers that could testify about the crimes of the Third Reich. Even now, 36 years later, Scherhorn could only grit his teeth in frustration when he thought of the fantastic stupidity of Himmler and Kaltenbrunner. Why hadn't those fools burned the documents, particularly *Plan Ya-4-Flug*. The most vital secret in the world, and Kaltenbrunner—*jener idiotisch*—had insisted on putting the documents in a stainless steel case and dropping it into the lake.

As American armor rolled closer to this last Nazi stronghold, the *Alpenfestung* became a madhouse of activity. Scherhorn still had dreams about those final days when he had still worn the black and silver uniform of the SD. SS men mingled and drank, exchanging plans, discussing the end of their world of conquest, a world that was now *kaput*. Crates of arms stood unnoticed in the snow, and heavy machine guns lay about, waiting to be assembled.

The "defenders" of the Alpine Fortress were far too preoccupied with their personal dreams of escape and the hiding of their loot to be concerned with weapons and many SS officers staggered about drunk. Some committed suicide, while others were busily engaged dying their hair, tending new mustaches, and posing for hurried passport photographs; and it seemed that everyone was carrying boxes and sacks to secret burying grounds.

Scherhorn, who had made plans with other officers of the SD, recalled vividly how he and four other officers had sat in a hut drinking cognac with Kaltenbrunner, awaiting word from Berlin. When the word did come, it was that Hitler had committed suicide and that the war was over. *Gut*, the plan had worked! Then Adolf Eichmann arrived unexpectedly from Berlin. No one was happy to see him, knowing that Eichmann, as chief of the Gestapo's Jewish Office, was one of the worst war criminals, who would soon be wanted by the Allies.

"What the hell do you want?" Kaltenbrunner snapped, staring at the dapper mass murderer.

"I'm going up into the mountains to the fortress," Eichmann explained, clicking his heels and giving the Hitler salute.

"I don't care where you go," Kaltenbrunner said. "Just get out of here and get lost. The show's over. Either lose yourself or commit suicide."

As the Americans and the Russians rolled closer to the last stronghold of Nazism, the SS hurriedly completed their plans. Treasure, documents, and secret weapons were buried in the mountain slopes and lakes, a very large share going into the cold waters of *Der Abfallkanne des Teufels*—The Devil's Trashcan.

Disguised as corporals in a *Maschinengewehr-Bataillon*, a motorized machine-gun battalion, Scherhorn and SD *Sturmbannführer* Emil Miesel had left the area, the two men splitting up after they reached Bad Ischl.

Major Miesel's luck had deserted him near Rome, Italy. Trapped by OSS agents, he had shoved the muzzle of a P-38 into his mouth and pulled the trigger. Scherhorn's fortunes had held. Thirteen months later, by way of the "Spanish Route," he was in Mar del Plata, Argentina. Eighteen months after leaving the Alpine Fortress and its madness, he was in Bom Jesus da Lapa, in the state of Bahia, Brazil—the new owner of a coffee plantation, bought with funds supplied by ODESSA. By then he had a personal history as Señor Jose del Rosa, born in Rio De Janeiro, in 1910.

Ernst Rudolf Muller was saying to an embarrassed Herman Kohne, "There are many things you don't realize, *mein junger Freund*. There are secrets in Lake Toplitz that must remain secret, at all costs, secrets no one must find."

Muller glanced at Herr and Frau Gunther. Sitting on a couch, the couple looked down at the floor, Ernest Gunther's hands trembling more than usual. Muller supressed a smile over the discomfort of Kohne who opened his mouth as if to speak, then closed it, as though deciding that silence could always be a partner of common sense.

Logic dictated what Kohne was thinking, and Muller put his thoughts into words. "Ya, you are wondering why, in all these years, we of ODESSA haven't removed those secrets from Lake Toplitz. We haven't because we can't. We can't because we can't move in equipment to do the job. The Austrian government wouldn't permit it. Even if the Austrians would permit our people to explore the lake, enemy agents would be quick to notice the activity."

"The BND and British SIS," Kohne said solemnly, relaxing and feeling less ill at ease.

"As well as the CIA and the KGB," Muller said. "The Russians in particular have contract agents in the area. Even scuba divers on vacation, who make dives in the lake, are carefully watched and checked out."

"We know that the West German government has put intense pressure on the Austrian Ministry of the Interior," amplified Victor Scherhorn, folding his hands in his lap. "On this basis alone, we can assume that the Cologne Historical Society expedition is only a front for an intelligence operation.

Ingrid Gunther spoke without thinking. "Herr del Rosa, how can you be positive that the West German government has forced the Austrians to comply and permit the expedition to dive in the lake?"

The old woman—she was 77—suddenly looked startled when she realized that her question might have violated ODESSA security.

Apparently it had not, for Scherhorn answered readily.

"We have our sources of information in the Austrian government, even within the Austrian SSS[4]. Fortunately, the BND and the CIA are not looking for any particular item in *Der Abfallkanne des Teufels*. They are only making a general sweep, a general search."

"It's all nonsense. This whole business is nonsense and a waste of time," muttered Ernst Gunther, his outspoken manner surprising not only his wife but Muller, Scherhorn, and Kohne as well.

Ernst Gunther picked up a rubber duck and began squeezing it with his right hand as he talked in a subdued monotone. "But it makes no difference. All of us . . . we are only living shadows, the remains of a dead era, an era that died with the Führer. Whether we live another five or ten years, what's the difference?"

Their senses reeling on the edge of astonishment, Muller and Scherhorn were stunned by Gunther's bold words. Herman Kohne's mouth fell open.

Lieutenant General Muller was the first to recover. "The difference is that we are alive and have a duty to unite all of Germany and crush the *kommuniste Schweinerei* that would subject the world to Marxism." Muller's voice rose in fervor, and his expression became messianic. "It is our duty to replace Communism with the order and discipline of the Fourth Reich."

Karl Scherhorn nodded vigorously, the bags under his eyes quivering with anticipation. "And when our descendants take over, the *Rassenprüfer*[5] will have enough work

[4]Secret Security Service: the Austrian intelligence apparatus
[5]Race Examiners: Under the Nazis, the *Rassenprüfer* were connected to the *Rasse und Siedlungshauptamt*, the Head Office for Race and Settlement, known by the letters RuSHA.

in the Soviet Union and the United States to keep them busy for years."

"*Nein,* not in the Soviet Union," Muller said coldly. "That backward nation is nothing but a giant cesspool filled with slop and the worst kind of diseased vermin. It will not be difficult to destroy the entire population with nerve gas, or slow starvation. At least we can use the corpses for fertilizer." He laughed a short, sinister laugh. "By God! The soil of the Soviet Union will become the most productive on earth."

"It's in the United States that the *Rassenprüfer* will have a fulltime job," thrust in Herman Kohne. "The *Amerikanerin* have the most mongrelized society in the world."

"Ya, brimming over with *Rassenschande*[6]," said Muller. "*Mein Gott!* Imagine! Treating millions of black apes as though they were human. What a degenerate society those *Amerikanerin* have."

"Don't forget the Latin trash constantly crossing the border from Mexico and pouring in from South America," Scherhorn said. "Sooner or later the decent white *Amerikanerin* will get sick of their government's stupidity and take matters into their own hands."

Muller disagreed. "I don't think so. The *Amerikanerin* have no self discipline. Their young men are morally weak and degenerate. Why they won't even fight for their own nation."

Herman Kohne's eyes became bright with enthusiasm. "Why not try and promote a war between the Soviet Union and the United States? We could take over after they destroyed each other."

Listening to the three talk, to what he considered madness, Ernst Gunther had his own bitter memories. He still found it difficult to believe that, more than 35 years earlier, he had been the number three official in the Lebensborn Society. The Lebensborn Society had 22 homes, six hospitals, 5 large estates and, at the end of the war, more than 25-million marks—taken from "enemies of the Reich," Jews in particular. During those days, he had been a proud and happy man. He had been serving *Der Führer* in what Adolf Hitler called "the struggle of the creative Teutonic-Aryan race."

Ernst Gunther, M.D., had believed in the theory of a

[6]Race pollution

"master race." After all, did not Nature herself exterminate the weak for the benefit of the strong and heathy? What was so morally wrong about deliberately breeding master stock, of mating suitable men and women who would produce a race of pure Aryans? Why he had even suggested to Reichsführer Himmler that the SS could import Norwegian girls to Bavaria for the purpose of transforming the Dinaric section of the Aryan race into a pure Nordic race by means of selective breeding. However, the Reichsführer had not approved of the idea, for reasons he did not disclose.

Yet even as the RuSHA racial machine was moving into high gear and as the war progressed, Gunther began to have doubts, began to see that the Lebensborn homes— supposedly maternity homes for unwed mothers—were nothing more than breeding stations, stud farms, where "racially valuable" unmarried women could be impregnated by members of the SS, the children of such unions to be the advance guard of a super race that would populate the German Reich that would last a thousand years. Officially, the aim of the "stud" program was what the Nazis called *Zuchtungsziel*, or target-breeding. Along with the program was a constant propaganda campaign that subtly stressed sexual promiscuity as being "honorable"—for the sole purpose of propagation in the name of the "struggle of the creative Teutonic-Aryan race."

Doctor Gunther had not been completely stupid. Along with thousands of other modern Nebuchadnezzars, he saw the handwriting on the wall. Germany could not win the war. With Ingrid Stressmann, the chief nurse at the Lebensborn "maternity" home in Frankfurt, Gunther began making his escape plans a year before the war officially ended. A week before the official surrender, he and Ingrid Stressmann quietly disappeared. With them went 281,000 German marks. With forged papers that identified them as Herr and Frau Ernst Gunther, of 1678 Kolonnenstrasse, Berlin, the pair made their way south toward conquered territory—just two more refugees among millions.

A year after the war, they left Freiburg, in southern Germany, and settled in Vienna, Austria, all the while terrified that the Allied War Crimes Commission might somehow learn about them and start a world-wide search. By then, *SS-Obergruppenführer* and *Waffen-SS* General Karl Wolff, Walter Darrem and the other "racial experts" had either been hanged as war criminals or else imprisoned. But the War Crimes Commission was not interested in little fish, especially minnows who had not been responsible for murder. No one bothered the Gunthers, who had purchased a *Bierstube* (or cafe) in Vienna and lived in a small apartment above the establishment.

Three and a half years later, the Gunthers (they had never married) had a caller. An agent of ODESSA paid them a visit. How were Ernst Gunther and Ingrid Stressmann like all of Vienna and the West German government to know that they had been part and parcel of the Lebensborn Society and had worked right along side of Max Sollmann, Gregor Ebner, Inge Viermetz, and other notorious Lebensborn officials, all of whom were serving long prison sentences, except Max Sollmann, the chief administrator, who had committed suicide during his trial?

Ever since that visit, Herr and Frau Gunther had been at the beck and call of ODESSA.

In 1978 Gunther had sold his *Bierstube*, retiring not only because of his age but because he had become a victim of Parkinson's Disease. Nonetheless, ODESSA did not release its hold on the Gunthers, at times using their apartment as a mail drop or as a stopover for special couriers.

Herman Kohne, who owned several whorehouses in the St. Pauli district of Hamburg, again said, "I still feel that a war between the United States and the Soviet Union would be to our advantage!" He looked expectantly at Muller and Scherhorn, expecting the two ODESSA officials from South America to agree with him.

Neither man did. Neither man made any kind of comment. They only stared at him. They considered him a good man—he did what he was told and was dedicated—but why tell him that ODESSA, through one of its front organizations, had already tried to promote a third world war by exploding an A-bomb in Egypt[7] and blaming the murder of millions of Egyptians on the Israelis. They had tried and had failed. The Brotherhood had been smashed. . . .

Forver concerned with cleanliness, Ernst Muller took a folded white handkerchief from an inner coat pocket, unfolded it and wiped his hands, his expression distant.

[7]Death Merchant #39: *The Fourth Reich*

A tiny smile frozen on his slit of a mouth, Karl Scherhorn let his eyes wander about the living room of the house. The room was furnished simply but in good taste, and it was bright and cheerful. On one of the bookshelves was a leather-bound copy of *Mein Kampf*. Next to the bible of Nazism was the Bible of Christianity.

Ridiculous! thought Scherhorn. The bible of a dead Jew and the bible of an Austrian madman. Both books, like its authors, were useless, but, in many respects, similar. Both demanded blind obedience and blind faith without facts. Scherhorn sighed to himself. This little house was pleasant. Dr. Gunther was fortunate to have been able to retire to Margareten, a suburb southwest of Vienna.

Carefully, Muller began to refold his handkerchief. He didn't look at Herman Kohne as he spoke. "I think, Herr Kohne, you will better serve the cause by confining yourself to the matter at hand. That means stopping the caravan."

Wondering about the secrets of Lake Toplitz, the solemn-faced Kohne pulled a road map from his pocket.

Chapter Three

The heat wave frying most of Europe did not bother the Death Merchant and the other members of the Historical Society of Cologne. The ten vehicles were air conditioned. It was the uncertainty of the mission that pricked at the nervous system of most of the men and the two women, the constant awareness that ODESSA would almost certainly strike again. That dark feeling of anxiety and apprehension did not burden Richard Camellion and Vallie West. They had lived in the shadow of death too many years to worry unnecessarily. They did not have any doubts; they were positive that ODESSA would make another attempt to stop the expedition. In the minds of Camellion and West, it was not a question of "maybe," but of when and where.

In antithesis to the two company men, Franz Heinz Ritter and the rest of the West German intelligence agents were troubled by a growing concern for the success of the operation. It wasn't that Ritter and his people weren't convinced that ODESSA would make another attack: it was not the where and when, but the *how* that kept their nerves in a constant state of agitation.

The two-day delay in Ottobrunn was another source of irritation, particularly because Herman Gunche and Walter Pieck had not been able to give any information of real value. All they knew was that they and the other gunmen had been hired by a Swiss named Bernd Steinitz. Why did Steinitz want the vehicles of the expedition destroyed? Gunche and Pieck did not know. Steinitz had not given his reasons.

As a security measure, the caravan changed its route. The expedition would not enter Austria by way of Salzburg. Instead, the ten vehicles would drive straight east and enter Austria through Braunau. Then, escorted by the Austrian police, the expedition would proceed to Linz, then turn south and head for Bad Aussee. No matter the route, the caravan would always be open to attack, even after the force reached Bad Aussee and proceeded into the dreary Dead Mountains. To make matters worse, there was no way of knowing to what extent ODESSA had infiltrated the Austrian police, not only SSS but the regular uniformed police at all levels.

The Death Merchant and Ritter had also arranged a change of the vehicles in the expedition. Two cars preceded the main body, the first car a mile ahead of the second vehicle. In turn, the second automobile was half a mile in front of the first car of the main body of the caravan. It was followed by another car and one of the two motor homes; then came the large industrial-type van, the tractor and trailer, and the second motor home. The last two vehicles were cars, the last car half a mile behind the first.

Radio contact between the ten vehicles was almost constant. As an added security measure, the Death Merchant was using the TX-transmitters as do-it-yourself "bumper beepers," outfitting the first two cars and the last two cars with a TX-T each and putting them in dashboard compartments. Each transmitter had been fitted with a field strength RF preselector that operated on a tuned resonant circuit and emitted UHF signals which were monitored on the TX-T central board within he van. At the first sign of danger, the man sitting next to the driver could shut off the TX-transmitter, the lack of a signal serving as a warning that all was not as it should be.

None of these security measures really satisfied Franz Ritter, who had insisted on a security measure of his own. Before the caravan had left Ottobrunn, he had demanded that Camellion post guards at night, inside and outside of the vehicles. The men could work in shifts, Ritter said. Marga von Roesch and Karen Weise, the two BND assistants, could sleep in one of the motor homes. Camellion had agreed; not only was Ritter's idea a good one, but it could not harm security.

Security was uppermost in Camellion's mind as he stared out of one of the blue-tinted windows and listened to Big Jim Flikkema discuss the approaching dives into Lake Toplitz with Bruno Wronkau: Even at this time of the year, the waters will be icy cold. I don't . . ."

The Death Merchant watched the fields roll by. At least they were travelling in comfort. Made by the German firm of Drössvelder und Fiebergrossen, the motor home was a palace on wheels, the interior all pushbutton, leather, chrome, and stainless steel. Owned by the Special Operations Section of the BND, the bus was more than a luxury vehicle. It was also a fortress on solid rubber tires. All the glass was bulletproof, and the inside of the walls was lined with cross-ply layers of Ballistic Nylon. There were also various secret compartments in which were stashed submachine guns, ammo, grenades, gas masks and other items.

"We could dive in the Arctic Ocean. It's the bottom of the damned lake that bothers me. We'll have to rig some kind of safety measure."

The second motor home was smaller; however, it too was armored. The smaller home on wheels could sleep two, the larger four, six if necessary.

Bruno Wronkau, who was the leader of the four West German Divers, slowly nodded. "We can solve that problem by having safety lines attached to each diver. They can signal at the slightest danger and be hauled to the surface."

The Death Merchant smiled to himself when he turned back to the group and looked at Flikkema and Wronkau, both of whom were side by side on one of the front sofas that could be turned into a bed. They were truly a Mutt & Jeff pair. Wronkau was pale-skinned, had a well-defined chin, long narrow nose and a head of bushy chestnut hair. Only ten times fatter than a thick toothpick, he was only five ft. three in. tall and looked as if a gentle breeze might blow him miles off course if he tried to walk down the street. In contrast, James Flikkema was six ft. five in. tall, had a deep tan and weighed 260 pounds—and not a single gram of fat. The sharp-witted West referred to Flikkema and Wronkau as "Sylvester the Cat" and "Tweetie the Bird."

"The diving is up to you divers," Gerhart Kausch said, leaning sideways in the low chrome-framed chair, crossing his legs. "But there is one factor you two had better consider and pass on to your crews. Any cases you might find could be boobytrapped."

"A nice, cheerful thought," grunted Flikkema.

"It's not all that bad," spoke up Franz Ritter, emphasizing each word. "In the first place, I doubt if you find any cases. Even if you do, the cases won't be opened until they've been hauled from the lake. With care, if you don't knock them around, there shouldn't be any danger in getting them out of the water."

"Ya, that's true," agreed Kausch, after a moment's reflection. "But we can't discount the possibility of one of the cases exploding below the surface."

"We'll worry about that problem once we get to the lake and when the divers find a case," retorted Ritter. He then blew his nose loudly, an indication that the air conditioning was again bothering his sinuses.

Richard Camellion joined in. "It seems to me we should give some extra serious thought to why ODESSA is trying to stop us from reaching the Devil's Trashcan—if there isn't anything of value in the lake."

With some slight surprise, Ritter gave Camellion an inquiring look.

"I thought we had covered that subject a few days ago," he said. "It's been concluded why O-Agents attacked us: ODESSA didn't have a choice. All Europe knows that Toplitz is supposed to contain Nazi secrets. Odessa has to consider its reputation. How would it look if ODESSA didn't fight back?"

"Look—to whom?" asked Vallie West, whose big frame was stretched out on the other sofa, his hands underneath his head.

Suspecting that the big American was subtly trying to provoke him, Ritter refused to show his annoyance.

"To certain South American governments that have given Nazi war criminals refuge all these years—Dr. Mengele for one, Martin Bormann for another—unless you believe that nonsense about Bormann's skull being uncovered in East Berlin a few years ago."

"Yeah, I know the skull was as phony as a politician's promise," Vallie said. "But the Bormann skull doesn't have any relationship to Lake Toplitz."

The Death Merchant asked, "Tell me, Franz, does the BND have absolute proof that the skull was not Bormann's? I was under the impression that even the teeth in the skull matched Bormann's dental chart?"

"The teeth did match the old dental charts, that's true," Ritter said, "but ODESSA made a small but very serious mistake. One of the teeth in the skull—I believe it was a molar on the left side—had been filled with a substance that wasn't used by dentists in Europe until 1962. Unless

31

Bormann had a time machine and had his tooth filled by a dentist in the future. . . ."

"Remember, Bormann was supposed to have been killed in 1945," interposed Gerhart Kausch.

"Precisely," declared Ritter. "The skull could not possibly have been his. The ploy was just another attempt by ODESSA to make the world believe that Bormann was dead. Your *Amerikaner* CIA knows this and so does the British SIH. Your own CIA had the information before the British."

"It's not 'my' CIA," the Death Merchant said with a slight chuckle. "If you think I'm a Case Officer, I'm not."

"Nor am I!" snapped Vallie West, as though "Case Officer" was an obscene title.

"It's the Yale and Harvard idiots with degrees in political science, economics, and other useless subjects that make a career of being kiss-ass paper-pushers. Most of them couldn't find their own two feet without detailed intructions on how to look."

"Instructions printed in large letters," added West with a belly-laugh. "It's men like us who go out into the field and get the damned job done."

"It's almost the same in the BND," Ritter said understandingly. "Most of our work in the field is done by *Vertrauensmann* agents—*V-Mann* for short, or 'trusted man' in English. Unlike your CIA, we don't hire career people on the basis of the number of university degrees they possess, or we'd get too many educated fools. Furthermore, our officers are trained to go into the field."

Gerhart Kausch quickly interjected in a severe voice, "We are not *V*-Mann agents. We are BND officers."

Vallie West sat up, his glance catching Camellion's for a moment, his eyes telegraphing, Yeah, we get the message. You krauts are officers. We are only contract-agents. Who gives a damn!

"Well, that's nice," Camellion said politely, hoping that West would add a comment or two. Vallie didn't. He merely smiled, an indication to Camellion that Vallie didn't consider the effort worth the time and trouble.

Just then the driver of the motor home began taking the big vehicle around a curve and the men paused to brace themselves against the pull of the momentum.

Once the motor home had negotiated the curve and was on a straight stretch of highway, Big Jim Flikkema leaned over, placed his folded hands between his knees and looked at Camellion and Ritter. Although he was a chemical engineer by profession and had his own business, his true passion was diving, and in pursuit of that great love he had gone underwater all over the world.

"Now that we've had a little lecture in case officers and *V*-Mann agents, suppose we get down and discuss more about security," he said in English. "Wronkau and I are concerned about the protection we'll have once we get to the lake and start the dive. "Other than us"—he nodded toward "Tweetie Bird"—"there are nine men in the German crew and two divers and two top men in the American crew. We have their safety to consider."

Ritter, rubbing a hand over the back of his neck, looked at the floor. "The Austrians are calling in extra state police," he answered in English. "They'll meet us and our escort in Bad Aussee. We shouldn't have any trouble."

"I don't like the Austrians," declared Bruno Wronkau. "I don't trust them. There were a lot of Nazis in that country."

Vallie West, now sitting up on the sofa, turned and caught Camellion's eye. The Death Merchant's expression remained neutral. He didn't care what kind of security measures Ritter and the other BND officers were counting on. He had made plans of his own and, if necessary, would exert his full authority. All he would have to do is radio Bonn.

"I hardly think the Austrian state police will machine gun us," Gerhart Kausch said drily, his gleaming bead eyes peering at Flikkema and Wronkau in their usual half-alarmed, half-expectant way. "We'll be protected by several hundred policemen, and helicopters will patrol the mountains in the immediate vicinity of the Trashcan. What more could we ask for?"

Far from being reassured, Flikkema rubbed the end of his chin.

"You're saying that all we have to worry about is getting to Toplitz, and that after we get into the mountains, our security will be airtight."

"It all sounds too easy to me," Bruno Wronkau said slowly, sitting up straight on the sofa.

Ritter, sitting in front of the curtain that fenced off the driver's compartment, looked past Kausch at the Death

Merchant. "I suppose you're going to say we should also have an army division standing by, just in case?"

Vallie West paused in lighting his Cambridge cigarette, his right thumb on the flint wheel of the Cricket lighter. "A damn good idea," he said with mock seriousness. "A German army division, I presume?"

Ignoring West and a chuckle from Flikkema, Ritter waited for a reply from Camellion, who was thinking that when Adolf Hitler attained power in 1933, the vitalization of Teutonic mythology demonstrated the peculiar German capacity to live in two worlds at once by constantly projecting an imaginary world onto reality. It was this "Germanness," this tendency to believe what one wanted to believe that made Ritter and the other BND officers unreliable.

"I have no complaints," Camellion said, pleasantly enough. "With the Austrian cops all around us, we should have locktight security." He saw the tightness around Ritter's mouth soften and the tenseness leave his face. "I hardly think that ODESSA will fly over and drop a nuclear device on us. On the other hand, I still think you're dead wrong about ODESSA being helpless after we get to the lake." He shrugged in an offhanded manner. "Why argue about it? Hell, you don't even believe there's anything of value in the Trashcan."

Ritter's surly face looked almost sorrowful. He opened his mouth, closed his mouth, thought for a moment, then said in a careful tone, "At one time the lake no doubt did have all kinds of secrets. The lake is in the heart of the former *Alpenfestung* region. But who knows what those damed Austrians found in 1963?"

Flikkema became very alert. "The Austrians have already conducted a search of the lake?"

Ritter nodded solemnly. "It really started as far back as the 1950s," he said, "with an Austrian named Albrecht Gaiswinkler, a former member of the Austrian Parliament."

Quickly and in bitter tones, the BND officer explained that Gaiswinkler had, for years, urged his government to conduct its own search of the mysterious lake and to end for all time the rumors, intrigue and sheer speculation.

Vienna remained silent. Even when a change of government put Franz Olah in charge of the Interior Ministry in March of 1963! Olah had been a good friend of Gaiswinkler and like the latter had been a socialist.

Then six men were found murdered in the Dead Mountains, close to the mysterious Devil's Trashcan. Supposedly, they had been German "tourists" on vacation. Each man had been shot with a 9-mm weapon, probably, according to the official Austrian report, a Walther P-38, the official sidearm of the German Army during World War II. Furthermore, an examination of each corpse revealed the lightning flash of the dreaded SS tattooed in the armpit of the right arm of each man."

"The SS killing each other?" Flikkema shook his head. "Or what version did the Austrians have?"

Ritter's mouth became fixed in a sort of snarl, the lips pulled back over the teeth. "Those *österreicher* (Austrians) gave the weak explanation that there must have been seven men. The idea was that the seventh man murdered the other six."

Flikkeman sort of smiled. "Don't tell me the seventh man committed suicide? Nobody would concoct that kind of story."

"Nobody did," Ritter said. "I don't mean that the Austrians said that the seventh man killed himself. They claimed that one of six must have regained consciousness and shot the seventh man, or shot him while going down. When all of Europe laughed at that ridiculous tale, the Austrians came up with another wild story. They said there might have been—get this—eight men and that the eighth man shot the other seven, then somehow made his way back to Bad Aussee, without anyone seeing him, and escaped."

Gerhart Kausch took off his sunglasses and said, "We could only guess at the truth." He laughed slightly. "Not 'us' because we weren't in the BND then. I mean that the BND of those times could only deduce what had taken place. At the time, there were two principal groups competing for the treasure reputed to be at the dark bottom of the lake. One of them, sounding like something out of a blood and thunder story, was a die-hard group of ex-Nazis, tightly formed into an organization called "The Spider." Their goal was to grab all the treasure they could before ODESSA could become fully organized and deal with them."

"The members of *Die Spinne* were considered renegades and traitors by ODESSA," Camellion said. There was no doubt in anyone's mind that he was not asking a question,

35

but giving a definitive statement. *"Die Spinne* was also after vital lists that furnished code keys to innumerable secret Swiss bank accounts where, from 1944 to the end of the war, Nazi agents had deposited the bulk of the Reich treasury. These accounts now contain about 40-billion dollars—counting the interest over the years."

Kausch, chewing the end of one of the temple arms of his dark glasses, turned and considered the Death Merchant with inquisitive eyes. Ritter regarded Camellion with a new but grudging respect. He realized that the CIA would have such information, but how could a contract agent be so remarkably well-informed?

Vallie West gave Ritter and Kausch their second surprise of the afternoon, and Bruno Wronkau who, although a master driver, was also a full officer in West German intelligence.

"The Spider people were also after the lists of Gestapo informers," he said in his heavy voice. "All those 'nice' men and women who had at one time or another collaborated with the Nazis, not only in Europe, but in nations all over the world."

"To use as blackmail material," said Big Jim Flikkema.

"Right on. Personally I doubt if Bormann—and it was he and his aides who did most of the planning before the war ended—would have given orders to drop any highly confidential lists into any lake. That pig was too clever. The CIA is of the opinion that all the lists were smuggled to South America, on microfilm, before the war ended."

Ritter appeared to be uncomfortable, and he was. He was not the kind of man who enjoyed contract agents of another world-wide intelligence service speaking on his level, giving out information he would have sworn they didn't possess.

He took out a pack of German Eagle cigarettes, and smiled weakly at Camellion. "I suppose you know the name of the other group that was fighting *Die Spinne* in Austria, and I don't mean ODESSA?"

"You should have asked me something difficult," Camellion said, smiling. "The other group was composed of Austrian resistance fighters. They were headed by Gaiswinkler. Their goal was to keep Spider from finding anything of value. They hoped to find it first and turn it over to the authorities for distribution among Hitler's victims and charitable institutions. Unfortunately they were no match for ODESSA. Idealists always stumble over their own morality and end up low man on the totem pole of life."

"The Spider didn't do so well either against ODESSA," grunted Gerhart Kausch. "ODESSA wiped them out and absorbed *Stille Hilfe*[1] and *Die Schleuse*[2], two SS escape-from-Europe organizations."

Ritter exhaled cigarette smoke and looked up toward the low cream-colored ceiling. "We can be positive that ODESSA will never get its hands on any of the Nazi loot stashed in Swiss banks. Way back in 1963 the Swiss passed a law freezing all those numbered Nazi accounts, making the money available to West Germany and to the poor Jewish victims of Nazi persecution. But none of this has any bearing on the supposed treasure and secrets in Lake Toplitz."

The Death Merchant could not be sure, but had he detected a faint sneer in Ritter's voice in reference to the Jewish victims? "Go ahead and finish your story about the Austrian government's search of Toplitz," he said to Ritter.

"You don't know what happened?" Ritter's eyebrows raised.

"No," Camellion lied.

"Scores of police swarmed into the Lake Toplitz region and hermetically sealed off the lake and the surrounding area," Ritter said. "A police boat began circling along the shoreline every hour. Scores of police . . ."

Ritter explained that police units went on 24-hour duty armed with automatic rifles, submachine guns, and side-arms. From Kiel, West Germany, the Austrians had obtained special underwater television cameras, as well as a team of experts to operate them. From Stuttgart came electronic echo-sounding equipment, sensitive to all metals except, strangely enough, gold and silver. A Hamburg firm sent a deep-sea diving bell; from Vienna came six highly trained and experienced frogman and four deep-sea divers and their rigs.

More than a hundred newsmen from all over the world sped to the resort village of Bad Aussee.

Reporters asked Minister Olah why the Austrian government had waited so long before conducting its own search.

[1]"Silent Help"
[2]"The Locked Gates"

"I'd rather not answer," Olah had replied, obviously not wanting to embarrass his predecessors in office. "I will tell you this. As soon as I become Minister, I laid plans for the search. The six men we found murdered merely accelerated everything."

The official Austrian search of the Devil's Trashcan began. From the very first, reporters were barred from the lake area and were made to depend on information from official statements issued at Bad Aussee by Dr. Paul Aschenbrenner, press officer of the Interior Ministry.

The search wasn't an hour old when Aschenbrenner tried systematically to laugh off all the lake legends, confirming the suspicions of newsmen that the Austrians were trying to pull a fast one and cover up something. After all, Vienna wasn't going to spend all that money just to stop fairy tales about buried treasure.

A rumor began making the rounds that a gigantic cover-up was in the making and that some incriminating documents had already been found and taken secretly to Vienna. Said one British journalist, "The massive efforts being put into the search operations contrast sharply with the airy pooh-poohing of the "treasure" story."

Quipped an American reporter with a sense of humor, "Something seems to be wrong in Austria, especially at Lake Toplitz." And so it would seem, for if the treasure was nothing but a wild myth as claimed by Dr. Aschenbrenner, why then did the good *Doktor* maintain a 24-hour open TV telephone and teletype circuit from Bad Aussee to Interior Minister Olah's desk in Vienna?

Cold weather set in and the search was called off. What had the Austrian government found in the Devil's Trashcan?

Several cases of phony English pound notes were brought to the surface, about $250,000 worth. Divers also recovered 35 printing plates for five-pound notes.

Announced Dr. Aschenbrenner: "Other than that, the search has turned up nothing but junk. We will search no more; already we have spent too much money."

Junk? Very few people believed the Austrian press officer.

"Simon Wiesenthal certainly didn't agree with Olah and Doc Aschenbrenner," remarked Vallie West. He got to his feet, walked behind the back of Kausch's chair and, heading for the built-in refrigerator, said, "Unless my memory is walking on faulty legs, I seem to recall his saying that he had a document in his possession which proves that the Germans decided to sink a lot of secrets in——"

"Not Germans—Nazis!" cut in Bruno Wronkau vigorously. "It was the Nazis who decided to hide secrets."

Weren't those Nazis also Germans, you fruit-loop? Vallie did not press the matter. He understood Wronkau's meaning: Germans in general were not Nazis in particular.

"OK, the higher-up Nazis decided to sink secrets in some lake," he said. He opened the door of the refrigerator and took out a can of *Weissbier*—beer brewed from wheat—then turned and looked at Wronkau and Ritter. "Unless you don't want to believe Wiesenthal, he claimed that while Toplitz was not specifically mentioned, he had very good evidence that this was the lake chosen." He pulled the tab from the aluminum can and started back for the sofa.

"Wiesenthal was full of shit," Gerhart Kausch flung out in anger. Almost springing up, he turned the chair around to face West, who was sitting down on the sofa. "Let me tell you—All of Europe would be better off if Wiesenthal and that damned Jewish Documents Center in Vienna would go up in smoke. He's a troublemaker and a constant pain in the ass." He dropped to the chair, all the while glaring at West who was sipping *Weissbier* and acting as if he were deaf.

Kausch turned toward Camellion, but the Death Merchant was faster.

"Adolf Eichmann would agree with you, if you could find him in hell," he said, his tone laced with amusement. "Weisenthal was certainly a troublemaker for Eichmann. He chased the master Jew killer for fifteen years before he found him in Argentina and tipped off Mossad[3]."

"Let's not play games." Kausch jerked his head toward the Death Merchant, his freckled face florid with anger. "If Wiesenthal had his way, any man who served in the SS or the German army would be classed as a war criminal."

"We're after the big-shot Nazis every bit as much as he is, but he picks on anyone. Who knows how many *Obergrenadiers* or *SS-Schutzes* were ordered by their superiors to shoot Jews, partisans, or whatever? What else could they do but obey? What would happen in the American army—

[3]The Israeli Intelligence Service.

39

in any army—if a little guy refused to obey orders. Wiesenthal's always snooping around, trying to find some poor slob he can turn into a 'war criminal.' "

"And don't call us anti-Semitic!" Ritter looked just like a shark must look when it strays across a choice morsel. "Hanging that label on anyone who disagrees with him is a favorite method of Wiesenthal. It's also a favorite method of the Israelis. But look what they're doing to the Arabs—treating them as bedbugs to be exterminated. They expect the world to kiss that ass because six million of them were murdered 35 years ago. They're running that damned 'Holocaust' crap in the ground."

"I wasn't calling you men anything," Camellion said, his smile ferocious. "You needn't give me a lesson on the use of the 'anti' technique. It's used all over the world by special interest groups and minorities."

"Your United States is a good example," Kausch said sharply. "As I understand it, if anyone says anything against your government's stupid policy of—what is it called when an employer must hire workers solely on the basis of race?"

"Affirmative Action." Camellion was frank. "This means that if a white American even whispers that any Black is less than perfect——"

"And should earn a grand a week because he can read on a first grade level and write his name!" thrust in Vallie West.

"——he's labelled a racist," Camellion finished.

"That explains it." Bruno Wronkau was delighted. "That explains why American products are considered junk in Europe, especially American automobiles."

"Having workers with little ability is only a part of the answer," Camellion said. He inhaled deeply; the three krauts were beginning to annoy him. Maybe he should remind them that Germany had started two wars within 67 years and had been badly beaten in both. *But we lost the Korean War and a bunch of pajama clad gooks chased us out of Vietnam . . .*

Vallie West took another sip of beer. He was waiting for Camellion to respond to the criticism of the sauerkraut boys when Michel Tirpitz's voice floated through the speaker in the ceiling.

"The *Amerikaner*—Henshaw—just called in. He said we are only twelve kilometers from Altotting. He wants to know if we're going to stop in that little town for the night. One of you had better come up here and talk to him. I've got him on hold."

Camellion stood up, adjusted his walking shorts, and tucked in his black silk shirt. "It's almost four o'clock," he announced. Altotting is almost a must for a night stop. And it's a nice little town."

"I'll smoke to that," Big Jim Flikkema said happily.

Vallie West belched, leaned back on the sofa, and took another sip of *Weissbier* while Ritter, getting up, picked up his yellow shirt from the back of the chair and, slipping into the garment, tossed his gaze at Camellion.

"We have practically four hours of daylight left. We could reach the Austrian border by eight o'clock."

"Sure we could, but have you stopped to think that maybe that is what Odessa expects us to do?" Camellion said, his expression becoming cold and distinctly threatening. "Or have you forgotten that is why we decided, back in Ottobrunn, not to stick to a schedule, but to hedgehop—from town to town?"

There was a hidden inference in Camellion's tone and manner that quietly warned Ritter—and Kausch and Wronkau—not to argue with this mysterious *Amerikaner* who killed with an expertise that was frightening, that could only be a special talent of a natural-born survivor. Besides, the three Germans realized that Camellion was right. Not only was it better to not adhere to a tight driving schedule, it was also safer to stop and settle down for the day in the sunlight.

Gerhart Kausch raised himself up from the chair to look as big and as imposing as possible. "I think we——"

"I'm going to talk to Henshaw," Camellion said, cutting him short. In no mood for a useless discussion, he brushed past Kausch and Ritter, strode toward the front of the large vehicle, parted the heavy curtain and stepped into the driver's compartment that, with all its controls and various buttons, reminded him of a control panel on an airliner. On either side of the blue-tinted glass was the Bavarian countryside, looking like a setting for Grimm's fairy tales.

The fields looked hot, but the mountains in the distance had a cool, calm, and enduring appearance, all in contrast to the nearby oaks and conifers which seemed sullen and lonely. Occasionally the large motor home passed a

41

thatched-roof, half-timbered medieval farm house, or men working in the sizzling fields.

Sixty meters ahead of the bus-like vehicle was a snug looking and stylishly compact Volkswagen Rabbit. A mile in front of the Rabbit was a Datsun, the first car of the caravan, driven by Ralph Waldo Duckworth. Riding with him was Harlan Henshaw, one of the two CIA Case Officers with the expedition, a fact known only to Camellion and West. As far as the other members of the expedition were concerned, Henshaw was one of the top men with the American divers.

Michel Tirpitz, a sinewy, hard-faced man with a quiet manner and brooding eyes, didn't as much as glance at the Death Merchant. The German merely removed the single head phone over his right ear and handed the phone and looped wire-mike to Camellion. The Death Merchant slipped the narrow band over the top of his head and adjusted the set so that the looped wire mike attached to the headphone was only four inches from his mouth. He pressed the small button on the headset, then said, "This is Camellion. We'll be spending the night in Altotting. Head right for the center of town. We'll give the natives a thrill."

"Check," Henshaw said. "All we need is a large enough area to park in. Anything else?"

"No, that's all—out." Camellion removed the headphone and mike set, handed it back to Tirpitz, and was turning to go when he saw the German reach out and switch off the TRIX transmitter receiver mounted underneath the dash.

"*Nein*, leave the radio on until we've parked." Camellion spoke in German. "We're not going to relax for a single moment."

Tirpitz, who had slipped the headset and mike back on, nodded and flipped the radio switch to ON.

The Death Merchant turned, parted the curtain and started back toward the living room of the motor home, thinking of how Germany—at least West Germany—had changed since the days of Adolf Hitler. Now, there was a sense of vitality among the Germans, plus an easiness about getting things done, because they no longer carried the burden of the past. The old history had been abolished; tradition, in general, was dead, especially noticeable when Ritter and his people spoke in German. Instead of the non-personal *Sie* for "you," they used the personal *du*—an unheard of practice in prewar Germany.

Ironic! How Fate changes side! West Germany was the most prosperous nation in all of Europe. The *Wirtschaftswunder* (economic miracle) had been of such magnitude that almost 3-million *Gastarbeiter* (guest workers) were in the country. These *Gastarbeiter* were not illegal aliens of the type that were costing Americans billions of dollars in lost taxes, crime, welfare, and medical assistance. The Germans had invited these foreign workers into West Germany because there were not enough Germans to fill the job vacancies.

Camellion once more thought of the farm houses they were passing. How easy it would be for agents of ODESSA to use one of the farm houses from which to launch missiles at the ten vehicle caravan with portable hand launchers.

He could almost hear the Cosmic Lord of Death grinning in amusement. Old Rattle Bones always won in the end, but in time, he too would go and eternity would be done with him.

Laugh, you bastard!

Chapter Four

This day was as hot as the previous day, the temperature in the upper 90s, the sun a sadistic taskmaster from which no one could escape, unless he or she retreated to air conditioning. There wasn't a single cloud in the sky, and the barometer was high.

The Death Merchant rode in the smaller "Aristocrat" motor home as the caravan moved east toward Braunau on the Austrian border. Camellion had chosen to ride in the Aristocrat because he wanted an opportunity to analyze the two BND female agents and Alfred Duselbeck and Gunther Helldorf, the other two BND agents who were known. Camellion had no doubt that either BND career officers or BND contract agents were hidden among the German divers and their top men.

Earlier, Camellion had learned a good deal about the two women and the two men from the way they walked and from their manner of speaking, plus other mannerisms. For example, Helldorf had a negative outlook on life, as revealed by his constricted gait. But Alfred Duselbeck was a middle-of-the-road optimist. He took long, free-swinging strides.

Marga von Roesch was the elder of the two BND women agents. In her mid-twenties, she was rather pretty, reserved, quiet mannered, and gave the impression of total efficiency. She was also predominantly introverted. She automatically kept her distance, feeling more comfortable when more "personal space" separated her from the person to whom she was speaking. Even when sitting, she was careful not to sit too close to another person, unless she couldn't avoid it. Camellion knew, too, that she was a careful, logical thinker.

Unlike Karen Weiss! The 22-year-old Weiss—attractive in a wholesome, athletic style—was extroverted, impulsive and gregarious. When she and another person were standing and talking, she moved in close and was not at all reluctant to express her opinions. Conversely, Alfred Luther Duselbeck—big, extroverted, and always carefully dressed whether in civvies or gray-green fatigues—had a nature that thrived on danger and excitement, an appetite for the spectacular and the unconventional. In Bonn, he had suggested that the force fly to Lake Toplitz in helicopters, forgetting how easily choppers would be destroyed by ground-to-air missiles. All right, how about balloons? An utter pragmatist, Duselbeck was concerned only with the "now," the present. To him, the past had never existed and the future would take care of itself.

But Gunther Helldorf, being half-Jewish, could not forget the past—all natural enough for a man who had lost his family and all his relatives in the extermination camps of Auschwitz, Belzec, Sobibor and Treblinka. Literally obsessed with the past, Helldorf was forever telling tales of Nazi horror, just as now he was explaining about a trainload of children that had left Warsaw bound for the extermination camp of Sobibor.

". . . news spread throughout the region that several thousand children were being sent to go up the chimneys. There was a crowd at every station, hoping that the train would stop. Most of the people intended to rush the train and save as many children as they could. The death train did stop at one small station. The crowd stormed the train, forced the door open and managed to grab a few hundred youngsters. None of the children were over twelve. Sometimes a child grabbed by eager hands was already dead and was put back while people searched for a living body. All too quickly the SS guards opened fire and killed scores of civilians with children in their arms. *Gott!* Not a single civilian or rescued child survived."

Beads of sweat glistened on Helldorf's lean face and his voice broke as he talked. "Early the next morning, partisans blew up the railroad tracks outside the Polish village of Piaskie. The train had to stop. The Partisans rescued sixty of the children before the SS monsters on the train forced them to retreat.

"When this news reached Globocnik[1], he went into such

---

[1]SS General Odilio Globocnik was in charge of two of the extermination camps in Poland—Majdanek and Sobibor. He committed suicide toward the end of the war.

a rage that he ordered the SS to kill every child on the train. The children were machine-gunned and their bodies tossed onto the sides of the tracks. The next day Globocnik's killers murdered 200 mothers with children in their arms in the village square of Piaskie. The bastards used flame throwers.

"To hurry up the business of what the Nazi swine called 'disinfection', all children under seven from the villages of Piaskie and Lomza were taken into the forest and 'disinfected' with a rain of hand grenades. Older children were sent into forced labor at the children's camp at Lodz. More than 3,000 children, between the ages of seven and fifteen, were interned there as 'anti-fascist war criminals'. I tell all of you—Adolf Hitler was evil incarnate. He must have been the Antichrist."

"Why torture yourself by dwelling on the past, Gunther." Sitting across from Camellion, Marga von Roesch spoke in a voice that was tender and sympathetic. "We can't change history. We can only learn from the past."

"We never have, or wars would have stopped centuries ago," observed Duselbeck, the tip of his tongue slowly exploring his lower lip. "I don't think the human race ever will."

"The Germans have—and no insult intended toward your nationality," Camellion said. "The Germans of today would never march to the beat of some would-be Hitler's drum. They'd laugh at him."

"Of course!" Karen Weiss gave a toss of her head, her blond ponytail flying from side to side. "The only people today who admire Hitler are the poor old veterans of the SS. They're harmless dreamers. They're laughed at so much they don't even march when they hold reunions. They stay indoors, sing songs, drink too much beer, talk about the old days of glory, and then their patient *Fraus* lead them off to bed."

Glancing at Weiss, Camellion vaguely wondered why the young woman was so careless about the way she dressed. In blue jeans that were almost ragged, and wearing a faded, short sleeved blue blouse, she looked as if a Goodwill truck had been dumped on her.

Alfred Duselbeck glanced at his wristwatch after which his brown eyes jumped to the Death Merchant. "It is 10:45, he said, a note of expectancy in his low voice. "We should be about twenty-four kilometers from the Austrian border."

"Yes, and close to that range of hills east of the road," Helldorf augmented. "A perfect place for an ambush. But if we know, and we do, ODESSA knows we know it. We are still going to halt and lose precious time?"

"We settled that at last night's meeting," Camellion said. He got up and, because the motor home was moving around a long curve, walked unsteadily to the door that separated the driver's compartment from the rest of the deluxe Aristocrat. Kurt Edlitz, the German who was driving, glanced sideways at Camellion, removed the headphone and mike set from his head, handed them to the Death Merchant and said, "I've been expecting to hear from Herr Henshaw for the last five minutes. Look around, we should be close to the hills."

The Death Merchant didn't have to look around. For the last ten minutes he had noticed that the countryside was becoming rough and uneven, the trees more scattered. The hills ahead, while definitely not a part of the *Kitzbühler Alpen*, those high, snow-capped Alps that meandered across part of southern Germany into Austria, were of the same rock strati of which the mountains, far to the south, were formed. Only 150 feet high at the tallest point, the mini-range didn't even have a name.

Camellion put on the headphone and activated the mike.

"Harlan, did some German 'Jolly Green Giant' move those hills?"

Henshaw's scratchy voice floated through the headphone, "I was only seconds away from calling you. Ralph is pulling off to the side right now."

"How far to the south are the hills?"

"I'd say about four-point-eight-two-eight-kilometers, or three miles if you don't understand metrics."

The Death Merchant smiled slightly. Not only did Henshaw have a sense of humor, but he had to be a damned good case officer. His had a typical CIA mentality—a dislike for any person who didn't have a lily white skin, wasn't Protestant, and whose native tongue wasn't the American brand of English. But like all good Company men, he never revealed his true feelings, except when around those he felt he could trust.

"You two sit tight," Camellion said. "The others and I will be up there shortly. And listen, don't get out of the

47

car and gawk at the hills through binoculars, or you'll tip them off. As things are now, they can't be sure why we're stopping."

"If ODESSA people are up their waiting, you mean!"

Not bothering to respond to Henshaw, Camellion spoke into the mike to the other drivers. "Have you others heard the conversation between Henshaw and me?" After the chorus of affirmative answers, he said, "Pull up behind the Datsun and park thirty meters apart. Stay in the vehicles until you see me and the others heading for the hills. Then get out and take refuge by the side of the road. Koerner, as soon as we're parked, pick up West, then come down the line and get me. Reply, please."

"Ya, I heard you Herr Camellion," Koerner replied in rapid German.

"Gut genug. Aus! Out!"

The Death Merchant removed the set, returned it to Kurt Edlitz and went back to the four persons in the forward section of the Aristocrat, where Gunther Helldorf had slipped into a GSG-9 combat suit and was straping on a holstered P9S 9-mm H&K auto pistol. He and Duselbeck and the two women glanced at Camellion in anticipation.

Duselbeck rubbed the center of his upper lip with the tip of a finger. "Well?"

"We'll be stopping in a moment," Camellion said. "The hills are only four kilometers away." Already dressed in green fatigues, he went to the aluminum Jensen case sitting on the floor by the chrome-framed aluminum chair in which he had been sitting.

"Five men are not enough." Duselbeck sounded determined. "I should go along and so should two or three others."

The Death Merchant, who had picked up the case and was opening it, paused and turned to Duselbeck. "Who would protect the caravan if all the men who go up into the hills get killed? No dice, chum. Five is enough."

Stubbing out her cigarette-sized cigar, Karen Weiss cocked her head to one side and studied the Death Merchant with curious eyes. "Going to search out the enemy does not seem to worry you?"

Worried? Why should I be? Today is not my time with Death. But you would not know that.

"No point in worrying about it," Camellion said. He slipped into the pair of shoulder holsters, each of which

48

contained a big custom model 200/International auto-mag pistol. "Going up there is like having cancer. Either you'll be cured or you'll die. Either we'll come back or we won't."

"I think that's a rather weird comparison," Marga von Roesch said. "People don't deliberately seek cancer."

"Let's say there are two ways to meet a difficulty: either we can alter the difficulty or we can alter ourselves to meet it," Camellion said. "In this case we've got to alter ourselves, and that means going into those hills."

He steadied himself as Edlitz brought the trailer to a stop and picked up the cartridge belt, with its pouches full of spare AMP magazines. Seven feet away, Helldorf was taking two Heckler & Koch 33A2 automatic rifles and two Gussett bags of clips for the 33A2s. Helldorf and Camellion, wearing camouflaged berets, were set to go by the time Vallie West opened the outside door of the Aristocrat and stepped inside the motorhome, a Demro Tac-1 American carbine resting from his right shoulder by means of a leather sling-strap.

The big man grinned. "You guys ready to go out and get shot at?"

The Death Merchant and Gunther Helldorf picked up their HK automatic rifles.

Artur Laskertitz, the German driver of the Audi, the last car in the line of ten vehicles, passed the Datsun and continued southward. Camellion, in the back with West, thought of the previous night. In his mind he had felt that there was a fifty/fifty chance that ODESSA would try a sneak attack. Accordingly, he had set up two TOBIAS (Terrestrial Oscillation Battlefield Intruder Alarm System.) systems in the town square where they had parked (much against the wishes of the *Bürgermeister* of Altotting. The Mayor stopped his protests when Franz Heinz Ritter shoved a BND identity card under his nose.

Developed by the Marconi Elliott Mobile Division, a TOBIAS system made use of passive geophones to give warning of the movement of men and vehicles and was specially effective for perimeter protection.

But nothing had happened. The only "intruders" had been a few of the curious townspeople. As they say in novels, the night had been "uneventful."

Sitting in the rear of the Audi with Camellion, Vallie

West said, "If they're up there, we should be able to flush them out with the AV launcher. It will send a grenade a thousand meters."

"They could be waiting at the other end of the hills, at the east end," said Gustav Koerner in German. A good-looking man in his late twenties, he had a devilish smile, the charm of a country lawyer, and always expressed himself with laconic precision. "Should they be at the east end, the grenades won't reach them. They could sit tight, wait for us, and blow us up as we got within range. We could very well be going to our own funerals."

"*Nein*, they're not at the other end," Camellion said with confidence. "My instincts tell me that they're spread out in a line, from west to east. They're not after one or two vehicles. They want to destroy all of us; and with hand portable anti-tank missiles, the job would be a snap."

"A group at each end and one in the middle," West commented. "That's how I'd do it."

"But you're not ODESSA," grunted Artur Laskertitz in high German, with a Berlin accent. "You have no way of knowing how that diabolical organization thinks."

"The hell I don't." Vallie stuck to his guns. "ODESSA is every bit as good as we are in this business, and it employs only experts."

"Well, experts don't mean anything," Laskertitz responded. "An expert is only someone who tells you something you already knew and makes it sound complicated."

"Maybe so, but I'd damn sure not want a piano player going with me up there," Camellion said. "I know what West and I can do with a firearm. I presume you and Koerner know how to shoot." He stared at the back of Laskertitz's head, thinking that the German would have been a nice looking fellow if he hadn't been as bald as an ice cube. The baldness was not natural. Laskertitz made a ritual of shaving his skull every morning.

No one spoke. Now the hills were only a mile away, their slopes only several hundred feet east of the blacktop. Would-be assassins couldn't have chosen a better position than the huge masses of granite that protruded from the earth like a twisted line of obscene boils. The slopes, covered in places with loose rock, bushes and small pine trees, were "shelled off," or exfoliated, and in places marred by open anticlinal folds. Still, the inclines were gentle gradations and, with some slight effort, one would be able to walk the hundred or so feet to the top. The summit of the connected chair of hills was covered with hundreds of boulders, some the size of a cottage, others as small as a barrel—the entire mess a veritable labyrinth of jumbled rock in which a small army could hide.

Presently Laskertitz asked, "Do you want me to park in front of the hills, say at the east end, or how do you want it done?"

At the same time, Gustav Koerner turned in the front seat and glanced from West to Camellion. "What assurance do we have that they won't open fire when they see us get out of the car?" There was more curiosity than fear in his voice. "Carrying weapons and dressed as we are, they'd have to be blind and double-stupid not to know that we intend to flush them out."

Gunther Helldorf, sitting hunched between Camellion and West, spoke up. "All of this is academic in my opinion. We're taking a very big risk. We all know it."

Laskertitz gave a slight laugh. "When we go up those slopes, we'll be—I believe that the American expression is—'sitting ducks'."

The Death Merchant was all business. "Pull off the road and park north of the slopes. From what I can see, there's more rock on the northside slant, and that means more cover. And the north side isn't very steep. We can practically walk up to the top."

Vallie West cleared his throat while checking a 9-mm Sig-Sauer auto pistol.

"Too many cigarettes, Val," Camellion joked.

"Koerner's got a point," Val said seriously. He proved he was aware of Camellion's line of reasoning by adding, "Yeah, I think they'll lie low and pretend not to be there, hoping we'll think the area is clear and then have the procession proceed. After all, knocking off the five of us would only warn the others."

Helldorf said, "They will see the launcher. If they guess how we intend to use it, we'll never reach the summit alive."

"You're a cheerful cuss, aren't you?" West growled, pulling out the second Sig-Sauer.

"But he's right," admitted Camellion. "I'm counting on their not guessing that we're going to use a spread pattern. In fact, I'm betting our lives on it."

51

"You had better be right, my American friend," Koerner said in a tight voice.

"*Achtung!*" announced Laskertitz. "I'm going to leave the road."

He slowed the car, turned the steering wheel to the left, and steered the Audi off the blacktop. The ride then became bumpy, the wheels rolling over uneven ground and small stones, the body of the vehicle rocking on its vibration-absorbing linkage couplings. Gradually, as the Audi drew closer to the northside slopes of the hills, the ride became rougher, the rocks larger and, in places, more piled.

Finally, Laskertitz stopped the car and turned off the engine.

"End of the line," he said. "Any farther and we'll damage the car."

"OK, let's get on with it," Camellion said, taking a pair of amber-colored sunglasses from his left breast pocket. "Val, you and I and Gunther will take the point. Koerner and Laskertitz will have their hands full with the launcher and the grenades."

The five men got out of the Audi: Camellion, West, and Helldorf carrying their long-guns in their hands. While they stared at the slopes only 75 feet away, Gustav Koerner and Artur Laskertitz went to the rear of the car, opened the hatchback and took two MP 5K HK submachines, two bags of spare magazines for the weapons, the launcher, and two bags of grenades from the small storage compartment. Koerner and Laskertitz shouldered the machine guns and strapped on the belted spare magazine leather containers. With Laskertitz carrying the grenade launcher and Koerner weighed down with the two bags of grenades, the two then joined the others.

Together, the five started for the slopes, West muttering with mock seriousness, "Right now I feel like a candidate for the purple chick award—with yellow belly clusters."

"What are you bumping your gums about?" Camellion tossed back. "Everybody has to be someplace in space and time. We happen to be here."

"Hippo crud!" mocked West. "There'll be pie in the sky when you die and that's another goddamn lie."

The Death Merchant adjusted his sunglasses and glanced up at the sky. "Val, did you know that the average human heart beats about one hundred-thousand times every day and that in a 72-year lifetime, it beats more than two-point-five billion times?"

"Yeah, and it takes 17 muscles to smile and 43 muscles to frown. But people frown more than they smile."

The three Germans did not comment. Privately, they felt that West and Camellion were *sehr seltsame volker*—very strange people—and now the Germans were convinced of it. All five might be stone dead in five minutes, but West and Camellion made jokes! Ach! Just as God does not play dice, one should not joke about, nor tempt, death. Worse, the two *Amerikaner* seemed to have a kind of self-immolation that made them anxious for combat.

At the beginning of the trip, Franz Ritter had privately remarked that *"Die Amerikaner sind unser Unglück."* Thinking about it now, Koerner, Helldorf, and Laskertitz were convinced that Ritter was correct in saying that "The Americans are our misfortune."

The five reached the base of the slopes and Camellion said, "Hold it. We have plenty of time." He pulled a hand-held MF602 FM/VHF 6-channel transceiver from its case on his belt, flipped the on-switch, pressed the C-4 button and held the mike end close to his mouth.

"Ritter, we're about to climb the slope and go to the top on the north side," he said in German. "You read me?"

"Ya, be careful." Ritter's voice was amazingly clear over the small transceiver. "ODESSA pigs are very tricky—as if you didn't know."

"Ja, wir werden." The Death Merchant turned off the transceiver, shoved it back into its case, and glanced at the circle of faces. The three West Germans looked anxious. Vallie appeared amused.

"Let's do it," Camellion said.

The five men began to climb the rough slope, a climb that was really only a lopsided walk, the difficulty not so much because of the slant but because of the unevenness of the hillside. In many places the five had to avoid grooves that were slippery and cuts that were three and four feet deep. They had to be careful of very loose rock and move around boulders—some half the size of the Datsun—perched precariously.

It took only fifteen minutes to reach the top of the hill which was shaped, more or less like a long mound. Rapidly they moved to the side of a large boulder of granite and looked around. Three miles to the north, the nine vehicles of the expedition resembled toys parked to one side of a wide black ribbon.

"A nice view," West said in an indolent manner.

All around them was the Bavarian countryside, the neat farmland laid out in squares, the farmhouses—models of Teutonic efficiency. A hot breeze whipped at the faces of Camellion and the other men. The burning star of the planet was one enemy they would never be able to whip.

They turned and looked south. A thousand feet ahead was the largest hill, it too covered with boulders and criss-crossed with cuts and other irregularities of terrain. Directly ahead, for several hundred feet, were boulders of various sizes and small stones of unstratified drift, some rounded, others subangular, their shape showing that the wear they had suffered had been affected by planing and bruising, rather than by rolling.

"How far do we move inward?" Gunther Helldorf looked at Camellion for the answer. The launcher was over his left shoulder. A cigarette dangled from the left side of his mouth.

Gunther Helldorf glanced from Helldorf to the Death Merchant.

"I'd say 45 meters, wouldn't you?"

Camellion shook his head in disagreement. "No, I wouldn't. If there's a group of ODESSA dirt bags toward this end, we don't want to bump into them. I'd say we move inward 19 meters, then start lobbing grenades."

"Yeah, sixty-five feet is about right," concurred West, lighting a Kent III cigarette. "Let's go and do it."

They moved south, Camellion, West, and Helldorf, in a line out front, eight ft. apart from each other, their eyes watching every rock and boulder ahead. Behind them came Koerner and Laskertitz with the launcher and the grenades.

At length, they came to three boulders set in a row, with the length of the last hunk of granite reversed, in that its ends were east and west. Smaller than the other two, this third boulder was only five ft. high.

"This is good enough," said the Death Merchant. "Go to work, Artur. Fire from behind the smaller boulder. Spread out six, each one three meters apart, and each one three meters behind its predecessor."

"How far from here do you want the first one?" Laskertitz asked.

"Start with 30 meters, then work back at an angle. Like I said, each one three meters apart and three meters back."

While Camellion, West, and Helldorf took positions at the end of boulders, Artur Laskertitz and Gustav Koerber, from behind the low boulder, prepared the Avery AV grenade launcher, Magazine-fed and semi-automatic, the weapon operated on the blow-back principle and had been initially configured to use all types of 1.5-in. riot control ammunition; however, the weapon had been modified to fire 4 O-mm grenades, so that now it was actually a battlefield launcher.

Laskertitz loaded the weapon with launch shells, then held the launcher at low level. Expertly, Koerner dropped eight 4O-mm "splinter" grenades into the binlike magazine protruding sideways from the middle top of the weapon.

Laskertitz adjusted the stock, put the weapon to his shoulder, measured the distance, lifted the barrel, measured the distance again, lifted the end of the launcher, and pulled the trigger.

BANG! Whoosh! And the first 4 O-mm grenade was on its way. It arced across the area and, landing behind a large boulder 27 meters (90 ft.) to the south, exploded with a roar that sounded like a German 88.

Vallie West chuckled. "Well, that's an eight ball in the side pocket," he quipped.

"Yeah, instant death in a hand basket," Camellion said.

Chapter Five

BLAMMMMM! The second 40-mm grenade exploded with a crashing roar. The grenades were not the ordinary kind. They were German GSG-9 grenades, each filled with 368 grams (or 13 ounces) of TNT. Unlike ordinary fragmentation grenades whose outer bodies are also the shrapnel, these GSG-9 grenades had 914 pieces of shrapnel contained within, and independent of, the sheet metal body, 914 tiny but jagged pieces of steel that could be flung outward with the lightning speed of a bullet.

The third grenade struck by the side of a boulder, detonated, and shattered the hot air with shrapnel, brain-crashing concussion and a blue-gray cloud of smoke. A few seconds later, while the explosion echoed back and forth across the Bavarian countryside, there was the distinct sound of small pieces of rock falling from the boulder next to which the grenade had exploded.

But the sounds that the Death Merchant wanted to hear were absent—not a single scream, not a single cry of pain.

Not even a tiny "Ouch!" Camellion could not help but wonder: *Is it possible that ODESSA isn't up here? No! I couldn't be that wrong.*

The fourth grenade exploded 36 meters (120 ft.) from the three boulders—and ten feet behind, and ten feet to the right of, the third explosion. This time there were several shrieks of intense pain, and lesser cries of fear and alarm.

The Death Merchant smiled slightly. So did West, who switched off the safety of the H&K sub-gun in his hands. Sweat dripping from his face, Gunter Helldorf muttered *"ODESSA Schweine, Schäume. . . ."*

Artur Laskertitz, who had also heard the howls of pain, worked as efficiently as a computer. He didn't send the fifty 40-mm grenade three meters back and to the right. Instead, he placed it and the one that followed in the same general area from which the screams had come. But the

56

fifth and the sixth explosions did not bring any cries and screams.

Gustav Koerner was dropping more grenades into the bin-magazine of the AV launcher when Camellion left the right end of the middle boulder and rushed over to him and Laskertitz.

"I want you to spread the next six in a line parallel to where the last two exploded," he told the two Germans. "Shoot off each one ten seconds apart."

"Why?" demanded Koerner, his eyes narrowing.

"West and I are going to move inward 22 meters," Camellion explained. "We know for sure that the enemy is up here. They'll stay put as long as the grenades are going off."

"What about Gunther?" Koerner asked, inhaling deeply.

"I'm leaving him here as an extra gun."

"And only you and the other *Amerikaner* will go forward?" Laskertitz's tone sounded suspicious. "And what do we do after we lay down the next six?"

"You wait until I or West contact you on the radio—and don't fire the first of the six until I give you the signal."

"Just you and West!" Laskertitz was insistent.

"*Richtig!* West and I have done this sort of things many times—and remember, don't fire the first grenade until I give you the signal."

Camellion turned and hurried over to West. In a low voice he explained the situation. West's only response was, "Helldorf's an unknown quality. I don't want any jerky turkey around me."

Val's combat suit, like the fatigues of Camellion and the three other men, was already soaked with sweat, the patches of wetness darker than the surrounding still-dry cloth.

"Yes, I know," agreed Camellion. He then walked over to Gunther Helldorf who was thirty feet to the left, at the left end of the east side boulder, and told the BND agent that "West and I are going to move ahead. You stay here and act as fire power for Artur and Gustav in case the O-men break through."

Helldorf did not argue. "*Ja, ich verstehe.*"

The Death Merchant returned to Vallie West. "Ready?"

"Sure, ever since we came to Krautland several weeks ago," West said. "Let's do it."

The Death Merchant turned and looked at Koerner and Laskertitz, both of whom were watching him, and nodded. Laskertitz immediately measured the distance, lifted the AV launcher, tilted the barrel, and pulled the trigger. *Whoosh!* Three seconds later the first grenade of this new batch of six exploded.

Camellion and West left the side of the granite boulder and crept forward, moving rapidly, moving with speed because both were experts in the Ninja and in the American Indian art of being able to move and breathe without being heard.

It was because they were experts that they didn't want Helldorf along, for to stalk properly requires countless hours of practice; otherwise any movements will be jerky and uncoordinated. The reason is that most people walk long-legged with their knees semi-locked. In this manner, when they walk, their heels hit the ground first, with the weight of the body timed with the foot touching the ground. This sets up a vibration that can be heard for yards.

Richard Camellion and Vallie West moved ahead by bending their knees and walking in a slight crouch, absorbing all vibrations by touching the ground with the balls of their feet, only then lowering their heels. Never did they shift the body weight to the advancing leg, nor did they allow body weight to go forward when they put down the advancing foot. By using this method, they internalized their locomotion and would be able to come to an abrupt stop, with the advancing foot only several inches from the ground; yet they would not lose their balance.

Another vital factor was correct breathing. West was better than most; Camellion was an expert. Most men slept seven to eight hours a night. The Death Merchant was fully rested with four. He spent an additional three hours doing Yoga breathing exercises, often indulging in Out-of-body-experiences.

The man not used to killing at close quarters has a tendency to hyperventilate because of fright and excitement; and excessive, rapid breathing does not a combat expert make. Intense emotions make the breathing shallow. Camellion and West controlled this automatic response by breathing into the lower diaphragm with quiet, smooth inhalations. From long practice, they held for three seconds, then exhaled with the same smooth cadance; and always they breathed slow and regularly and constantly from the abdominal region. To insure a high oxygen supply, they timed the breathing with the pace of their movements. They breathed in on the first two steps and out on the third.

Camellion and West had two other instincts going for them—both were natural born killers; both were master survivors.

Only eight ft. apart, Richard and Vallie crept swiftly in a southern direction. Due to the intervening rocks, there were those times when they were closer to each other, or farther apart than eight feet.

In front of them the 40-mm grenades roared off, each explosion tossing steel-slivered shrapnel and rock rubble to the hot winds. The explosion of fifth grenade brought a single high-pitched scream that was soon lost within the echo of the savage blast. The shriek had been to the left of Camellion and West, 21 meters (70 ft.) ahead.

The Death Merchant stopped, waited until Vallie came from around the right side of the boulder, and point to the left, toward the southeast. Vallie nodded, and as the sixth and the last 40-mm grenade exploded, the two moved in a low "cat-spring" crouch toward the area from which the scream had come.

Now that they were so close to the enemy, it was vital that they not make the slightest sound—almost an impossibility because of the loose ground rock, much of it piled and similar to shale. Now, too, hearing was of prime importance.

Experts use a "clock position" to determine sound. A sound at 9 o'clock is loudest to the left ear and more faint to the right. The noise will also get to the left ear first. But if the sound comes from 12.00 hours—12 o'clock—it will reach both ears at the same time and usually with the same intensity. The same applies to a sound from 6 o'clock. However, sounds from directly in front and from the rear can be confused. Sounds from the back might be fainter than noise from the front. The only answer to this dilemma is instinct and experience. And more experience.

Out of necessity, West and Camellion were forced to slow down. They had to because of the time required to cross a small area thick with layered "leaf" rock. Each time each man put down a foot, he had to be extremely careful. He had to be positive that the rock would not snap under his weight. One loud *pop* could and would warn the enemy. From the south there was not the slightest sound, except for the moan of the hot wind and an occasional piece of rock sliding from a boulder whose surface rock had been weakened by one of the exploding grenades.

Camellion and West were both relieved once they had crossed the area of loose, layered rock and were approaching two very large boulders. The one to their right was as big as the largest of the two motor homes. It sat there defiantly, a tremendous chunk of granite three meters high. The boulder to the left was just as tall at its right end, but its top sloped so that its left end almost touched the ground. Between the two boulders was a ten-foot space.

Their H&K and TAC-1 carbine ready to fire, Camellion and West entered the natural passageway which was almost 15 ft. long, the width of the top of each boulder. Since the last scream had come from the southeast and not too far ahead, the Death Merchant moved to the right end of the boulder to the east, motioning for West to get behind him. Should Vallie have been at the left end of the other boulder, he could not have crept to its forward end corner without being seen—provided someone was watching.

Camellion moved up the passage, came to the edge of the boulder and looked the edge. To the left was an open area, open in the sense that it was free of large boulders. The biggest rock wasn't any larger than a football.

Three bodies lay spread grotesquely on the rocks, two of the corpses on their backs, the third face down, all three as broken and as bloody as mannequins slugged with sledge hammers and splattered with red paint. Their clothes— shirts, slacks, and wide-brimmed hats (no longer on their heads)—were tattered and ripped.

There was a fourth man. His clothes were in fairly good condition, except for his right side which was a mass of blood. He was crawling on his hands and knees, moving to West and Camellion's right, his left leg dragging.

"What do you see?" hissed West.

"Take a look." Camellion stepped back so that Vallie could take his place at the corner of the boulder. All the while, the Death Merchant kept a sharp eye on the area directly ahead of him and West, watching the tops of the larger boulders and the sides of the smaller ones. Behind the boulders, farther to the south, were tall rocks that, leaning sideways, could only be classed as pinnacles, their sharp points poking at the hot sky.

West, now at the corner, was elated. "Hot dog damn! One of the grenades must have landed almost in their laps. We'll finish off the other dirt bag when we cross." He inhaled sharply. Ahead and to the left, two men stepped out from the side of a boulder. Both wore dark glasses, walking shorts, were naked to the waist and so suntanned that their skin was walnut-colored. Each carried a Vz61 Skorpion machine pistol.

"We have company," Val whispered. "Two of them, armed with Skorpions. Hold it! Three more have stepped out. All five are headed for the goof on the ground."

Standing behind West and several feet to Vallie's right, Camellion—even as West spoke—saw two more men step out from the side of a boulder that was straight across from where he and Val were standing. In that split-down-the-middle moment, the two ODESSA gunmen looked north and spotted West in the shadow. It was not their first look at death; it was their last.

Camellion and West opened fire. Vallie sent fourteen 45-caliber ACP slugs from the TAC-1 carbine, the full metal jacketed projectiles stinging the enemy agents like the tip of a bullwhip. Three men died within a second. The other two had only the space of several eye-blinks to realize they were being turned into dead men. Shock then slammed shut their consciousness and they toppled to the ground.

The 5.56-mm projectiles fired by the Death Merchant cut into the chests of the two men straight across from him. Killed instantly, the men slammed against one of the boulders, then slid slowly to the ground, leaving long blood smears on the granite.

"Those seven must have been the group at this end," Vallie said. "Damn it, we had to fire, but now the other two groups have been warned."

"So what else is new?" Camellion said in a steady voice.

"Yeah, but what's our next move?"

"All we can do is sit tight and wait."

"I don't like it. The group in the middle and at the south end knows what's going on. The shots warned them."

Vallie was only half right. The loud chatter of the HK and the carbine had indeed warned the two other groups of ODESSA gunmen. He was half wrong in that the middle and the south groups were no longer in their proper places.

Much earlier, Reinhard Geissler, the leader of the ODESSA contingent, had seen the Audi leave the road and had guessed the Death Merchant's intention. Geissler had been with the south end group, not far from the four helicopters. He had immediately contacted the middle and the north end groups by radio and had told them to sit tight. Help was on the way.

Geissler and his group had linked up with the men in the center of the hills. Both groups had then moved north. They had been only 13 meters south of the seven men—all that remained of the north end group—when Camellion and West had terminated them.

No fool, Geissler knew that the enemy was in front of him and his men, and only a short distance away. Accordingly, he sent some of the men to his right, toward the east. They would circle around while he and the rest of the ODESSA force distracted the enemy from the south.

Camellion and West knew they were in trouble when they spotted three heads looking around boulders, then quickly darting back out of sight. Neither the Death Merchant nor West bothered to waste precious ammo or time by firing at targets that couldn't be seen, that no longer were there. Instead, both men moved back and shoved fresh magazines into their weapons. West then took a position at the northwest corner of the smaller boulder. Camellion, moving behind the boulder, crept to a position where the slope of the top was only inches above his head.

A blast of Skorpion machine pistol fire cut into the passageway between the two boulders, the scores of 7.65-mm projectiles striking the west end of the boulder shielding West and Camellion. The air became alive with screaming ricochets as projectiles struck the granite, then either zinged off into space or else struck the east end of the larger of the two boulders. Some of the flat-nosed, hard-core lead struck so close to West that several sharp chips of rock stabbed him in the right cheek, so that he was forced to withdraw completely behind the boulder, all the while cursing in half a dozen different languages. He dropped to one knee, quickly thrust the barrel of the carbine around the corner and began pulling the trigger, firing off five rounds to prevent the enemy from making a charge.

"Here they come!" Camellion yelled, his voice low and

calm. "It's going to be like Saturday night in a Turkish

The two ODESSA groups charged together. The gun-
restaurant."

men who had circled around raced in from the east, firing
short bursts from Skorpion machine pistols and other automatic weapons. At the same time the group to the south
raced zig-zag fashion across the area, their Skorpions and
Schmeisser MP40 submachine guns firing at such a steady
rate that West didn't dare try to thrust the T-1 carbine into
the passageway and get off more shots. But he was ready,
waiting for the lag-time he knew must come.

The Death Merchant was in an equally dangerous position. Projectiles from the east-end ODESSA group cut into
the top northern edge of the boulder, the screaming, ri-
cocheting slugs generating a cloud of dust and chips that
rained down on the Death Merchant as he crept three feet
to the east. He didn't need a sky-writer to tell him that the
O-agents had neatly trapped him and Val in a pincers, not
that he and West hadn't really anticipated such a maneu-
ver. Yet they had to do what must be done and were doing
it, gambling that they were better than the enemy.

And I don't intend to let them get away with it!

Lag-time overcame the O-gunmen coming in from the
south and West, now standing, jumped out and fired a
long, sweeping burst. A micro-moment later, lag-time fell
over the group pouring toward the boulder from the east.
For only a second the firing stopped, and a second was all
that the Death Merchant needed. He reared up and, with
the HK A-R on full automatic, raised the weapon, pulled
the trigger and moved the automatic rifle from side to side,
hosing down the attacking men with streams of hot 5.56-
mm projectiles. Slug-stabbed in their chests and stomachs,
four men were swept into eternity by the long blast, one
giving out a short howl of agony as a three-bullet impact
knocked him back, spun him around, and sent him crashing to the ground.

As Camellion fired and saw his slugs hitting targets, he
noted that three other agents were already on the boulder,
almost to the middle of the top that sloped toward the east.
Within seconds they would fire down on Vallie . . . *and
on me! Damn this clumsy rifle. In close, it's only good as a
club.*

Men with less experience might have panicked, or else
they might have tried to kill the four gunmen with the HK

automatic rifle. The Death Merchant knew better. He dropped the rifle, pulled the twin M-200 International Auto Mags from their special shoulder holsters, switched off the safety catches and jumped to the left as one of the men on the boulder triggered off a long burst from a Heckler and Koch 53KL sub-machine gun.

The Death Merchant's ducking to the left saved his life. The stream of full-metal-jacketed 9-mm projectiles sizzled by him to the right, two almost leaving burn marks on the deltoid muscle or outer side of his right arm.

Evald Halm, the poor slob who had fired the HK 53KL chatter box, paused in confusion for a mini-moment, not sure whether he had hit Camellion. As Paul Strik-Strikfeldt swung toward Camellion and started to shift his 9-mm Walther sub-gun, Halm decided that every single one of his slugs had missed the fierce-eyed man below. By then it was too late for both Halm and Strik-Strikfeldt.

The Death Merchant jumped back and to the left, raised both AMPs and pulled both triggers simultaneously, the huge stainless steel weapons booming like midget cannons.

"OH, UHhhhhhhhh!" A Lee Jurras 137-grain .357 magnum bullet, travelling at 2150 feet-per-second, bored all the way through Halm's stomach, blew apart the 11th dorsal vertebra of his spine and shot out through his back into the wild blue yonder.

The .357 bullet from the right AMP went upward and struck Paul Strik-Strikfeldt in the chest, the pure lead core of the projectile "flowing" on impact, the mushrooming slug cutting through the Austrian's body and leaving behind a gory tunnel the size of a new-born baby's fist.

Knocked off their feet by the Super Vel jacketed soft-point slugs, the corpses of Halm and Strik-Strikfeldt were sagging when the Death Merchant swung the long barrels of the AMPs toward the last gunmen on the boulder, a pudgy puke-face who, dressed in blue jeans, brown shirt and boots, was down on his knees, at the edge, about to aim his Skorpion M-P down at West.

Vallie's earlier long, sweeping blast had killed three of the group charging from the south. The only ones who had remained behind were Reinhard Geissler and Fredrich Hohehorst, both of whom were actually "junior" members of ODESSA, their fathers having been SS officers in the *Das Reich* division of the *Waffen SS*; and both knew that the Audi could hold six persons at maximum. But they had

64

heard only two weapons firing. Where were the other four men? Geissler and Hohehorst were bosses. Why should they take chances? Let the hired help do the fighting.

Hans Lippolz's fighting days were over, and so was his life. One of the "hired help," Lippolz had not quite swung the sights of his machine pistol to West when Camellion muttered "Eight ball in the side pocket" and pulled the triggers of both Auto Mags.

Instant annihilation! One .357 JSP bullet bored into Lippolz's right hip. The slug shattered the illium (or hip bone) and, going upward at a sharp angle through his colon and stomach and part of his liver, shattered the 12th rib on the left side and rocketed out of his body. But it was the second projectile that killed him quicker than ten-year-old news. Splat! The bullet struck him in the right temple. Skull, brain and blood exploded outward in one big cloudy mess.

The Death Merchant grinned. *It beats practicing on coconuts!*

Camellion's killing of Hans Lippolz saved Vallie's life in more ways than one. The double dynamite impact of the two .357 AMP slugs knocked the headless corpse of Lippolz off the edge of the boulder into the passageway between the two huge chunks of granite. To West's good fortune, the dead body of Lippolz fell on Julius George Dempke and Johann Scheubner and sent both men falling and cursing to the ground. A third man, Rudolf Eichorn, tripped over one of Dempke's leg, and he, too, lost his balance and fell, his left hand releasing its hold on the forearm of the HK MP5 A3 submachine gun.

During those brief moments, West had put aside his Demro Tac-1 carbine and drawn his two SIG auto-pistols. Now, as the Death Merchant darted toward the passage way to lend a hand, West heard the commotion and knew this was his opportunity to take advantage of Lippolz's confusion. Vallie didn't know exactly what had happened, and so he had no way of knowing during that millisecond that other O-gunmen were racing around the corpse of Lippolz and the other men who had fallen, were on their feet and all primed to kill.

Vallie wasn't killed on the spot for several reasons. Not only was he much faster than the ODESSA goons, but even a rank beginner could handle auto-loaders faster than machine pistols, which were actually small submachine guns.

The two SIG automatics exploded, Peter Wallenberger and Wilhelm Katz taking the first two slugs. Katz bought the "Big Forever Sleep" in the lower chest. Wallenberger yelled and dropped his Skorpion when Val's 9-mm hollow point pinned him in the gut and gave him the last belly-ache of his life. A third 9-mm bullet, from the SIG in Vallie's left hand, bored into the right side of Rudolf Ei-chorn who was stumbling to his feet. A loud "Ohhhhh!" jumped from his mouth as he twisted slightly and fell on his face.

But Oscar Svaboda and Karl Redlich, the two assassins behind Katz and Wallenberger, were experienced street fighters and proved it by their quick thinking. During those passing moments, they couldn't fire at West because the falling Katz and Wallenberger were between them and the big Company man. Svaboda and Redlich knew from expe-rience that by the time they tried to duck around the two doomed men, West would get off shots at them. Svaboda and Redlich did the only thing possible: while Katz and Wallenberger were sagging, the Czech and the Austrian pushed the two unconscious men at West, who tried to dodge the dead weight of the two bodies but was not suc-cessful. One of Katz's shoulders struck him in the chest. Wallenberger fell sideways against his stomach, groin, and upper legs. Vallie, staggering back slightly, his left arm pinned by the sagging and dying Wallenberger, attempted to raise the right SIG automatic and fire at Svaboda.

While Redlich did his best to get around Katz and Wal-lenberger and stitch Vallie's left side with half a dozen rounds of Skorpion slugs, Svaboda suddenly found himself in serious trouble. Because of Katz, sagging against West, Svaboda couldn't fire. Very quickly, he released his left hand from the machine pistol, edged sideways and franti-cally grabbed Vallie's right wrist, twisting with all his might. The Czech was a very powerful man and his grip was as tough as two-inch armor plate. West soon found the SIG twisted from his hand.

Karl Redlich might have succeeded in exterminating Vallie West, except for one little thing—a chunk of .357 Auto Mag lead that the Death Merchant flung at him. The JSP projectile mushroomed in the German's left side above his belt, and knocked him sideways to the rear of a sweating, snarling Svaboda, who now was pressing a knee into Katz's back in an effort to keep West's left arm pinned with Katz's body.

By now, the Death Merchant was at the north end of the passageway between the two granite monoliths, as furious as a burned grizzly dancing on cactus. Richard's left Auto Mag boomed and Victor Liebknecht, about to aim down on him with a Foote submachine gun, was smashed against the east end of the larger boulder. The big .357 magnum slug has stabbed him in the right side and had blown away his ribs, lungs, and heart.

Time was against the Death Merchant. ODESSA agents were all around him, so close than none fired, fearing they might hit each other. Two grabbed his wrists to disarm him. A third, only four feet in front of Camellion, started to swing the barrel of his H&K SMG toward Richard's stomach.

Better to lose the AMPs for now than get a gutfull of slugs!

Camellion relaxed his arms, permitted a surprised Max Hindemith and Adolf Aufricht to force him to drop the AMPs, and came up with his left leg in a powerful front-snap kick, knowing that if he missed . . . *I'll be a cold cut!*

His aim, however, was perfect. The tip of his short boot crashed against the underside of Bauer's HK 53 SMG, ripped the weapon from the man's hands and sent it flying upward. Camellion didn't give the astonished Paul Bauer a chance to recover. His next front-snap kick grabbed Bauer in the groin, the smash of such power that it fractured the would-be-killer's *mons pubis* bone. Bauer let out a howl of agony that sounded like the wail of a lost soul falling into hell, the long cry unnerving the barrel-shaped Aufricht and the ugly Hindemith who had a face that would have frightened Godzilla.

"*Kiai!*" The Death Merchant's bloodcurdling karate scream decreased their confidence even more and, for a hint of a moment, made the two krauts relax their hold somewhat on Camellion's wrist. But they still hung on, except Adolf Aufricht, who jerked his right hand from Camellion's wrist, doubled it into a fist, and tried a stright-in jab at the side of Camellion's neck.

Lightning quick, the Death Merchant ducked the blow, jerked his right arm free of Aufricht's left hand and—while

Hindemith tried desperately to twist his left hand with both hands—slammed a terrific *sun* punch to Aufricht's chin, staggering the man. His hand moving so fast it couldn't be seen, Camellion followed through with a *Teisho* strike, the heel of his right hand crashing into Aufricht's nose and flattening it to the thickness of thick tissue paper. Aufricht was *kaput*. With blood spurting from his nose and his face possessed of a crucifixion agony, he wobbled back, making *Uh Uh Uh* sounds.

Oscar Svaboda was also making noises, but of rage and frustration. Although he still held onto the Skorpion machine pistol with one hand and still imprisoned Vallie West's right wrist with his left hand, he could not fire the chatter box because the body of the now dead Katz was between him and the Company man. Afraid of the SIG in Vallie's left hand, Svaboda pressed against the small of Katz's back, keeping Val's arm pinned. Similarly, West, keenly aware of the machine pistol, pressed with his left knee against the stomach of the dead Katz. Val's biggest concern was that, sooner or later, Svaboda would realize that he could fire through the corpse and that the slugs would still sting . . . *me right into the next world. If there is one!* Val also realized that even if he could bring up the SIG auto-pistol, he wouldn't be able to swing up and sight in faster than Svaboda could pull the trigger of the Skorpion machine pistol.

But, old pro that West was, he had more combat tricks than a politician has promises on the eve of an election. He let his fingers unwind from around the butt of the SIG and managed to free his index finger from against the trigger and from within the trigger guard, all the while preparing for his next move. Either it would work or it wouldn't. He relaxed his left knee against the stomach of the dead Katz and, almost simultaneously, stamped on Svaboda's left instep with the heel of his right boot. A gamble! All of it a self-wager that the agony in the gunman's foot would detour his concentration from the deadly little Skorpion.

The tactic worked beautifully. With the metatarsal bones of his foot broken, the big Czech jumped and screamed in agony, his body sagging to the left. His fingers relaxed around Vallie's right wrist, and for that split second he didn't notice that the corpse of Katz was sliding to the ground. That narrow line of time was all West needed. His left hand streaked out; his fingers clawed around the stubby barrel and the front end of the Skorpion and forced the SMG far to his left. The movement was so sudden and violent that it broke Svaboda's trigger finger as Vallie twisted the the automatic weapon from the agonized man's hand, the broken digit pulling against the trigger for a single moment. The Skorpion roared, six slugs spitting out of the barrel and shooting skyward. Fortunately for Vallie, the edge of his hand was two inches back from the muzzle.

Oscar Svaboda was also a pro. Instantly he realized how he had been tricked and shifted his full weight to his right foot. At the same time he tried to slam Val across the bridge of the nose with a right knife-hand chop, an attempted blow that Vallie easily ducked.

"Stupid!" snarled Vallie. He dropped the Skorpion, grabbed Svaboda's right wrist with his left hand, jerked on the arm, pulled Svaboda toward him and, with his left arm, went to work on the doomed man with a series of *Hiji* elbow strikes. The first left elbow smash came down like a sledge hammer on Svaboda's right shoulder. Snap went the clavicle—Svaboda yelled in pain. He gave a kind of strangled gurgle when the second *Hiji* strike broke his nose. Staggered beyond recovery, Svaboda's mind spun in black, hopeless panic. But not for long. Vallie polished him off with a "Tiger Mouth," an inside right-hand, that squeezed Svaboda's Adam's apple to the top of his trachea. Svaboda, with air rushing through his nose in a loud whistle, began to sag. Choking to death, he would be dead in 20 seconds.

Vallie didn't take time to stoop down and pick up the two SIG auto-loaders. Instead, he reached for one of his backup weapons in a Bianchi belt-slide holster on his left side, a Smith & Wesson M-15 Combat Masterpiece.

The Death Merchant turned his attention to Max Hindemith who released his left arm and soon discovered that he had a lot to learn regarding the martial arts. When he saw Camellion extend his right foot a step, Hindemith feigned a left spear-hand thrust and a right *Seiken* forefist punch. All the while he was supremely confident that his tall, blue-eyed opponent would not expect what would follow. Very swiftly—but as slow as a crippled snail to the Death Merchant—Hindemith rotated his body to an almost complete 180 degree position and attempted a left-

69

legged, reverse-hook kick, a very stupid move because such a kick lacks power and is used almost exclusively as a high kick to the face.

The Death Merchant almost smiled—*The halfwit fell for it!*

He grabbed Hindemith's left foot with both hands and twisted to his right with such force that Hindemith's leg was almost dislocated, with such force that Hindemith was thrown off balance. He fell heavily on Julius George Dempke, who was getting to his feet, a Wz63 Polish machine pistol in his right hand. Dempke again went down, this time flat on his face, Hindemith on top of him.

To the right of Dempke and Hindemith, Johann Scheubner had just stood up and was swinging an Italian Franchi submachine gun in Camellion's direction.

Camellion—at the moment he was kicking Hindemith in the side of the head—ducked to his right and his right hand reached for the weighted ice pick in its special holster strapped between his shoulder blades, a few inches of the weighted steel handle protruding a few inches above the collar of his combat fatigues. However, he never got a chance to throw the special weapon anymore than the bearded Scheubner got a chance to fire the Franchi music box.

Vallie West's snub-nosed revolver cracked twice in rapid succession. Scheuber jerked and jumped. His eyes went wide. He stared, each eyeball frozen in shock. Then his mouth went slack and he died and dropped . . . two bullet holes in his narrow chest.

There were only two other ODESSA hired guns left in the passage between the two boulders. Seeing how quickly the others had died—and killed only by two men—Werner Bauhoss and Heinrich Kopf were so terrified that naked fear, while quickening their reflexes, had seriously impaired their judgment.

With what resembled a gurgled squawk, Bauhoss turned his HK MP 5A2 submachine gun toward Vallie West.

The burly Kopf, using a VP70M machine pistol, with stock attached, decided to liquidate the Death Merchant.

Camellion and West didn't know it, but not all the men from the east group had charged the two enormous boulders. Hermann Durtizwizzer and Theodor Rohmmer were not cowards. The two bedbugs who walked like men were not only sneaky, their line of reasoning was very logical: it was better to be the mop-up squad than to be in the first line of sacrificial victims.

During the 4.17 minutes that had passed, the two skulkers had heard the firing but had not seen any of the action. They had stayed down behind a boulder. Now, on the assumption that the other ODESSA agents had the situation in hand, Rohmmer and Durtizwizzer got to their feet and started trotting toward the boulder whose top slanted from west to east.

Neither expected any serious trouble. Neither ever knew what hit them. They were halfway to the end of the boulder when an automatic rifle and a submachine gun roared from several hundred feet to the north. Each man, struck by a dozen or more projectiles, was knocked off his feet, dead the instant he started to fall.

Artur Laskertitz lowered his MP 5K submachine gun. Gunther Helldorf smiled and relaxed with his HK 33A2 automatic rifle.

"Nice shooting," said Gustav Koerner.

"Ya, but I don't think the two *Amerikaner* will thank us for killing those two swine," Helldorf said.

Camellion and West saw Bauhoss and Kopf sighting down on them. Val threw his body to the right, snap-aimed and fired the S&W Combat Masterpiece twice as Bauhoss' H&K machine gun snarled and a stream of slugs cut the air only several feet to Vallie's left.

The Death Merchant, however, had not had time to draw any of his backup sidearms, two .25 Bauer autos in ankle holsters and a .38 S&W military and police revolver in a flapped holster on his left side. Nonetheless, he was not entirely helpless. Just as Heinrich Kopf stopped moving the machine pistol, Camellion flung himself to the left, his right hand going to the handle of the icepick strapped beneath his neck.

Kopf was pulling the trigger of the machine pistol, which had been set to fire three round bursts, when Camellion's right arm snapped back then came forward and down, the icepick leaving his hand in a low trajectory. The first three bullets zipped by Camellion, missing him by a good three feet. The icepick did not miss Kopf. Camellion had aimed the giant needle so that it would make contact with Kopf's body below the VP machine pistol whose stock was against the gunman's right shoulder.

Blood trickled from the corners of Kopf's mouth. Strength fled from his arms and the machine pistol fell from the ground. Kopf doubled over; his eyes rolled to the back of his head, and he toppled forward, hit the ground and rolled over on his back. The icepick was buried up to its handle in the upper part of his stomach.

There was another crack from Vallie West's .38 revolver, and Julius George Dempke, trying to crawl out from underneath the dead Max Hindemith whose neck Camellion had broken with a *Uchi-Soku-To* kick, flopped dead on his face, a bullet hole in his forehead.

The world is full of pain and losers, and these lice have lost!

The Death Merchant—careful not to step to the north, outside the natural passageway—hurried back to where the two M-200 Auto Mags lay on the ground.

West first turned and glanced toward the south, hearing the approach of Koerner, Helldorf, and Laskertitz. Then he walked over to the Death Merchant and grinned.

"It's like the Lord said to King David, 'Go get 'em,'" Val said with a half laugh. "And David got 'em. I think it was the Moabites that Dave got. I'm damned sure it wasn't the satellites." He looked around at the corpses. "Well, there's a little less evil in the world, not much less, but a tiny bit less."

The Death Merchant, reloading the AMPS did not reply. *Damned little! Even the "nice people" are ruthless savages. Sixteen million cats and dogs will be put to death this year because nobody wants them. A hundred and eighty thousand baby seals will be clubbed to death—and many skinned while still alive—this year, simply because they have beautiful fur! To hell with the human race!*

Only a short distance to the south, Reinhard Geissler and Fredrich Hohehorst found it difficult to accept what had happened. *Mein Gott!* Everyone had been slaughtered.

"What are we going to do?" Hohehorst whispered to Geissler and ran a hand through his dark brown hair, that looked as if it had been combed with an eggbeater. "The two of us can't fire missiles at the cars below!"

Geissler, thin-lipped and cold-eyed, took off his dark glasses and wiped sweat from his face with the palm of his right hand. Almost savagely then, he turned and glared at the frightened Hohehorst.

"We're going back to the helicopters, you dumb ox. There isn't anything else we can do, and the faster we get there the better off we'll be."

"But what will Kohne say?"

"The hell with him."

The two men edged back from the boulder, got to their feet and began running in a southern direction, every now and then glancing over their shoulders.

Richard Camellion didn't bother to mention to the three Germans that they had disobeyed orders by leaving their previous position. Nor did he waste time with other trivia. Again he and West took the point, and the group of five moved south, expecting trouble at any moment.

Twenty-two minutes later they heard the rotor of the four helicopters. A fourth of a minute later, they saw the four choppers lift off—a half mile to the south.

"They're Sikorskys," Camellion said, looking up at the sky, his left hands shielding his eyes against the fierce sun. "Sikorsky S-64s."

"The same type that is used by the Austrian border police," Helldorf said ominously.

Chapter Six

True to their word, the Austrians were waiting in force three kilometers outside of Braunau, only 18 meters the Austrian side of the border. The *Staats Ordnungspolizei* had a variety of internal security vehicles. Other than the blue Porsche sedan, in which rode Oltwig Haffner, an Under Secretary of the Austrian Interior Ministry, and his two assistants, there was an armored GKN Sankey AT-105 vehicle, a Glover Land Rover escort vehicle, a Glover Thracian special support vehicle, a Shortland MK-3 armored car, an eight-ton Gonderfled troop carrier (capacity: 30 men and two drivers), and a Hotspur armored Land Rover that served as the command car of the Austrian state police column.

The formalities were held in the open, under the boiling sun, between the front of the Shortland armored car, the first vehicle of the Austrians. Present were Oltwig Haffner, his two assistants, and Franz Heinz Ritter and Artur Laskertitz who, officially, were the duel heads of the Cologne Historical Society of Cologne University. Big Jim Flikkema, representing the American divers, was also present.

Richard Camellion and Vallie West, standing beside the Aristocrat motor home, watched the proceedings with interest—first the round of handshaking, then Ritter and Flikkema submitting permits, passports, visas, and other official papers.

West lighted a Cambridge cigarette and looked around the countryside, at the well-kept fields and the tops of the taller buildings of Braunau, to the southeast. Far to the south, miles and miles to the south were the dim, snowy peaks of the *Kitzbühler Alpen*—the range of Alps that meandered across southern Germany into Austria. Farther to the south, but still a part of the Alps, were the Dead Mountains and the *Alpenfestung* region.

"So, this is Austria," West mused, "the romantic land of

castles and coffeehouses, Strauss waltzes and apple strudel."

"You'll like average Austrians," Camellion said, watching Ritter and Haffner and the other men in the official
group ahead. "They're an easygoing, gracious people, a
manner that's a reflection of their *Gemütlichkeit*—their
love of good living, their habit of regarding life as a sort of
theatrical spectacle."

"They sound like Parisians, the way you describe them."

"And just as sophisticated, at least in Vienna. Being land-
locked as they are, they're both parochial and international. It was inevitable. For centuries the Austrians lived
under the same sky roof with people of a dozen different
languages and nationalities. That's why the Austrian makes
such a wonderful host. He welcomes the foreigner because
the foreigner is foreign." Camellion suddenly laughed.
"Speaking of apple strudel, Val, you'll love Austria—the
way you like to eat. Four meals a day is the Austrian custom—breakfast, lunch, afternoon tea, and dinner; a second
breakfast of beer and sausages at ten in the morning can be
added to this. And some of the best coffee in Europe. The
Kaffeehäuser serve coffee in forty or fifty different ways, all
the way from the heavy black *Mokka* to white whipped-
cream-coated *Schlagobers*."

Vallie pushed back his camouflaged beret and fixed his
intense eyes on the group between the Datsun and the
Shortland armored car.

"Crocodile crap!" Val muttered. "I agree with Bruno
Wronkau. I don't trust the officials. The only reason we're
here is because The Company twisted the arms of the West
Germans and the krauts put some kind of pressure on the
Austrians to give permission for us to poke around inside
Lake Toplitz. I'm only wondering what kind of pressure
the krauts used. Hmmm . . . two more Austrians are
joining the group. The one joker must be the boss-man of
the column."

Camellion and West watched with interest as two men,
who had gotten out of the Hotspur armored Land Rover,
joined the group. Bareheaded, both men wore bright blue
trousers and light blue shirts with shoulder tabs of navy
blue. Red and yellow stripes ran across the top of the tabs.

Walking ramrod straight, the larger man—slightly over
six ft—had a lantern jaw, viscid fishy slits for eyes, and
gave the impression that he wore his masculinity in the

same belted holster that contained a Walther P-38 auto-pistol. Camellion sized him up as a man who would be quick to use his fists.

The smaller man, older by ten years than the larger man who was in his early thirties, moved with a quicker step. Of medium height, he was half-bald, wore sunglasses, and was smoking a stubby pipe. But he didn't look right. Camellion determined that it was the size of his chest and disturbingly wide shoulders that hinted at his being deformed.

"They look like they're arguing," West said. "I wonder if it's about the four choppers we saw or what happened on the hills back yonder?"

The Death Merchant continued to watch the knot of men. The mouth of the larger man in uniform was going at typewriter speed, and he was motioning with his hands. A slight smile slid across his lips. As soon as he and Val and the three Germans had returned to the vehicles of the Cologne expedition, a report of the intended ODESSA ambush had been sent in special code to Bonn and, in a code provided by the Austrian intelligence service, to Vienna. Included in the report had been a detailed account of the battle and how Camellion and the other four had found three one-man portable launchers and German Cobra missiles. Had the ODESSA gunmen used the Cobra missiles, all ten vehicles of the expedition would have been blown into flaming junk.

Ritter, Flikkema, and the Austrians talked another 12 minutes, after which the Austrians returned to their vehicles, and Ritter and Flikkema started back to the Aristocrat.

"Let's get out of this heat," suggested West. "This is just like Arizona or New Mexico."

The Death Merchant responded in German. "*Nein*. With this high humidity it's more like southeast Texas. You get used to it once you make up your mind that there isn't anything you can do about the heat."

He followed West into the motor home and closed the door. Several minutes passed and Franz Ritter and Big Jim Flikkema entered the motor home. They wiped perspiration from their faces and went directly to the refrigerator.

"What's the T.O.?" Camellion asked, his odd-colored blue eyes fastened to the two men.

76

"T.O.?" Ritter paused at the small door of the refrigerator, turned, and looked at Camellion.

"Table of Operation," Camellion explained.

"Wait till we get back and I'll start at the beginning."

In another minute Ritter and Flikkama were relaxing in easy chairs, cold cans of *Weissbier* in their hands, as Ritter explained that all had gone well with the Austrian delegation. Herr Oltwig Haffner had been very cooperative, stating that his government was prepared to give all the protection and assistance that the expedition would need.

"Did he mention the four choppers we reported?" Camellion, drinking carrot juice laced with *Deidesheim,* a rich German wine, leaned forward and stared intently at the muscular BND man.

"*Nein,* he did not. But Major Blotz did. He――"

"The straight-as-a-broomstick joker in uniform?" asked West.

"Ya, Major Felix Blotz. A career professional. He's in command of the *Österreichisch* armored column. The other *dumm Esel* is Captain Fedor Axmann. He's nothing more than a 'yes' man."

"What did Blotz say?" Camellion said.

"He said that he hadn't received any reports of strange helicopters in any area."

West said, "The helicopters could have flown into Germany, or by flying low, they could have slipped across flat country, zipped up and flown off somewhere in the *Kitzbühler Alpen.* Not that we'll ever know."

Ritter made a sour face, took a sip of beer and looked at the Death Merchant. "Major Blotz didn't like the idea of our being armed to the teeth with automatic weapons. He even demanded that we turn over our weapons to his troopers."

The Death Merchant frowned heavily. An angry expression fell over West's bronzed face.

A little laugh came from Big Jim Flikkama. "We told them in very polite language to go to hell. We said that before we'd give up a single bullet, we'd turn around and return to Germany, and then tell the world why."

Ritter added, "We intimated that we had to retain our weapons because we doubted the ability of the Austrians to protect us." He shrugged. "Why should they be afraid of our weapons. We are honest people." He grinned. "Or could they have something to hide and were only using the weapons as an excuse to keep us from diving?"

Forever the optimist, Alfred Duselbeck spoke up with enthusiasm: "I doubt very seriously if ODESSA will try anything else. Twice the Nazi swine have tried, and twice we've slaughtered them. They know we'll be expecting another attack and will be prepared."

"I'll smoke to that," said Jim Flikkema, who had been studying West and Camellion's face.

Camellion's expression remained grave. "To my knowledge, there isn't anything more dangerous than active ignorance," he said placidly.

"And fanatics," West said, "crackpots with an overabundance of ignorance and confidence. Hitler is a good example. ODESSA is another. Unfortunately, ODESSA is only ignorant when it comes to moral values. They have more than enough confidence and plenty of bucks. No, gentlemen, I can't see ODESSA calling it quits just because we'll be in Austria. Mark my words, they'll make another attempt; and if we become complacent we'll join the ranks of the actively ignorant."

The Death Merchant put down his glass, now empty. He was about to speak when Ritter said, "The T.O., as you call it, is for the Austrian *Ordnungspolizei* to escort us all the way to Bad Aussee and maintain a high security profile while we dive."

"I assumed that, but what's the order of procession?" the Death Merchant said. "Did Major Blotz agree to the radio contact arrangement?"

"They had better have some of that armored stuff behind us," growled Vallie West. He lighted another Cambridge from the butt of the previous cigarette he had been smoking.

"They will have," Ritter said. He paused and glanced out one of the windows as Kurt Edlitz, the driver of the motor home, got the Aristocrat under way. The armored car and the armored Land Rover will be first in line. Next will be Haffner. Then us, in line the way we are now. The four other vehicles of the order police will follow our Audi."

"Communications?" inquired the Death Merchant.

"Major Blotz again said that for his men to switch to our band was a fine idea." Ritter snickered. "It surprised the hell out of me. I expected him to disagree with anything we might suggest, going on how he raved about 'dangerous weapons.' "

One leg over the arm of a chrome-framed chair, Duselbeck said, "We'll have to watch what we say over the TRIXs. One of the Austrians could be an informer for ODESSA. With all the money that ODESSA has, they could bribe angels."

Camellion chuckled. "Christian or Jewish angels? Or isn't there a difference?"

Deep laughter rumbled from Ritter. "No difference, none at all. *Ach!* A Christian is just another kind of Jew who thinks he has a better insurance policy to get him past the Pearly Gates."

Jim Flikkema, not as much as smiling, gave his opinion—which had nothing to do with angels.

"Personally, I don't see why we should waste time by going out of our way to get to Bad Aussee. First we go east, all the way to Linz. We turn at Linz and head southwest. Why that route means another 276 kilometers." He sighed and gestured with a hand. "Sure, I know. The longer route offers less danger of an ambush; the terrain is less mountainous. But once we get 20 miles south of Linz, we'll be in high country. We know it. ODESSA knows it."

"All very true," Camellion said. "By taking the longer route, instead of cutting southeast, we eliminate about half the possibilities for an ambush. We couldn't change the route now if we wanted to. . . . The Austrians wouldn't go for it and we couldn't blame them."

The motor home slowed and began to move at a snail's pace. Through the wide window across from him, Camellion could see that they were passing the four armored vehicles of the Austrians that would make up the rear of the column.

Camellion was beginning to get impatient—*All ODESSA has to do is sneeze hard in our direction and we'll turn Austria into a cemetery!*

A distance of 276 kilometers is very short, by today's standards. But only if one is moving at a normal rate of speed, say 50 to 60 miles per hour. At no time did the 16-vehicle caravan exceed 20 miles per hour. Why? Because Major Felix Blotz didn't want any of the vehicles to ram into each other. The Shortland MK-3 Armored Car did not go beyond the 20 MPH limit. Neither did any of the other fifteen vehicles, since none of them could pull out of line.

Every six kilometers the entire column would come to a halt and the Austrian police would scan the flanks for the least sign of danger. The Shortland MK-3 armored car would move slowly ahead for several kilometers, the electronic Laske D-14 mine detector extended from the MK-3's front bumper, probing for mines.

That first day the column spent the night in Griesknechen, a large village where—at a dinner hosted by Major Blotz—the food was excellent, especially the *Backhendl* (young chicken breaded and fried in deep fat to a golden brown). Major Blotz also insisted that they all try a finely-textured sponge cake called *Guglhupf, mit Schlagobers* (whipped cream in coffee).

The column was on the road again the next morning at 09.00 hours, and by 16.00 hours was pulling into Linz, the townspeople rubbernecking. Another night and more good Austrian food.

By 15.00 hours of the next day the seventeen vehicles were 32 kilometers southwest of Linz, the line of vehicles moving upward. The column would not actually reach the lower foothills of the *Totes Gebirge*—the Dead Mountains, a part of the *Kitzbühler Alpen*—until it was a few kilometers past the tiny resort town of Temberg. Nonetheless, indications of mountain country approaching were clearly in evidence. On both sides of the road the fields were small and the landscape more irregular, rougher, much of it good for only pasture. Patches of useless, rocky ground became more and more common. Gradually, as the miles rolled slowly by, the pines and firs began to put most of their growth into wide, thick masses of ground-level branches. Higher on the trunks, the branch buds on the windward side had been sheared off, for in winter ice particles were as sharp as razors, the fierce winds from the Alps driving ice and snow with hurricane force.

In the larger motor home, the Death Merchant was not the least bit interested in the Austrian countryside. He had seen the same sights in the American West, in Canada, in parts of Europe, and in the lower Andes in South America. A tree was a tree, a mountain was a mountain—No matter where you saw it.

Other than Camellion, Ritter and Kausch, Major Felix Glotz, who had developed the habit of dividing his time between his Hotspur command rover and the two motor homes, was also in the big bus, at the moment explaining that some of the farms in the general area had been in the same family for hundreds of years.

"Those people actually living in modern Austria were very fortunate in 1918, when the Allies carved up the old Hapsburg empire to satisfy the national yearnings of the Serbs, Czechs, Italians, and other former subjects of the Hapsburgs. The people within Austria kept their homes and remained under the same government.

Relaxed in one of the easy chairs, the Death Merchant said casually, "I have never considered home a place or locale, certainly not the place where one is born. Home is where one is happy."

"The Hapsburg empire is ancient history," Ritter said with morose disinterest.

Major Blotz—heavy-boned and thick-waisted—regarded the Death Merchant with a thoughtful, steady gaze. "Where is home for you, American?"

He's on a fishing expedition. He's after information. "Home?" A hint of a smile crossed the Death Merchant's face. "Home is wherever I happen to be, Major. Right now I'm in Austria."

Blotz smiled diplomatically. "Ah, yes, I see. A man of the world." His tone was suave, and in no way did he indicate whether he might be dissatisfied with Camellion's reply.

A sly glint crept into the eyes of Gerhart Kausch who was sitting to Camellion's left. "I should think our American friends would be happier in this part of the world than in their own United States," he said with deceptive gentleness. "Most European news magazines are in agreement that American society is becoming more mongrelized. Your government lets in 150,000 Cubans and blacks from Haiti, not to mention a few hundred rice farmers from southeast Asia, all of whom breed faster than rats." He laughed harshly. "If the American government doesn't change its ridiculous policy, twenty years from now the trash on welfare will outnumber the hard-working European-Americans supporting them with their tax dollars."

Franz Ritter, on the sofa across from Camellion, chimed in happily.

"Everyone agrees that Castro made a fool out of President Carter, whose refugee policy was costly, unrealistic, a spit in the face of the American unemployed, and gave the whole world a big laugh. And if our own intelligence reports are correct, Castro intends to swamp the United States with another hundred-thousand of his scum to relieve chronically disastrous and rapidly worsening economic conditions in Cuba. Frankly we Europeans find it all very amusing. Now the North Vietnamese and Castro have fifth columns in the U.S.—all of them disguised as economic refugees."

Camellion hooked his hands on the open collar of his military safari shirt and decided to get a rise out of Cyril Purdue, who was seated to his right.

"Fudge! Castro didn't make a fool out of Carter, no sir," he said. And when he saw an expression of surprise drop over Ritter's face, he finished with, "After all, it's impossible to make a fool out of an unrealistic idiot, and any man who trusts the Soviet pig farmers is the worst kind of unrealistic idiot!"

The two West Germans and the Austrian were momentarily struck dumb by the Death Merchant's unconstrained frankness. This was not the case with Cy Purdue, the second CIA Case Officer with the expedition. A tall man, Purdue carried his 187 pounds easily and deceptively. He could move very fast, but always lightly and without sound. He had thick brown hair, graying slightly at the temples, and a small, neat mustache. The Company man would never know, but the Death Merchant had a lot of respect for him. Purdue was Ivy League, career CIA, all six-feet-one-inch of him. He could have remained safely in the American Embassy in Bonn; yet he had volunteered for this mission and had readily agreed to follow the orders and/or decisions of Camellion, a "lowly" contract agent. Camellion also respected Harlan Henshaw, another "government employee," as he referred to himself. Henshaw, too, had volunteered.

Purdue, who ordinarily said very little, now exploded with words, yet in a manner that was calm and easy, without his appearing to be a fanatic about Americanism. "As a native-born American (*And white Protestant!* Camellion mused), I take exception to your insults against our President. He is not a dictator." Turning, Purdue glared at Camellion who, with a straight face, continued to stare ahead, out the window, the one behind Ritter and Blotz, both of whom were on the sofa-bed.

"You should have mentioned that any bill the President might want can be vetoed by Congress," Purdue said to Camellion. "I suggest you put the situation in perspective and quit putting all the blame on any President."

Right on, Junior! Right on! The hell of it is that Blotz and the two krauts are right. Our transport protection system is ripped apart. Our borders are indefensible. Our weather is being tampered with by the pig farmers. We're at the mercy of the Arab blanket riders and doing nothing about our national defense. Our measuring system is all that's holding us together. Convert to total metric—which is another ripoff and the product of Washington paperpushers—and the world will swallow us alive in one gulp.

Camellion recalled a study that Courtland Grojean had told him about before the affair in Scotland[1]—*Project Blue Barometer.* This study, from a high-powered California think tank, predicted a very somber future for the inexorably declining "democratic" West. The study pointed to a "Balkanization" of the Atlantic nations and noted that one of its consequences—fiscal and monetary debauchery—may have already weakened and despoiled the wealthy and advanced nations to the point where they would not be capable of fighting, let alone winning, a major war.

Cy Purdue smiled pleasantly at Ritter and Blotz. He even leaned forward, looked past Camellion and grinned at Gerhart Kausch, who was secretly hoping that Camellion and Purdue would become involved in a verbal fist-city.

Purdue then said in rapid-fire German, "*Und mein en Herren,* I should like to remind you that it was Uncle Sam who twice saved Europe from German domination in two world wars. As you will recall, Major, even though you were to young to remember, Hitler and his gang had their heels on Austria's throat until we Americans invaded *Festung Europa.* Or would all of you have preferred to grow up under the swastika?"

Major Blotz's face retained its grave expression, but in his eyes was a peculiar sort of irony. Coolly he lighted a

---

[1]Death Merchant #39: The Fourth Reich.

cigarette and, ignoring Purdue, blew smoke toward the rounded ceiling of the motor home.

Ritter, pulling gently at his right ear lobe, said sourly, "We're not here to discuss politics. I suggest we shelve the subject of the American government and discuss the matter that has brought us all together." He turned to Major Blotz. "As I recall, Major, you were saying earlier that the so-called mystery of the Devil's Trashcan was only a myth."

"A myth perpetuated by the world press." Blotz's voice was hard. He did not look at Purdue who was secretly seething over what he considered the other men's truculence and insulting behavior.

"It's true that a score of men have died over the years, trying to find this supposed treasure, but actually very little has been found. So far, all the intrigue, plotting and snooping has been rewarded with only death in the form of fatal accidents . . . and mysterious disappearances. But real treasure?" The Austrian chuckled. "A lot of nonsense. Gentlemen, I assure you: all of us are wasting our time, and Cologne University is wasting a lot of money."

"Major Blotz, I suggest you get all your facts straight," Camellion said, his odd-colored blue eyes directed quizzically at the Austrian.

The beginning smile left Blotz's lips, and his nostrils flared slightly. "I do have my facts correct," he said tightly. "Nothing of real value has been found in Lake Toplitz."

"I wouldn't call three chests containing 19,000 gold doubloons, worth $300,000 on today's market, 'very little'," Camellion said. "Those three chests were hauled out of Toplitz in 1951—by the Austrian government."

"Oh yes, yes. . . ." Blotz nodded. "I forgot about those three chests."

Purdue spoke up, his voice sounding accusing. "It is definitely known that Kaltenbrunner brought with him to Alpenfestung land a fortune worth millions. Official records of the SS list it as $10-million in U.S. currency, five small boxes of precious stones, fifty chests, each weighing a hundred pounds, full of gold articles. He also has another million in Swiss francs, and his personal stamp collection valued at more than a million dollars."

"And let's not forget dear old Adolf Eichmann," Camellion said. "He was supposed to have buried almost $8-million worth of negotiable currency and other valuable in a slope called Blue Mountain Pasture before he left on foot over one of the mountain passes, I admit, however, that this has not been confirmed. But right after the war, the American OSS did find one case that Eichmann buried. It contained 53 pounds of pure heroin."

"I think it's a damned waste of time to even discuss it," Gerhart Kausch said . . . nonsense. And we're all forgetting Dr. Hoettl." The slight pause before the name of the SS major, who had been a close friend of Eichmann's, gave relevance to his words. Kausch went on, "Dr. Hoettl maintained to the day he died that there wasn't any treasure in Toplitz."

The Death Merchant astonished even the two West Germans by saying, "Who can believe Wilhelm Hoettl? He was a damned traitor. He swore an oath to Adolf Hitler but turned out to be working as an undercover agent for Allen Dulles' OSS. He was also a chief Allied prosecution witness during the war-crimes trials, for which he was called a 'dirty double-dealing son-of-a-bitch' by Hermann Goering. I agree with Goering."

Cy Purdue swung around and stared at Camellion. Kausch, Ritter, and Blotz were too stunned for the moment to speak. Finally, Ritter found his voice.

"Your sympathies lie in a strange direction, my friend! Whose side are you on?"

"Don't be a fool, Ritter," growled Camellion. "You know the answer. I agree with Goering only because I believe that when a man takes an oath, he should keep it. Hoettl was like a lot of the German generals who conveniently made their oaths of loyalty fit the situation. It was 'Heil Hitler' while the *Wehrmacht* was winning. It was 'Let's kill the son-of-a-bitch!' when the generals saw defeat staring them in the face. A man should keep his word— even to a maniac like Hitler."

Major Blotz cleared his throat loudly. "Naturally, everyone is entitled to his own opinion," he said equitably. "As I view the situation, what we have been discussing is irrelevant to the approaching dives. But I still maintain it's all a waste of time, manpower, and money. You won't find anything of value in Lake Toplitz. As I said, it's all tall tales generated by the media."

Franz Ritter appeared annoyed and his voice proved it. "Herr Blotz, it sounds somewhat ridiculous for you to sit there and insist so dogmatically that *Der Abfallkanne des*

Teufels is devoid of anything of value. It is fact that the Nazis dumped a lot of crates in the *Alpenfestung* region."

Blotz cleared his throat again and looked uncomfortable. Ritter went on, "In 1945, when the Americans arrived in the area, they found thousands of English five-, ten-, and twenty-pound notes floating on the River Traun. Some of the boxes dumped in the river had burst open under the battering of the current. The bills were rescued and laid out to dry. The river was dredged for more bills and a hurried call was put through to U.S. counterintelligence agents."

"Which doesn't prove anything about Lake Toplitz," Blotz said with a shrug.

"Let me continue. Twenty-three cases were recovered from the River Traun. They contained notes with a face value of eighty-million American dollars—and every single note was a perfect counterfeit. The villagers of Redl-Zipf told the Americans about other 'wonders' that could be found in the *Alpenfestung*. They spoke of deep caves built by starving men and women driven with whips. Some of the villagers even told about hundreds of cases that were dumped into the Devil's Trashcan."

"It was in one of the caves that General Patton's XII Corps found the greatest art collection ever assembled on earth," Camellion said. The cave was about twenty kilometers southwest of Alt Aussee. There were rare and priceless books, antiques of all kinds, furniture and tapestries, fantastic assemblies of marble statues, Renaissance armor, rare musical instruments, plus 5,348 paintings by the old masters—the whole lot stolen from museums all over Europe." Camellion's laugh was low and sinister. "Hitler, the biggest con artist and art thief who ever existed, had stolen all this for the museum he intended to build in Linz, after the war."

"I was not aware of that cave." Major Blotz's lips barely moved. His eyes remained pinned on the Death Merchant.

"Der Führer had determined that if he couldn't have these art objects, no one else would have them either. One large crate marked *Marmor Nicht Stürzen*[2] was crammed with high explosives and kept at the entrance of the cave and triggered to blow up the works if anyone discovered

[2]"Marble—do not touch!"

the covered-up entrance. For some reason or another, the device failed to go off."

Cyril Purdue glanced over at Ritter. "I'm interested in the funny-money found floating on the River Traun. Wasn't that counterfeit money part of a Nazi scheme to wreck the value of the British pound?"

Ritter finished lighting an Eagle cigarette, inhaled deeply and blinked rapidly at Purdue.

"It's simple enough. Since the villagers of Redl-Zipf kept telling the Americans about all the cases in Lake Toplitz, the Americans went straight to that damned lake. One diver went down, caught his lifeline in a tree branch and drowned. The other diver who went down with him surfaced and reported the monstrous false bottom of logs and water-claimed tree trunks." Ritter reached down and flicked ash from his cigarette into an ashtray on the floor of the motor home. "But the Americans were determined. They used explosives to blast holes through the floor of wood. But the holes closed up almost as fast as they were made, and no diver was going to risk getting caught under that platform of trees. The Americans gave up the search.

"As for counterfeit money, this was Operation Bernhard, by which the Nazis hoped to undermine the currencies of both England and the United States by having special agents distribute the money all over the world. They hoped all this would hasten the defeat of the Allies. Actually about three hundred-million-dollars worth of counterfeit pound-notes were put into circulation. *Ach!* The bills were so good that for years, not even experts at the Bank of England could tell them from the genuine article."

"I take it the Nazis didn't produce any American money," Purdue said, "or else didn't get a chance to circulate any of it."

"No one ever found out, as far as I know," Ritter said. "It is known that the bills were first produced at Sachsenhausen concentration camp. Then the SS, in charge of the operation, moved the printing plant to the concentration camp at Ebensee, Austria, about 36 kilometers from Lake Toplitz. When the situation became grave and the SS realized the war was lost, they dismantled the plant and ordered everything hidden. Some of the crates were dumped into the River Traun, but during the night of . . . I forget the date. I only remember that it was a night in April of

1945. During the night a convoy of trucks drove the remaining type, printing presses, banknotes, plates, engraving tools and other equipment to the Devil's Trashcan and dumped the entire works into the lake."

Major Blotz looked puzzled. He leaned back, recrossed his legs, and hooked a thumb over his belt buckle, on which was an embossed silver Austrian eagle. "But, is there any concrete proof that the SS dumped the printing plant into the lake?" he asked, frowning.

"At this point, I think we should mention Herr Wolfgang Loehde." The Death Merchant slowly moved his right hand over his forehead and, in one closet of his mind, wondered if the two foreign contract agents in Bad Aussee had learned anything of value.

Cy Purdue turned and eyeballed Camellion. "Loehde! The name rings a big bell. Wasn't he an editor of the big West German magazine *Stern*?"

Stupid! Don't you do your homework? Of course not! You were holed up in the Embassy in Bonn, behind the East European Nations Desk, reading and filing reports before you asked to go out into the field.

"Ya, he was," Kausch said. "He——"

"Loehde was the only man ever to get permission from my government to search Lake Toplitz," cut in Blotz quickly. "I remember that he did find some steel cases. I also recall that it was Loehde who wrote a long article in *Stern* explaining why we Austrians waited so long to search the lake, because of the technical difficulties and the tremendous cost. Keep in mind, gentlemen, we're a small nation with a small budget."

Ritter said, "Loehde began his search of Toplitz in the summer of . . . it was either 1958 or 1959. I forget which. I do know that it was during the summer. You have all noticed how the temperature has declined steadily with each few kilometers. By the time we get to the Trashcan, the temperature will be in the upper sixties or lower seventies—perfect for working. But at night, the temperature can drop to the fifties.

"Getting back to Herr Loehde, he brought frogmen, salvage experts and engineers with him. Patiently and systematically they combed the lake. They located the much-rumored cases and hauled up eight of them. They were crammed full of expertly forged five-pound notes, around $35-million worth. Loehde had proven his story."

"Franz, don't forget the ninth case," Kausch said, his tone sounding as though he might be chastising Ritter. "This ninth case was filled not with counterfeit money but with papers and documents of various kinds. There were even diaries of various SS officers. Just why the SS would want to preserve this incriminating evidence is a mystery to me."

The Death Merchant's memory—he had almost total re-call—clicked all six trillion circuits. "The ninth case was marked B-9," he said. "According to Albrecht Gaiswink-ler, the B-9 case was part of a shipment his brother saw dumped into Toplitz on May 3rd, 1945."

"What happened next?" asked Purdue. "I mean, did Loehde find anything else."

Ritter glanced at Major Blotz, then captured Purdue with his gaze.

"*Nein,* nothing else. Very suddenly, Henri Nannen, *Stern*'s publisher, called off the search—'effective immedi-ately.' Need I tell you what happened next? As you might imagine, rumors began flying all over the place, to the ef-fect that Nannen had either been bribed or forced to quit by powerful forces who wanted the secret of Toplitz to re-main hidden forever."

Gerhart Kausch jumped in. "But Loehde said it was all a lot of bunk. He said that the reason the search was called off was that *Stern* was being scooped by other publications about the lake."

Again, Purdue revealed his ignorance by saying, "Rub-bish! How the hell could the other papers and magazines scoop *Stern* when Loehde was right there at the lake?"

Damn it! Something is wrong! Purdue can't be that stu-pid!

Kausch leaned forward, and looked past Camellion at Purdue. "Herr Purdue, *Stern* is a weekly publication. Every-time the *Stern* people hauled up a case, a mob of report-ers and photographers on the bank would race off with the story. But *Stern,* as a weekly, had to wait a week before publishing the results of its own find. As Loehde wrote la-ter, why spend more money and then get scooped out of the story? The *Stern* people packed up and went home. And that was the end of it, except for a man getting mur-dered now and then in the vicinity of Toplitz.

Camellion's laugh was low and faintly amusing. "Like Karl Bruckhardt!"

"Oh yes, that one!" Ritter said, rubbing the tip of his nose. His eyes narrowed to mere slits. "You have a re- remarkably good memory, Herr Camellion. The official report said that he had been drinking with his buddies!"

"Hold on, damn it!" Purdue spoke in a loud, irritated voice. "Who the hell is—or was—Karl Bruckhardt?"

The Death Merchant felt like grabbing Purdue's Adam's apple with a *Koko* "tiger's mouth" hold, one of the deadli- est in the *Go ju-Ryu* school of karate. This jerk can't be for real. Or maybe you have to wind him up to get intelligent answers? Oh no! That's it. He's putting on an act. *He had damn well better be, or by the time I'm finished with him he'll feel like a walnut without its insides!*

Ritter said very patiently to Purdue. "Karl Bruckhardt was one of the 'hard-hat' divers who was with the Austrian government search. Bruckhardt complained bitterly about the search, insisting to the press that a lot more of the stainless steel cases could have been brought to the surface if the Austrian salvage people had used the proper equip- ment. Bruckhardt said that all that was needed was a heav- ier winch and a stronger cable. But, according to Bruck- hardt, the Austrian government refused to furnish a bigger winch and cable." Ritter turned his head slightly and glanced at a tight-lipped Major Blotz. "The search was called off and Bruckhardt returned to his native Vienna. Two weeks later he was found murdered in an alley—shot three times with a nine millimeter job."

Major Blotz straightened up and shook his big head from side to side. "A drunk! Bruckhardt was an alcoholic," he said vehemently, an expression of distaste twisting his features. "Not only was he an alcoholic, but he was a big mouth know-it-all who made a lot of assumtions and then went around telling it to the press as fact. It was, and is, people like Bruckhardt who have caused all the ridiculous rumors about Lake Toplitz . . . the same kind of halfwits who generated the story about the SS wiring a cave en- trance to explode . . . who believe in 'alien beings' and flying saucers."

The Death Merchant watched Blotz somewhat in the same manner that a biochemist would study a newly dis- covered virus under an electron microscope. The man was neither a fool nor an actor. In his own blundering way, he was merely trying to save his country from embarrassment.

What would Major Blotz say—What would all of them

say—if they knew that Vietnam was the result of a plan to prove to the Soviet Union that we could be just as savage as they were and are? What reply would they make if they knew how certain renegade American officers had wired a certain mine in France?[3]

Flying saucers! Definitely. Truth, simple truth, is very often a hundred times more strange than the wildest fiction! Who would believe the story about the Sandorians[4]? First the public must be conditioned to such mind-boggling facts. The first step is to condition the millions, over a period of years, with visual and auditory behavioral modification programs. You use the mass media to plant the tiny seeds that will grow into the flowers of acceptance. Step two: Assessment. Is the public ready? Yes? Very gradually, you release the news that *we are not alone.* You talk about a "non-human" base discovered on the moon. Something else is found on Mars. Leak to the press that . . . possibly . . . some UFOs are alien spacecraft. All the while there are the motion pictures about "encounters" and "crashed flying discs."

Or suppose they knew who really killed John F. Kennedy?

And what would be their comments if I told them that Josep Broz Tito—Marshal Tito—had been murdered by the Russians in 1942 and replaced by a Czarist officer named Wladimir Lebedev, a Tito look-alike?

He was suddenly aware that Ritter was studying him in an odd manner and that Kausch was saying to Major Blotz, "Herr Major, you're wrong about Karl Bruckhardt. He didn't drink."

"You must be mistaken!" Blotz said stiffly, drawing himself erect on the sofa. "Police records show that he was arrested numerous times for drunken brawls."

Kausch did not press the issue. Ritter said offhandedly to Camellion, in a voice that was gently probing, "I thought for a moment you had left us. You were here, but your thoughts were not."

Camellion shrugged elaborately. "I was thinking of the recent advance in genetics. I was wondering if geneticists could cross a French chef with a pigmy, would they get a short-order cook?"

[3]Death Merchant #42: *HIGH COMMAND MURDER*
[4]Death Merchant #30: *THE SHAMBHALA STRIKE*

Before any of the men could laugh or comment in any way, Michel Tirpitz's voice came loud and clear through the disguised speaker in the ceiling of the motor home, "Herr Major Blotz, Hauptmann Axmann is calling you from your command vehicle. He said it is extremely urgent."

Without a word, Major Blotz got up from the sofa-bed and hurried to the driving compartment.

Ritter locked eyes with the Death Merchant.

"Now what?" said Purdue to no one in particular.

Gerhart Kausch muttered in German, "Wouldn't it be ironic if these Austrian *Staats Ordunungspolizei* turned out to be agents of ODESSA?"

"I doubt if anyone of us would die laughing," Camellion said.

Chapter Seven

Try as they might, Richard Camellion and the three other men could not hear what Major Blotz said over the mike to Captain Axmann. The Austrian major talked too low. Camellion and the others knew his secretive manner had to be force of habit, since Tirpitz could hear every word he said, and so could the men sitting next to the drivers of the other vehicles.

In a few minutes the heavy blue drapes parted, Blotz left the driver's compartment, walked back quickly to the sofa-bed and sat down next to Ritter, his worried expression like a mask. Briefly he glanced at Ritter, then at the other interested faces in front of him.

"As you know, that was Captain Axmann on the radio," Blotz said matter-of-factly. "As I told you, I have men stationed all over Bad Aussee. Some are in uniform; others are in civilian clothes. Some are even disguised as tourists."

"Major, please get to the point." Gerhart Kausch was not as patient as Camellion and the other men.

"Two men—they were supposed to be tourists from England—registered at the *Schloss Hofen*, a castle-hotel in Bad Aussee. When one of the housemen was taking their bags up the stairs, the handle of a suitcase came off. The case fell down the steps, came open and a dissembled machine pistol fell out. It was an American Ingram. Even Austrians must have permits to own firearms. Machine pistols are never permitted under any circumstances. You gentlemen are the exception."

The Death Merchant spoke in German. "*Herr Major* what happened to the two *Englishchvolk*?"

"The houseman raced to the manager. The manager called two uniformed *Staats Ordnunspolizei* stationed in the lobby. In the meanwhile the two men ran down the steps and tried to escape through the rear of the hotel. The two policemen caught up with them as they were going out the door. There was a gun battle. One ODESSA terrorist was killed. The other is seriously wounded and has not regained consciouness. One of the *Polizist* was killed. The other was shot in the leg. The bone is broken, but he is not in any danger.

"When did this happen?" Camellion asked gently.

From Ritter came, "ODESSA terrorist you said. Is there proof?"

The granite-visaged police major frowned deeply, but his tone was mild. "Not quite half an hour ago." He turned and glared at Ritter. "ODESSA—ya. Who else would bring machine *Pistoles* into Bad Aussee? There was another American Ingram in the suitcase of the other gunmen. Each man carried a 9-mm Heckler & Koch *Pistole* on his person."

"It doesn't surprise me, and the shoot-out shouldn't surprise any of you." Cy Purdue stretched out his legs and slumped deeper into the chair. "ODESSA is not going to give up without a fight. Logically none of it makes sense— ODESSA's going to all that risk and trouble to prove a point."

"Ya, Herr Purdue, I agree." Kausch nodded his head vigorously. "ODESSA planners are very clever and cautious. Once we are at the lake, how can they possibly hope to stop us. Why we're practically a small army!"

"There will be three times as many *Polizei* guarding you at the lake," Major Blotz said quickly. "Every man will be armed with an automatic weapon, have plenty of ammunitions and will even have a gas mask."

"What names were on their passports? If——"

"Double-ditto to passports," Camellion snapped, his voice having a deep, unworldly timbre. "Anyone with a buck can obtain a forged passport and a visa. What did we learn in Ottobrunn from Pieck and Gunche? Nothing of value. They were only scum hired to pull triggers, hired by another bedbug who was supposed to be Swiss and whose name was Steinitz. Bunk!"

"You're right," Ritter agreed. "What bothers me is why ODESSA should go to all this trouble. The only possible answer is that there is something of tremendous importance in the lake, something we are not supposed to find."

The Death Merchant's lips spread in a welcoming smile. "ODESSA can't bring whatever it is to the surface, and they can't have us doing it. I have a gut feeling that it's something that was dumped in the lake by mistake."

"We'll know in a matter of days, *meinen Herren*," Major Blotz said thoughtfully. "We'll reach Bad Aussee by tomorrow afternoon. We will spend the night in Bad Ischl. Herr Haffner and his people from the Interior Ministry will leave us once we reach Bad Ischl."

As the long line of vehicles crawled up the road, each kilometer taking them higher, the temperature continued to drop and the terrain became more mountainous. Lunch was an hour-and-a-half stop at the village of Temberg whose buildings were pure Middle Ages.

The seventeen vehicles moved out of Temberg where two Austrian helicopters had been waiting—Sikorsky S-64s. The two chopper gunships, armed with rockets and electric machine guns, would monitor the high rocks on either side of the road. Later, the two helicopters would patrol the Dead Mountains in the vicinity around Lake Toplitz while the divers were submerged.

After lunch, Camellion and Cy Purdue had gone to the Datsun to ride with Ralph Duckworth and Harlan Henshaw. But even as the vehicles had gotten under way, the Death Merchant had jumped Purdue about his "utter ignorance about the Toplitz Project."

"Zip your mouth for a moment," Purdue had growled. The CIA Case Officer had then proceeded to rattle off facts and figures about Lake Toplitz, some of which had surprised Camellion. For example, Albrecht Gaiswinkler had worked for the OSS, then later for the newly formed U.S. Central Intelligence Agency.

Camellion congratulated himself. Purdue had been putting on an act, or as he, himself, had explained it—"Ritter and his BND boys think that you and West are the Company on this expedition. Let them. If they want to suspect me of being a C-Nick, let them think I'm a dumb Company man. I don't mind. Do you?"

No, Camellion did not. . . .

They passed a large forest fourteen kilometers south of Temberg, a sunshot cathedral of calm ignoring man and his little stupidities. All around was a raw and wild cragginess. New-mown pastures were gone and so was the oppressive heat.

Bad Ischl . . . where the Emperor Franz Josef, the last Hapsburg monarch of the Austrian-Hungarian Empire, had spent his summers. He had died in 1916, after a reign of 68 years, leaving his domain in the midst of the trauma and famine of World War I. The Austro-Hungarian Empire fell to pieces two years after him. In old Austria the population had been 52 million. In the Austria of 1981, the population was not quite 8 million.

Like a wagon train of America's Old West, the vehicles formed a square only half a kilometer south of the village. The night of the full moon passed without incident. There was only the quietness of the mind and the soft whispering of the wind through the trees.

With the Shortland MK-3 armored car moving out first, the expeditionary force left the next morning at 09.00 hours. Richard Camellion and Vallie West rode in the back seat of the Datsun, with Duckworth who was driving, and Henshaw who was acting as radio man.

"The barometer was four points lower this morning, Duckworth remarked, carefully watching the rear of the armored Land Rover, "and did you notice the line of dark clouds to the northwest?"

"Huh! All we need is a nice thunderstorm," Henshaw said, "although I suppose a short one wouldn't hurt anything."

In spite of his English ancestry, Harlan Henshaw, with his swarthy complexion, was often mistaken for a Sicilian or a Turk, and sometimes even a Syrian. Gangling and painfully tall, he usually walked with a stooped posture which made most people think he was older than his 34 years. His carrot-colored hair, worn medium length, was always carefully combed, and his short beard gave him a mild air of distinction. According to Grojean, Henshaw was a first-rate analyst. According to the Death Merchant, "a first-rate analyst" was a pain in the rear end.

Wearing the narrow headband with a single headphone and mike attachment, Henshaw shifted his body around, put his left arm across the top of the front seat and looked at West and Camellion. Before he could speak, the Death Merchant said, "Did you check this car for hidden transmitters before and pulled out, and are you positive your mike is off?"

"Yes to both questions. I'm positive to the nth degree."

Henshaw made no effort to conceal his annoyance. "We'll be in Bad Aussee shortly. I'd like to know when and how we make contact with 'Whip' and 'Bloodstone,' the two FCAs? And I don't mind telling you that both Purdue and I resent your being the only one who knows how contact is to be made. But I suppose Operations has its reasons."

Operations doesn't trust paper-pushers, that's why! "Let's get something clear right now, Henshaw. I don't give a damn what you resent. To me—"

"—And me!" inserted West.

"—you and the others are necessary trigger-fingers, nothing more. And don't ask me the names of 'Whip' and 'Bloodstone'. I don't know who they are. If I did, I wouldn't tell you."

"I don't give a damn if they're Little Orphan Annie and Alley Oop. I only want to know how they'll contact us."

The Death Merchant put a Procaine IH3 vitamin pill in his mouth and washed it down with a sip of peppermint tea poured into a cup from a stainless-steel thermos. West, smoking a Cambridge cigarette, continued to stare at Henshaw, making the CIA officer feel uncomfortable. Nor did West and Camellion fail to notice that, every now and then, Duckworth's eyes would dart to the rearview mirrow, as if he expected the men in the back seat to blow off the back of his head.

"Whip and Bloodstone will know when we arrive in Bad Aussee," Camellion said. "We're like Barnum and Bailey. Everyone in Bad Aussee will know it when we hit town. Whip and Bloodstone will contact us at twenty hundred hours this evening. We'll pick them up on the Transvertex in the van."

"Who knows? Maybe they'll have something of value for us." Henshaw turned around to face the front, then attempted to joke about the mission. "Anyhow, I have every reason to believe that we'll succeed and get back home to our wives and kids."

The Death Merchant finished drinking the rest of the peppermint tea in the cup. Vallie West said dryly, "By God, you're as much of an optimist as Helldorf. Such an attitude can get your head lopped off. You'll end up saying, like Marie Antoinette, 'Operator, I've been cut off!' "

Henshaw, who had lighted a cigarette, took a nervous puff and bristled, an expression of resentment flashing over his face. "That's a hell of a statement to make. If I didn't

97

have the hope of coming out of this alive, I wouldn't be here. Maybe you two have some kind of death wish, but I don't. I don't think the rest of us have one either."

"You're not getting my drift," West said evenly, adjusting his sunglasses. "The difference between me and Camellion and the rest of you is that if we buy the big one, we won't be disappointed." The mocking tone vanished from Vallie's voice, and he became very serious. "Frankly, if I were married and had children, I wouldn't be in this business."

"A wedding is really a funeral where you get to smell your own flowers," drawled Camellion. He then proceeded to screw the cup onto the thermos. "I tried marriage once. I almost had a nervous breakdown from boredom."

"At least you're serving your government," Duckworth said stiffly. From the tone of his voice, he might as well have said: *At least you two bums and killer-happy hoods are doing something useful.*

A wiry but well-muscled individual, Duckworth had a lot of curly black hair, had a prominent forehead, dark brown eyes that were always suspicious and a narrow mouth with deeply etched lines on either side of it. Highly educated, he could read Kant in the original German and Voltaire in the original French. His only trouble was that he confused education with intelligence.

Camellion yawned, gave Duckworth and Henshaw a pathetic look, and placed the thermos in a leather Tripmaster tote.

Vallie West's deep laughter filled the car, his large frame shaking with mirth. Duckworth's unsteady gaze shot to the rearview mirror. Henshaw, startled, started to turn around, then changed his mind.

"We're serving ourselves," Vallie calmed down long enough to say. "Those witless policy makers in the State Department haven't the sense God gives to a Mongolian idiot. Can you imagine serving a government that had a flibbertigibbet like Jimmy Carter for President. He's the midget-minded moron who said that Andy Young '*is our national treasure!*" You gentlemen remember Andrew Young, don't you? He's that wonderful humanitarian who said that one day the Ayatollah will be considered a *saint!* That's rich—serving our government!"

The Death Merchant said in a cold and condemning voice, "Apparently the two of you don't keep track of history very well, or don't you realize that for the last thirty years there has been a continuous erosion of American power? And it's due to constant concessions to and defeats by the communists. Washington even goes out of its way to make sure the Reds make fools of us."

"Bunk. That's a lot of garbage!" Although quick with a rebuttal, Henshaw sounded unsure of himself.

"No, it's not, and you know it," Camellion said easily. "Only you don't like to admit it to yourself. I could give you fifty examples. I'll give you only one: the Kama River truck factory built in the Soviet Union in 1980. Two U.S. financial institutions put up 90 percent of the $2-billion loan needed to construct the plant—the Chase Manhattan Bank and the Export-Import Bank."

"But," started Henshaw.

"Shut up and let me finish. That $2-billion was guaranteed by the United States Government. Well, my fine Company friend, should the pig farmers in Mother Russia decide not to pay back the loans, the *American taxpayer* will pay off *their* debts!

"There's more. The Kama plant has the world's largest industrial computer system, thanks to U.S. technology. The plant can produce almost 250,000 vehicles yearly, everything from scout cars to tanks and troop carriers—all due to idiots in Washington, D.C.!"

Both Henshaw and Duckworth jumped to the defense of the American government, the angry words rolling out of their mouths.

"Washington knows what's going on!" snapped Henshaw. "The Soviets have a lot of hardware, but they don't have the finely-tuned technology. Well, damn it, we do!

"Our professionalism is better!" Duckworth almost shouted. "The American military is——"

"Shut up, Duckworth," Camellion said, his voice gentle, almost lilting. "Your ignorance is matched only by your belief in myths. Major wars are always fought by amateurs. It's the professionals who do the planning but very seldom the dying. The millions of soldiers in World War II weren't professionals. Neither were the GIs in Korea or Vietnam. They were butchers and bakers, farm boys and mechanics, clerks and factory workers—all amateurs, all cannon fodder."

Vallie West laughed again, this time a light laugh. "Hell, you guys will be telling us next that governments learn from the examples of history. People learn, but governments never do. By the time the men and women in government see their mistakes, it's too late and they're out of office. A new crop of dimwits takes over and the same mistakes are repeated. It was weakness and gutlessness that brought on World War II. We've got less spine today, which explains why World War III is just around the corner in a few more years."

"With the Soviets!" Henshaw said.

"With the Soviets," West said firmly.

"And the pigs will lose," Camellion said. "The U.S. and Red China will band together and turn the Soviet Union into a wasteland of death and destruction."

Henshaw and Duckworth, looking pained, paused to reflect, pure instinct telling each man that Camellion and West had him out-gunned with facts and figures. Henshaw made the best choice: he would remain silent. Duckworth wanted to know. The only way to find out was to ask.

"I'll say one thing for you two, you're honest about it," he said whole heartedly. "Does contract work pay all that well?"

"It does when you're as experienced as West and I," the Death Merchant said, toying with Henshaw and Duckworth. Duckworth was an agent of I.N.R., the U.S. State Department's Bureau of Intelligence & Research. Company men refer to other American intelligence agencies as "The people across the street." In contrast, other U.S. agencies refer to the CIA as the "Pickle Factory." Why "Pickle Factory"? No one seems to know.

"You see, we're experts at what the human race does best—killing!"

"It's more than the money with us," Vallie said, lightning quick to pick up on what the Death Merchant was doing. "With us, violence and killing is like smoking. Once you get the habit, it's almost impossible to break."

"This war you spoke about," Duckworth said. "Why all the concern, if we Americans and the Chinese are going to annihilate the Soviets?"

"I didn't tell you the rest of the sad tale," Camellion said. "After the Russians are destroyed, the Red Chinese will sweep across Asia into Europe. With that will come the total destruction of the United States—a full-scale nuclear war. History will sweep the world clean and the survivors will begin all over again. It's all part of a cycle. It has happened before. It will happen again."

Just to be on the safe side, Henshaw and Duckworth snickered slightly, each man trying to decide whether Camellion was sincere or subtly trying to make fools of them. With an odd-ball like Camellion, how could you tell?

In spite of his realism and talent for accepting facts, Vallie West felt chills creep and slither up and down his spine. He was positive that the Death Merchant was serious. Worse, Camellion had a track record of being right.

After a long pause, Henshaw said brusquely, "Since the Russians are already in Afghanistan, I suppose you're going to tell us that the war has already started?"

"No. The real beginning will come when the Soviet Union moves either into Iran or Turkey. The Bear wants the Mediterranean more than the Indian Ocean. India is too populous and too close to China. Should the Soviets move into India, such a move would be a tactical blunder. If the Soviets don't move into Iran but strike against Turkey, then probably, at the same time that the pig farmers move west, the Iraqis will move east into Iran. There'll be plenty of excitement for all of us."

West's mouth formed a tight satisfied grin. "Yeah, you bet. It's going to be worse than even the heartbreak of psoriasis. . . ."

Chapter Eight

Bad Aussee: Located in central Austria, in the Traun Valley.

The resort town (resident population: 6,240) is the former center of the Salzkammerhof salt region. Salt mining is still important. The Kursthalle salt mine, still in operation, is only 4.1 kilometers east of the town. Bad Aussee also has two fourteenth and fifteenth Century churches and is well known as a health resort—brine baths—and a holiday center, skiing in winter, mountain climbing in summer. No one, however, ever went near Lake Toplitz. The sinister reputation of the Devil's Trashcan made sure visitors stayed away.

Due to the numerous security stops the caravan of vehicles did not reach Bad Aussee until 11.52 hours. Uniformed *Staats Ordnungspolizei* were as thick as starving ants at a picnic. The townspeople and the tourists were even thicker, the entire procedure resembling a parade with everyone in the area lined up at the curbs to watch the vehicles pass by, their mood laughing and boisterous.

"I feel like I'm standing naked at a convention of nuns," growled Vallie West, watching the people on the sidewalk. "I just wonder how many of those waving at us are secretly working for ODESSA?"

Two more vehicles joined the procession: another Gonderfled troop carrier and another Thracian special-support vehicle—as Major Blotz informed everyone on the TRIX communications system.

"We are being escorted to our base camp by Captain Alois Kalls and Lieutenant Bernard Webbler of the state order police," announced Blotz from his command car. "As all of you know, we'll establish our base of operations three kilometers southwest of Bad Aussee."

Harlan Henshaw said, "Gentlemen, I suppose one can say we've arrived. . . ."

"Not quite," said the Death Merchant, "not until we're actually at Toplitz."

"See the photographers on the sidewalk," Henshaw said. "We're going to be in every paper in the world."

"No need to worry," Camellion said. "They can't get a clear picture of our faces through the tinted glass of the car."

The base site was a somewhat rocky pasture, four kilometers south of Bad Aussee, that offered a scenographic view of the gloomy *Totes Gebirge*. At a distance, they looked like any other mountain range, but when one studied them through binoculars one could see that they weren't so much forlorn as they were rugged. One could almost feel their silent deadliness and sinister treachery.

The Dead Mountains were not noted for their height—the tallest peak was only 8744 feet (2665.1712 meters)—but for their extreme ruggedness. It is because of the scraggliness of the Dead Mountains that climbers, amateur and professional alike, come to practice and perfect techniques on the highly dangerous slopes and bluffs, on giant ledges and overhangs that appear to be poised more on hope than on any solid foundation.

The vehicles parked in the form of a cross, the horizontal line intersecting the exact center of the perpendicular line. Half the vehicles parked horizontally faced the north, the other half the south. Half the vehicles parked perpendicularly faced the east, the other half the west. To the southwest of the cross, the order police set up five large tents and a generator for electricity. One tent was a field kitchen; the other four would house the 150 police who would make sure that reporters and curious townspeople and tourists would not pass the barrier eight miles (12.872 km) to the northwest. Beyond the black and yellow X-frame fence was the road that concentration camp slaves had widened, the rocky road that led to the Devil's Trashcan.

Security was checked and double-checked, not only by Major Blotz, Captain Axmann, and Captain Kalls, but also by Vallie West, Cy Purdue, Gerhart Kausch, and Gunther Helldorf, the latter four wanting to be positive that every possible direction was under a gun. Attack from above? The two Sikorskys were overhead, flying back and forth over the Dead Mountains.

103

In addition, the Austrians had brought up three Mobile Surveillance System vehicles. Each Land Rover was fitted with a TV-surveillance JA-1 700 series low light level camera which was attached to a motorized pan and tilt unit on top of a three-meter motor driven hydraulic mast. The three cameras continuously scanned the mountains, Bad Aussee a short distance away, the surrounding pasture and lower foothills.

14.00 hours. The West German divers and the American divers, and their tenders, or top men, held a meeting in one of the tents, one in which camp cots had not yet been set up. Also in attendance were Camellion and Franz Ritter, Major Blotz and Captain Axmann.

Bruno Wronkau tapped a topography chart of Lake Toplitz. The rectangular chart was spread out on a large folding-type aluminum table, the four sides weighted down by various items to prevent the large fans placed around the tent from blowing the chart from the table.

"Gentlemen, there it is," Wronkau said, "the Devil's Trashcan, all 600,000 square yards of it." He glanced speculatively at Big Jim Flikkema who was standing across the table from him. The other men, gathered around the table, glanced from Wronkau to Flikkema, who was wiping his face with a red and blue bandana. The temperature was only 72 degrees and the fans were blowing at full force; yet tension was making everyone perspire.

"Let me see the inventory of the equipment first," Flikkema said to Wronkau. "That was in your department, Bruno. I was still in the United States when you assembled the equipment."

"Ya, I have it." Wronkau reached down, picked up a small attache case, opened it, took out several sheet of paper and handed them to Flikkema.

The giant of a man looked at the sheets. The inventory was neatly typed in English. Everything was listed very efficiently.

I. Needs—to locate the treasure:
  A. Four small (approximately 20') boats with outboards.
  B. Personnel and equipment for each boat:
    1. 3 men : operator, sonar, magnetometer.
    2. Bottom-scanning sonar with recorder.

3. *Towable magnetimeter with recorder.*
4. *8 radios—MF603/673, CRS type.*
5. *Marker buoys with radar and sonar targets and dye.*

C. *Checkout teams as below:*
  1. *3 divers, all qualified for Scuba, hard hat, and mixed gas.*
  2. *A tender for each diver.*
  3. *A divemaster.*
  4. *Complete Scuba gear.*
  5. *Deep-dive gears*
      A. *Heated suits—plain rubber.*
      B. *Three helmets with phones and lights.*
      C. *Deep submergence-lockout bell/chamber.*
      D. *24 tanks each of helium, oxygen and baralyme.*
  6. *Deck decompression/recompression chamber.*
  7. *Diving physician—specialist in hyperbaric medicine.*
  8. *Main expedition boat.*

II. *Needs—to recover any object and/or objects from lake:*
  A. *Lift bags.*
  B. *Lift bags, extra.*
  C. *Surface winch.*
  D. *Surface air supply, Scuba back up (pony bottle).*
  E. *Tie off tanks with stopwatch and tables.*
  F. *Ascent/descent lines (10).*

"Very good," Flikkema said. He gave a pleased Bruno Wronkau a brief glance and turned to page two: It read:

Scuba gear

I. *Six Masks:*
  A. *Low volume.*
  B. *Velcro strap for easy adjustment.*
II. *Fins.*
  A. *Sized for power.*
III. *Snorkel (for safety). Quantity: 10.*
IV. *Wet suits (9); Dry suits (electrically heated)—(9).*
  A. *Cold water hoods, gloves, hard-sole booties.*
V. *Weight belts (10)*
  A. *Approximately 1 pound of lead per 10 pounds of body weight.*

VI. Buoyancy compensator:
  A. 50 pound lift capacity.
VII. 9 diving watches; 9 spares.
VIII. 9 Depth gages:
  A. Capillary and oil-filled (four of each type).
IX. Compass:
  A. With side port for "compass lock" position.
X. Knives (10) Heavy and strong for cutting, prying, hammering, etc.
XI. Regulator (9)
  A. Double stage (single hose type) with:
    1. Submersible pressure gage.
    2. B.C.—low pressure hose.
    3. Octopus second stage.
XII. Tanks: (22, including spares):
  A. Twin 80's—80 cubic feet of air of 3000 psi/aluminum alloy.
  B. Cryogenic Scuba.
  C. 25 Pony bottles—supply each: 5 minutes of air at 60 feet.
XIII. Lights:
  A. 20, including spares: 100,000 candlepower.
  B. Narrow beam.

A satisfied look on his face, Flikkema handed the sheets of paper to the Death Merchant who was standing next to him, then smiled in appreciation at Bruno Wronkau. "A good job, Bruno, very good. I do have some questions, first of all, who's going to act as Divemaster, and,"—he looked at the grim German faces around the table—"which one of you is a doctor? None of our people are."

"I'm the *Doktor*, Herr Flikkema." Josef Messner, the man who spoke was across the table to Big Jim's right. He was a portly individual with a double chin and long sideburns. "I am attached to the German Navy. My speciality is hyperbaric medicine."

Wronkau went on, "As for the dredge, I included it on the list for technical reasons. We both know there isn't any dredge. Even if we could get one up to Toplitz, the lake is not suited for the use of a dredge. Why the operation alone would take many months. "As for the Divemaster"—Tweetie Bird shrugged his bony shoulders—"who would you suggest?"

"Him—Burton Waller." Flikkema jerked a thumb toward a bull of a man who was to his right, a man who had his short sleeves rolled up half an inch to reveal powerful biceps. Gray haired, he was in his early forties and had a sun- and wind-whipped look about him.

"United States Navy," Flikkema said. "A twenty-year man, retired for four. Tell them, Burt."

"I was both a diver and a tender," Waller said, his voice naturally gruff. "I've dived all over the world, and I've worked in places a lot more dangerous than Lake Toplitz."

Bruno Wronkau nodded slowly. "I see. Ya, you are an expert, Herr Waller. But may I point out that Herr Zarkes"—with a turn of his head he indicated a tall, but stooped man who was in his middle sixties—"has almost thirty years of experience. He began his career with the Nazi submarine service in World War II and continued to work in deep-dive salvage until he was 46 years old. After that, he worked as a diving supervisor."

Flikkema thought for a moment. It was plain that Wronkau was of the opinion that his man, having more experience, should have the job. But Richard Camellion's orders had been explicit. An American had to be included.

"I think I have the solution. We'll have two Divemasters," Big Jim said, "provided it's all right with you and with them."

"Why not? They'll both have to work as tenders anyhow." Wronkau looked from Fredrick Zarkes to Burton Waller. Both men nodded. Only Waller, however, smiled slightly.

"I have a question," Camellion said. He handed the papers to Flikkema who returned them to Wronkau. "While I've done some diving, I'm not an authority like you men. Correct me if I'm mistaken, but isn't the cryogenic[1] gas concept still in the experimental stage and considered dangerous?"

"I was about to mention that same point," Flikkema agreed, his expression questioning, as he fixed his eyes on Bruno Wronkau. "I won't use a cryogenic tank, nor will I permit any of my divers to use one."

"Both of you are correct," admitted Wronkau. "I only included them on the list because they will give us 12 times as much air as the twin 80s. We can use the other tanks if you want." As the German master diver was speaking, he

[1]Refers to gas stored at extremely low temperature.

kept watching Gene Slack and Herbert Paggett. The two American divers were leaning over the table studying the relief map of Lake Toplitz and reading the various notations printed in both English and high German. The expression on the faces of the two men was a clear signal that they were not happy about something.

"Spill it," cracked Flikkema, who had also noticed the storm clouds on the faces of the two men. "What's your beef."

The stocky Paggett, very fair skinned for an outdoorsmen, stared hard at Big Jim. "We're using the wrong methods for the right objective," he complained. He swept a hand toward the map dotted with numerous red Xs. Each red X marked a tangle of logs. "Look at all those logs and other debris. Using scuba gear in that mess would be suicidal!"

"Where's the diving platform and the hoist for the bell?" demanded Gene Slack, a sandy-haired man in his late twenties. Where's the infrared TV cameras? We going at this backassward!"

Franz Ritter and Big Jim Flikkema turned and gazed at Richard Camellion. "It's time we tell them," Ritter said harshly.

The Death Merchant turned and looked at the two American divers.

"There is a diving platform," he said casually, "and it has a crane that will lower the diving bell. We Americans brought three television cameras with us. As for scuba gear, I myself——"

"You mean there's a platform already?"

Camellion held up a hand and silenced Herbie Paggett. "I mean that for the past week, West German and Austrian engineers have been assembling the platform—and I agree with you about SCUBAS in the lake."

"Well why in hell weren't we told before now," grumbled Paggett. "I know, I know—'for reasons of security.' But even if we use the hard helmet suits, what do we do about the logs and mud? After all these years, there must be twice as many logs. The mud must be ten feet deep."

"Don't forget cross currents," said Slack. Wearing only walking shorts and low-top boots, he was a very hairy man, his muscular legs as mat-covered as his chest.

"There aren't anymore logs now than there were when the war ended," Ritter said. "The logs don't fall in by themselves. It was the SS who had the trees in the area cut down and dumped into the lake on top of the most valuable cases."

Major Blotz's voice had a nervous edge. "Everyone avoids the lake like a plague, even the foreigners who come here to climb those damned Dead Mountains or to ski. We keep an eye on Toplitz. We have for years. I can assure all of you that no one has been dumping anything in the lake."

Slack and Paggett didn't appear to be satisfied.

"Jim, what's the setup for standby divers?" Slack asked.

"Better yet, what's the overall OP?" asked Paggett. "What about the boats for the sonar and the magnetoneter?"

"First of all, we have four twenty-foot-long aluminum boats with outboards," Flikkema said evenly. "Bruno, tell them about the other two vehicles not listed on the inventory sheets."

Wronkau sighed and placed his hands flat on the table as he spoke. "While we were on our way to Bad Aussee, two West German Navy landing craft were being transported to Lake Toplitz on large flatbed trailers. They are self-propelled wheeled vehicles designed to transport cargo and personnel, either on land or water. In German, we call such a vehicle *Meerschaufel*. It means 'sea shovel' in English."

Camellion interjected, "The German sea shovels are similar to our BARC amphibious resupply cargo barges, but the German craft are about a third smaller. We'll use one sea shovel as a command craft. The other will make the sweeps with the magnetometer. The command craft will also control the TV camera." His blue eyes first fastened on Flikkema, then went to Bruno Wronkau. "I surmise that's your Operational Plan?"

Wronkau and Flikkema smiled.

"*Ach, mein Herr*, you are more than an amateur diver, much more," Wronkau said warm heartedly.

The Death Merchant returned the German's smile with one of his own.

"Better than a novice, but far from being a professional."

Peter Schroetter, one of the West German divers, cleared his throat to get attention. "How is the American diver-delivery vehicle to be used?"

Big Jim Flikkema supplied the answer. "Well, the DDV

can operate at a maximum depth of three hundred feet, or 91.44 meters." He gave Bruno Wronkau a quick glance. "I think we should use it as an underwater scout. We'll have a swivel light of 300,000 candlepower, and we'll be equipped with sonar."

"Yes, I agree," Wronkau said with a nod.

Schroetter crushed out his stub of a cigarette in a metal ashtray.

"I wouldn't count too much on the underwater vehicle if I were you," he said, vigorously scratching the back of his head, "and I doubt if we can complete the job in a month."

"It's not your place to think!" Wronkau's face contorted in anger. "Your job is to follow orders."

The Death Merchant felt like laughing. He didn't. He only thought that while these Germans were good men and not Nazis, they still possessed that well-known Teutonic trait of following orders—*If they had lived under that maniac Hitler, no doubt they would have marched people off to the ovens if ordered to do so!*

Schroetter wasn't the least bit fazed by Wronkau (There's hope for him yet!) "Following orders doesn't mean I can't have an opinion," he said fiercely. "When the Austrians searched the lake, they hoped to complete the entire search in two or three weeks. The way I understand it, they managed to scan only 17,000 square yards of the lake bottom with the TV camera. The camera itself only had an observation radius of one square meter; and the electronic echo sounder only covered a quarter of the lake's surface, or about 120,000 square yards. I use 'yards' so that you Americans can understand better."

Major Blotz drew himself up straight and reddened slightly. Captain Axmann made an angry face.

"Under the circumstances, my government did the best it could," Blotz said slowly and deliberately, "the best it could with such a small budget."

The Death Merchant surprised everyone by saying, "I can understand the difficulties with a budget, *Herr Major*. Yet there are some features of the Austrian search that are most perplexing."

"I demand an explanation!" demanded Blotz, having no choice but to ask for one. "I'm getting sick of all of you slandering my government and hinting that we deliberately covered up something."

Camellion's laugh was light. "Don't be so touchy, *Herr*

Major. After all, the search was botched up. For example, the TV camera was attached to a cable that was only 316 feet or 96.3168 meters long. I ask you: how could the camera spot anything of value in a lake that, in some places reaches a depth of 800 feet—243.84 meters? Even the divers had——"

"The deepest parts of the lake are the most likely places to search," cut in Ritter. "It's reasonable to assume that the SS chose the deepest parts to dump their secrets."

"Not necessarily," Camellion said. "We can't be sure. First of all the SS scum were in a hurry. Unless they had a chart of the lake, a relief map of its bottom, they didn't deliberately dump anything of value in the deep sections. Any cases below the 500 foot mark would be at that depth by accident."

Ritter frowned in disagreement. "*SS-Obergruppenführer* Kaltenbrunner was very meticulous in such vital matters."

"Camellion, you were saying about the Austrian divers?" Big Jim ran a hand through his thick, curly brown hair.

"I was going to say that the Austrian divers had equipment that would take them down only to 240 feet, 73.152 meters. The diving bell was never used. Dr. Aschenbrenner said it wasn't necessary."

As the Death Merchant talked, he could see that Major Blotz and Captain Axmann were becoming more angry. He surmised that neither man was making a comment because they knew he was speaking the truth.

Camellion continued. "Getting back to the television camera, even if the cable had been the proper length, the camera couldn't have spotted anything of value. After all these years any cases of value would be covered with at least five to six feet of mud."

Major Blotz spoke in a loud voice. "I suppose there is going to be a miraculous parting of the mud when you Americans and your German friends use TV cameras?" Contempt began to color his tone. "Or would you have us believe that you can work some kind of underwater miracle?"

"The summer insect cannot speak of ice," Camellion said, smiling at an emotionally off-balanced Major Blotz. "The frog in the bottom of the well should not talk of the heavens."

Neither Major Blotz nor Captain Axmann had time to

ponder whether they were being insulted. Big Jim Flikkema's words got in the way of their angry thoughts.

"There won't be any miracles. We'll use only common-sense." Flikkema's manner was easy and nonchalant. "Sure, we'll use the TV cameras, but only after we detect something with the magnetometer. With the proper coordination, we should complete the job in three weeks."

"Three weeks or three months—The results will be the same," Blotz growled. "It's a waste of time and money, no doubt Central Intelligence Agency money.

While some of the Germans and the Americans looked startled, Major Blotz's attempt to trick Camellion into admitting Company involvement failed.

The Death Merchant chuckled, then smiled broadly at a caught-off-guard Major Felix Blotz.

"Tch, tch, tch . . . *Herr Major*, with your wild imagination, you should be writing fiction. . . ."

22.00 *Hours.* Huddled around the RT-67/GRC receiver/transmitter in the air-conditioned van, Camellion and West, Purdue and Henshaw waited for the message from Whip and Bloodstone. The transvertex SR-22 Cipher device connected to the RT transceiver did more than transmit ciphered speech; it also decoded incoming ciphered speech, this complex process accomplished by adding a pseudo-random pulse series, usually referred to as a superimposition series. The same superimposition series was added for deciphering, after which the signal was converted back to normal speech. Anyone picking up the message on the same VHF band would hear only gibble-gabble.

The superimposition series was controlled by an actual key setting which could be altered by the operator and would, therefore, be known only to him and to the party broadcasting from the other end. The key on the Transvertex in the van had been turned to 789.28675. Whip and Bloodstone would also have their set turned to the same number.

The driver's section of the van was sealed off from the rest of the interior by a steel wall, in the center of which was a small oval-shaped door. The van was actually more heavily armored than a Brink's armored car.

Two lights burned in the main section of the van, a shaded blue light over the RT-transceiver and Transvertex SR-22, and another shielded blue bulb over the two powerful transceivers watched over by Barry Polley, who was a communications expert and a Company contract agent.

The air conditioner hummed softly.

An exhaust fan in the ceiling whispered.

Vallie West, watching the fan pull cigarette smoke toward the ceiling, leaned back in the short-backed chair and sighed. "For the life of me, I can't understand why the Germans had to bring those two women along. Huh! 'To keep records!' No wonder the krauts lost the war. With all the record keeping they had to do, they didn't have time to fight."

No one answered Vallie. Camellion was studying a note pad on which he had written several sentences. Purdue was absorbed in playing electronic gin, an LCD spellout display showing his shuffles, deals, and scores. Next to Vallie sat Henshaw, engrossed in honing a Gerber Mark I. Survival knife on a ceramic sharpener. In front of the two large shortwave sets, Barry Polley was reading a paperback book entitled *Six Gun Samurai*.

"Damn it to hell, have all of you gone deaf!" Vallie snarled aggressively. "I was talking about the two Fräuleins. You know—women! You know what women are. They're creatures with nice looking lumps in the right places and no hoses between their legs."

A sideways grin formed on the Death Merchant's mouth. Startled, Purdue and Henshaw looked up and stared at West.

"How the Germans keep recrods is none of our business," Camellion said. "Karen and Marga don't interfere with us in any way. Why should we concern ourselves about them?"

Vallie was puzzled. "Jolly, jolly. But if you're right and ODESSA has more little goodies in store for us at the lake, who will take care of Karen and Marga?"

"They'll be on their own. I rather suspect we'll all be."

"God damn it, how can you sit there and say ODESSA will attack?" Henshaw's words were quick and alarmed as he shoved the Gerber knife into his belt. "There'll be a couple of hundred order police around that lake, all armed with autmatic weapons. Light and heavy machine guns! The works. ODESSA is one of the cleverest organizations in the world. Those dmaned ex-Nazis are a lot of things, but their worst enemies, the Israelis, wouldn't even dream of calling them foolhardy or stupid. ODESSA has lost its opportunities to stop us."

"He's right," Purdue said emphatically. He was going to continue, but the low voice from the RT-67/GRC transmitter stopped him.

"This is Whip and Bloodstone, calling Sanchez. Will wait one minute, then repeat."

"By God, we got them!" Henshaw said excitedly.

Camellion flipped the Activate switch of the Transvertex SR-22, picked up the pencil-type Dynamic mike and held the silver end close to his mouth.

"Sanchez here." He glanced down at the words written on the pad. "There are no roses on the hillside. The fields are bare. The snows are deep."

With the speed of light the Transvertex scrambled the words and fed them into the transmitter which broadcast the vocal gobblegook via the whip antenna on the roof.

The rather harsh voice replied from the transceiver:

"Tell us about the bouquet."

"There are no bouquets."

"Tell us about the bouquet."

"Incorrect, there are no bouquets."

"Correct. There are no bouquets."

"Report," Camellion said.

"We haven't learned anything of value. Many of the older people of Bad Aussee were either Nazi Party members or Nazi sympathizers. We estimate there are at least five thousand tourists in the area, but we haven't detected anything suspicious about any individual. Any questions?"

"No. Follow your instructions. Sanchez ending the transmission. Acknowledge."

"Acknowledged."

The Death Merchant put down the mike, switched off the Transvertex and the RT-transceiver, and sighed. "Mercy, mercy, Mother Percy. It's been a waste of time with Whip and Bloodstone."

"Damn, damn, Mrs. Hammm," West said simply. "We weren't counting on those two anyhow. So what's the difference?"

"I didn't think those two creeps would report anything of value," Henshaw said priggishly. "Hell, you know what they're doing—living it up with the girls, screwing themselves silly."

The Death Merchant gave Henshaw a small look of

slight pity, took out a small bottle, opened it, took out some pills, put them into his mouth and washed them down with a sip of iced coffee laced with a jigger of brandy."

"Look, what are all those pills you are always taking?" asked Purdue, his voice demanding.

"Choline, vitamin E., Procaine hydrochloride and a few little other odds and ends,"[2] Camellion explained with a grin. "Care for a few?"

"No thanks." Purdue shook his head vigorously.

"Val, have you seen the moon tonight?" Camellion addressed West.

"A blood moon," West said.

[2]Dietary supplements for keeping the brain's circulatory system in good condition.

Chapter Nine

Wein (Vienna, the capital of Austria, as it is more familiarly known, is noted for many features. There aren't any slums. There isn't a housing shortage. Smog is nil, and the fear of communism does not exist. There are no serious problems in drug addiction or juvenile delinquency. Flowing down from the Styrian hills, the drinking water is the best in Europe, clear and icy cold on even the hottest days.

Few Americans realize it, but Vienna is ruled by a socialist administration. Even fewer know that Wien is the foremost socialist metropolis in the world (i.e., within the Western sense of the world "socialist"). The *Gemeinde Wien* (municipality) is noted for the multiplicity and quality of its good works—medical clinics, baths, schools, hospitals, institutues, and such enormous housing projects as the Karl Marxhof, and the George Washingtonhof, named after two well-known revolutionaries in history.

Another little known fact is that most Viennese seldom see the Danube which flows five kilometers northeast of the city. Nor is the Danube "blue". It has always been, and still is, a yellowish-brown.

Vienna is still a soft, discreet city, still retaining its own peculiar gloss and sophisticated varnish. The old Vienna of Freud, Adler, and Mahler is gone; however, there is still a backdrop of imperial magnificence. No capital in the world is so lavishly and majestically laid out, with the exception of Paris, Leningrad, and the old Peking. Nonetheless, Vienna has lost much of its substance, if only because the Nazis murdered its Jewish citizens, who helped make the city one of the most dynamic and creative capitals of the world.

Vienna is definitely not noted for harboring Nazi war criminals. As a rule, the known members of ODESSA avoid the city because Israeli Mossad agents keep a close watch on foreign visitors.

116

Ex-*SS Gruppenführer* Ernst Rudolf Muller and ex-*SS Standartenführer* Karl Victor Scherhorn were not worried about Israeli intelligence agents. The two high officials of ODESSA had been too cautious to have taken an airliner to Schwechat Airport, 17 km southeast of Vienna. Coming from Turkey, the two ex-Nazis had flown to Munich, weeks earlier. From Munich, they had been smuggled into Vienna, arriving in Austria in a motor home driven by an elderly couple who were fanatical ex-Nazis.

In an ODESSA safe house on the *Obere Donaustrabe,* in the Leopoldstadt district of Vienna, Muller and Scherhorn knew they were beyond the reach of Mossad agents and agents of the other intelligence agencies of the world. In particular were they safe in this house, which was the home of Herr Wilhelm Rupert Holtz, a high official in the Austrian *Staatts Ordnunspolizei.* Any orders that were re-layed to Major Felix Blotz from the State's Ministry had to cross the desk of Colonel Holtz. All orders transmitted to Major Blotz were relayed to Muller and Scherhorn by Holtz, whose father had been an *SS-Hauptscharführer* (Sergeant-Major) in the *Waffen SS Germania* devision.

Envy in his eyes, Scherhorn watched Muller who was eating an *Obers Omelet,* a cold sugared crêpe folded over half a pound of cream whipped as solid as a pillow. Muller always had the appetite of a starving horse; yet he never gained an ounce. In contrast, Scherhorn had to watch his diet and force himself to avoid pastries, or within months would look as though he were in the ninth month of pregnancy.

"I tell you, Ernst, we are taking a tremendous risk," Scherhorn said after a lengthy silence. "You know as well as I do that unless our own agents within the Order Police have a lot of luck, the attack from the mountains will fail. Kohne and those crazies with him can't succeed by themselves."

He got up from the leather glider chair, went across the room to the tiny bar and picked up a bottle of *Gumpold-skirchner,* a white wine. Scherhorn hated being cooped up in this sub-basement room where he and Muller had to sleep on folding cots. *Mein Gott im Himmel!* He had clos-ets in his home in Brazil that were almost as large as this room with the white painted walls.

"Victor, you worry too much." Muller's fork paused in

mid-air and he carefully wiped whipped cream from the corners of his mouth with a napkin. "All that is needed is for the attack to succeed to the extent that it prevents the Americans and the West Germans from diving into the lake. I doubt if there will be another expedition, if this one fails."

"I totally disagree," Scherhorn said, pouring *Gumpoldskirchner* into an ordinary water glass. "Within hours of the attack, the wire services of the world will be broadcasting the news. Even if the attack succeeds, it will only make the CIA and the BND more determined. To save face, they will have to mount another expedition." He corked the bottle and turned to face Muller who had resumed eating. "Whether the attack succeeds or fails, all it is going to do is prove that ODESSA exists and that there is some secret in the lake that the 'old Nazis' don't want revealed."

Scherhorn picked up the glass and started back to his chair.

Muller swallowed another mouthful of omelet before replying.

"I agree with you, but the decision was not ours. The High Command said to use any methods available to prevent the diving—and damn the publicity." He shook his fork at Scherhorn. "Ya, we lost the gold bullion in France, but in this round we outguessed the CIA and the BND. We should congratulate ourselves. Gathering those fanatical idiots and sending them into the caves a month ago is going to be our salvation."

Scherhorn leaned back in his chair and smiled slightly. "And why report to the High Command in Peru that sending those 200 men into the Dead Mountains was Kohne's idea? He most certainly will die in the suicide attack."

"Precisely, *mein Kamerad*," Muller said sinisterly. "Remember the campaign on the Eastern Front? Remember how some of those young SS fanatics attacked the *Russischen Soldaten*? Kohne is that kind of fool, an idiot who thinks he is fighting for a 'great cause.' Kohne, Geissler, Hohehorst, the whole lot of them—all lunatics!" He glanced down, put his fork into the *Obers Omelet*, and a sly smile played over his mouth. "Naturally the majority of those fools will be killed, but that is not our problem. Our only objective is to prevent the case with Plan Ya-4 Flug from being found and brought to the surface."

Scherhorn took a sip of white wine. "Damn Kaltenbrunner! I hope he's kissing the devil's redhot ass! The only copy in existence and he had to put it in one of those damned cases." He stared at Muller and his voice grew more savage. "If it weren't for Kaltenbrunner, we wouldn't be in this mess. Why at this point, we don't even have any reassurance that those fools in the Dead Mountains haven't been discovered by the Austrians. I even consider it a minor miracle that they succeeded in getting to the caves, even though they travelled in groups of twos and threes. Ya, a miracle."

"Don't be foolish," Muller said crossly. "Who would notice a few climbers here, or four or five there? No one, especially the Austrians. You know the proverbial fecklessness of the Austrians. They live from day to day and don't care."

"At least we know that the Austrians haven't found any of the important caves," Scherhorn said, "the ones used as storage depots, or Holtz would have reported it. I only wonder if the weapons and ammo will be usable after all these years?"

Having finished eating, Muller pushed back his plate. "Why not? Machine pistols, ammunition, grenades—all were sealed in airtight containers." He laughed in amusement. "*Ach,* Victor. You were there at the *Alpenfestung.* You saw the equipment being carried into the caves and then sealed."

Scherhorn took another sip of *Gumpoldskirchner,* then said stiffly, "I remember very well. The confusion was terrible. I'm counting on the modern weapons brought in by the 200 halfwits who are willing to die for the 'glorious Fourth Reich'. Well, we should know in a day or so when the news of the attack bursts upon the world." He paused, thinking. "There must be no connection with us. You have made the proper arrangements for Herr and Frau Gunther?"

Sadistic delight glinted in Muller's eyes. "The day we leave Vienna, Herr and Frau Gunther will burn to death when their house catches fire. Hermann made arrangements before he left for the *Totes Gebirge.*"

Well satisfied, Muller tilted back the wooden chair and began to hum *Deutschland über alles . . . ber alles in der Welt. . . .* Germany over all . . . over all in the world. . . .

119

Chapter Ten

Standing by the side of the Glover Land Rover, Richard Camellion let his eyes wander slowly over the area. Ribbons of coppery clouds filled the sky. The temperature was 72 degrees Fahrenheit. A strong wind blew. A drop of a few more degrees and the air would have been chilly.

Three to four kilometers to the northwest were the lower reaches of the Dead Mountains which, technically, were a part of the Styrian Alps.

"Formidable looking, aren't they?" commented Vallie West, who was standing next to the Death Merchant, leaning against the vehicle. "They remind me of the Superstition Mountain'," Camellion said. "The entire range in Arizona is known collectively as Superstition Mountain. The early Spanish explorers called them *Sierra de la Espuma* 'Mountains of the Foam'. As for the name Superstition, no one really knows how it came about."

"Yeah, well why call the mountains 'Superstition Mountain' when it's not one mountain but a range of mountains?"

"The reason is that when viewed from the southwest, the entire mess of rock looks like a mountain. To the Apaches that vantage point was all that mattered, hence the use of the singular. It really doesn't make that much difference."

There were times when West felt like belting Camellion in the mouth. Rick was too intensely analytical, his mind too probing. Too damned intellectual! Vallie told himself. Superstition? Vallie thought of the time he had visited Camellion's *Memento Mori* Ranch in the Big Thicket region of southeastern Texas. Never again! During the week too many mysterious things had happened. Vallie had heard strange noises in the night . . . subtle whispering, and shadows, caught for only a moment from the corner of the eye, shadows that didn't behave like shadows. Vallie was positive that Camellion dabbled in certain ancient and secret sciences. He didn't know what these sciences were, nor did he want to know.

"There are a lot of caves in those mountains," Camellion said, surveying the *Totes Gebirge*. "Major Blotz swears that most of them have been searched, the poor fool."

"I don't think he's lying," West said. "He simply won't consider the possibility of any caves being sealed. Besides, you know how the Austrians go about any venture. Haphazard planning and a 'so-what' attitude."

For a long moment the two men studied the Dead Mountains. Within that chain of black and smokey-gray rocks were thousands of peaks, cliffs, bluffs, mesas, all connected in a tangled mass that was one of the most desolate and forbidding areas in all the world.

The line of armored vehicles was between the mountains and the majority of the rocky plateau where the Cologne Historical Society expedition had established its base of operations. There were 15 large tents for housing and feeding the members of the expedition and the Austrian order police. South of the tents were three helicopter pads built of lumber and concrete, and a long tin shed where diving suits, air tanks and other equipment was being double checked.

Three fourths of a kilometer to the east of the tents was Lake Toplitz, the sinister Devil's Trashcan, a grim body of black water shaped like an enormously fat frankfurter bent in the middle, so that the northern end pointed west.

During the three days that the expedition had been at the actual site of the lake, Austrian engineers and workmen had built a long, wide wharf at the southeast end of the lake. The diving platform, 125 feet long and 85 feet wide, was moored at the end of the long pier. The diving platform consisted of dozens of hollow tanks welded to a framework, on top of which had been bolted a steel floor. A jib crane was mounted at one end of the platform, the weight of the crane offset by three heavy anchors at the opposite end of the platform. The four aluminum 20-foot boats were tethered to one side of the pier, against the piles of which the waves of Lake Toplitz broke into white foam, for the surface of Lake Toplitz was not calm, the mountain wind constantly tormenting the water.

In front of the tin shed rested the Edis diving bell with its lockout chamber. It rested on a six-wheeled platform that, powered by an electric motor, could be driven at a rate of 5 MPH.

Beyond the diving and work platform were the two

Meerschaufels, the two "sea shovels". Moored next to the two West German cargo and personnel transports was the Underwater Propulsions, Inc. diver-delivery vehicle; it was powered by a 36-volt, permanent magnet DC motor fueled by six, 6-volt batteries.

West—dressed like Camellion in flannel-lined Chino pants, West German *Bundesgrenzschutz* field jacket and black paratrooper boots—adjusted his Bianchi Pistolero gunbelt rig with two holsters, each holster filled with a Safari Arms Match Master .45 auto loader.

"You know, Rick, the Austrians don't have the precise efficiency of the krauts, but you have to hand it to them," Vallie said. "They've done ninety-five percent of the work since we arrived in Bad Aussee. In three days, they not only packed up everything in the pasture below but got us up here, set up camp, built the pier and all the rest of it."

"Well, our people drove our vehicles," the Death Merchant said, his tone giving Vallie the distinct impression that Camellion was reluctant to give the Austrians any credit. "Waller did one fine job of driving that tractor and trailer. Of course, the road did twist and turn all over the place, but it was plenty wide, due to the poor concentration camp devils who widened it, thirty-seven or thirty-eight years ago."

With a deep chuckle, Vallie reached for his cigarettes. "I was thinking of how insulted Blotz and the other Austrians were when you insisted that our scuba divers check out the bottom of the diving platform for timed explosive devices. Did you really think the guys would find anything?"

"No. Time bombs on any of the floats would be too obvious," said Camellion, looking up at the sky. "I've a hunch that ODESSA has something very special in store for us. As for Blotz, he's not so bad, even if he is a klutz."

"He's still not as bad as Axmann," Vallie said, reaching for his cigarettes. "I got Axmann figured as a jerk who wouldn't give a crutch to a crippled crab if he owned the Black Forest. I don't trust him. That baldheaded joker is always looking you straight in the eye. He's been a prick somewhere along the line, but I can't figure out where."

The Death Merchant did not reply. He watched as Flikkema and Ritter, Wronkau and Captain Alois Kalls hurried toward him and West.

Reaching Camellion and West, the four grouped around them.

"Herr Camellion, you are positive that neither you nor Herr West will be making any dives?" asked Ritter. "Herr Wronkau and Herr Flikkema must know before they make the diving schedule and assign the men."

"You haven't changed your minds?" Big Jim said. "If you have, now is the time to say so."

"We haven't," Camellion said, frowning. "It's a matter of decompression. We all know that the deeper a diver goes and the longer he stays down, the longer it takes to decompress."

"You're right about that," Big Jim said. "If a diver goes down an hour in the DDV, and cruises around, say at 300 feet, he will have to sit for 18 to 20 hours in a decompression chamber."

"Ya, that is true," agreed Wronkau. "But even a scuba diver can go down to a depth of 30 meters, or a hundred feet, remain there for 25 minutes and then come directly to the surface, as long as he comes upward at a rate of 18 meters or 60 feet per minute."

"Exactly," Camellion said. "Suppose trouble starts up here and Val and I are cooped up in a decompression chamber? Furthermore, we're not talking about a mere hundred feet. Hard-hat divers or boys in the bell might have to go down five hundred feet or more, provided we find something. For that same reason, the time involved in decompression, I'm not permitting any of you to make any deep dives."

Lightning flashed in Ritter's icy cold eyes and his jaw became a concrete block of determination. "Herr Camellion, you are not the dictator of this expedition. I also have something to say about who might dive and I think——"

"I'm not interested in your views," Camellion said sharply but in a low voice. "Trot on over to the van and"—he gave Captain Kalls a quick glance—"check with the officials of the Cologne Historical Society. They'll tell you damned fast that any final decision is on my shoulders."

"We'll see about that!" Ritter snapped, his voice laced with intense anger. He turned and began walking briskly toward the van parked toward the east end of the lineof vehicles.

Bruno "Tweetie Bird" Wronkau stared after Ritter for a moment, then turned back to Camellion, consumed with concern, confusion, and resentment; yet he sensed that the tall *Amerikaner* was not a man to make wild statements.

Wronkau also sensed that Ritter had only gone to the van to save face.

Captain Kalls, a lean, tall man in his twenties, folded his hands behind his back and looked amused.

"Gentlemen, it is irrelevant to us who dives into the lake," he said, as if enjoying the situation. "Exploring the lake is not our job."

"Well now, is that a fact!" Vallie said with deliberate seriousness, thinking that Kall's English was remarkably fluent, though his broad Austrian accent gave his speech a deeper resonance, making him sound impressive and rather distinguished.

Big Jim Flikkema shifted from foot to foot. "Deduct the men who can't dive and that leaves us with five divers, three Germans and two Americans," he said mildly. "And there's no problem with tenders."

"The O.S.P. is still the same?" Camellion leaned back against the Glover Land Rover and folded his arms.

"Why should we change it?" Wronkau's gruff voice was stubbornly insistent. "The plan is foolproof."

Commented Flikkema, "One might say that the Operational Scan Plan can be compared to a straight line being the shortest distance between two points."

West blew out smoke, dropped his stub of a cigarette and ground it out with the toe of his boot. "Uh huh. You're saying there is only one practical way to scan the lake?"

"You got it, Val. Each West German 'sea shovel' will use a magnetometer and sonar. One craft will work the east side of the lake, the other the west side.

"These magnetometers," put forth Vallie, tugging at his left ear. "I rather gather that they don't actually pick up any metal? I mean the way a small magnet would grab a nail?"

"A magnetometer only detects the presence of metal," Flikkema patiently explained. "The registering meter . . . well, it's like a signal strength meter on a radio. The larger the mass of metal detected, the stronger the signal on the magnetometer, both in sound and on the meter."

Camellion sounded thoughtful and introspective. "We're almost certain that the SS dumped a lot of advanced weaponry into the Trashcan, weapons that were ahead of their time for those years. Scuba- and hard-hat divers can't go down each time we detect a mass of metal, or we'd have all

124

the divers sitting for days in decompression chambers. I trust that's where the TV cameras and the bell comes in?"

"You're absolutely correct," Flikkema said. "Each TV camera can scan 14 sq. ft. in infrared. What the cameras can't see, the two men in the Edis bell will. The bell has four ports and side lights of 250,000 candlepower. The nice part about using the bell is that the divers can go down to the deepest part of the lake and be hauled right back up to the surface, then leave the bell without going through hours of decompression."

"You mean unless the divers leave the bell through the lockout chamber while it's on the lake bottom?" Vallie said.

"Right," said Big Jim. "Say the divers were down at 500 feet and left the bell for several hours and worked at that depth. In that case after they were hauled back to the surface, they'd have to stay in the bell for a day and a half."

Wronkau looked from Camellion to West. "So far we have oversimplified the procedures," he said stiffly. "First, the small aluminum boats will make a grid search with sonar and locate any likely spots. If a spot looks promising, a buoy will be dropped and a checkout team sent down. Scuba men if the depth is not more than 30 meters. If the depth is greater and the magnetometer indicates a likely target spot, the TV cameras and the bell will take over."

"Depending on the find"—Flikkema took over—"hard-hat divers or dry-suit scuba boys can leave the bell through its lockout chamber."

Bruno Wronkau was suddenly tense. "Should we use the bell for the actual recovery operation, then I must insist on three men going down in the bell." He gave Flikkema a searching look. "We both know that for each hard hat a tender is needed and that a Divemaster monitors each diver's time in the water. Either Waller or Zarkes will have to be the third man in the bell, should recovery take place below 121 meters or 400 feet."

"Why 400 feet?" inquired Vallie West.

"We can use regular hard-hat divers down to that depth," Wronkau explained. "Below that depth the bell would be best. There aren't any problems. Two scuba men, using closed breathing systems, will not have any difficulty in leaving the bell." The German thought for a few moments, then added, "We must realize though that there are dangers in any deep dive."

Wronkau went on to explain that there was air embolism. AE could be caused by a diver's holding his breath during ascent, in which case the air would rapidly expand and blow a hole in the man's lungs. Along with the hole, air bubbles would form in the blood, bubbles that could move to the brain, cut off the blood supply and either cripple or kill the diver.

"There's O_2 poisoning—oxygen poisoning," Wronkau said, looking at Vallie. "A hundred percent oxygen is not significantly toxic when breathed at depths of less than 33 American feet for a short period of time. But the oxygen becomes toxic at 85 meters. Let's see . . . in American feet, 85 meters. . . ."

"Two hundred and eighty feet," Camellion said promptly, his expression as stone-faced as ever. "That's 85.344 meters."

"Another way of explaining oxygen toxicity is to explain it in terms of atmospheres—pressure of air," Flikkema said. "Under two atmospheres partial pressure, oxygen turns poison. This means that pure oxygen at two atmospheres, or air at ten atmospheres, will poison the diver."

"Where do you find ten atmosphere," Vallie said, "six or seven hundred feet down?"

"Oh no! Ten atmospheres is about 297 feet"—he glanced at Wronkau—"or 90 meters. You see, we're speaking about atmosphere pressure in the diver's lungs. For instance, let's say that a diver has to work at the 500-ft. level. OK. The air mixture has to be just right. To keep at the safe level of one atmosphere, the gas mixture has to be 6.81 percent oxygen and the remainder helium. At 200 feet, 17 percent oxygen. At the deepest part of the lake—800 feet—the percentage would have to be 4.25 percent oxygen and 95.75 percent helium."

"*Ya*, that is right," Bruno said quickly. "But the mixture at 800 feet, that is . . . 243 meters, will not support life above the 60-foot level."

There were other dangers which Flikkema and Wronkau explained to West and Camellion. Such as carbon dioxide poisoning, caused by breathing impure gas, or the failure of CO_2 absorbent (granular baralyme) in closed or semi-closed SCUBA gear.

"Most of the time carbon dioxide poisoning is caused by damp, overused or channeled absorbent," Flikkema said, "although overexertion or holding the breath to conserve air while diving can also trigger CO poisoning."

There was carbon monoxide poisoning that occurred when more then 0.002 percent CO was present in the breathing medium. The CO then combined with the hemoglobin in the blood, displacing the oxygen which the hemoglobin usually carries to the tissues. Anoxia of the tissues was the result, even though the lungs themselves are capable of supplying adequate oxygen to sustain life.

The cause was an air compressor that contained flushing or lubricating oil. Such a compressor would often produce compressed air containing carbon monoxide. A compressor used in an enclosed space, or with its air intake close to its exhaust, would also produce compressed air containing dangerous amounts of CO.

"Depending on the depth a diver works, nitrogen is added to the gas mixture," Flikkema said. "That leads us to a nitrogen 'drunk' or nitrogen narcosis. This is caused by nitrogen under pressure. A rough rule of thumb is that every 50 feet of depth is like one dry martini."

"Or a small glass of good Schnapps," Wronkau interjected with a laugh.

"Yes, but the catch is that you don't feel the effects until about 130 feet. At 200 feet you feel like you've had half a bottle of Schnapps. This is why deep divers use helium instead of nitrogen. Just the same, even helium will act the same way. We don't have to worry about that. We're not going down any 2,000 feet."

Surprisingly, the least that divers feared was the bends—or Caisson's compressed air illness. If a diver ascended too rapidly, the air would come out of solution within the tissues and joints in the form of bubbles, these bubbles putting pressure on the nerves and other structures and interfering with proper function of blood circulation. Result? Pain, paralysis, asphyxia, or, if the bubbles are large and numerous enough—death.

"The cause is simple," Wronkau said roughly. "Not obeying the diving tables, especially on repetitive dives within a 12-hour period, or if you dive when sick, or if you're overweight, or overly fatigued."

"Or after drinking too much," Flikkema said. He smiled softly, thoughtfully. "I'm not worried about any of the divers; they're all professionals. The West German made

Draeger Lt Lund II. Scuba equipment is the best. The same goes for the other equipment."

The Death Merchant said, "Have the air tanks been checked?" He punched holes in the mountain air with the trigger of his right hand. "We don't dare underestimate ODESSA. If they had the chance, no telling what kind of gas they would have put in the divers' air tanks."

While Wronkau shook his head, as if to say that Camellion was the worst kind of paranoid, Big Jim Flikkema explained that each Scuba tank had been checked and its contents analyzed. "I can assure you that each tank contains only pure oxygen or pure helium; and we've double-checked both air compressors. Just in case someone around here might be in the pay of ODESSA, we'll make another check before any diver goes down tomorrow when the grid search starts."

Intoned West, "Purdye and Duckworth are guarding the diving equipment. "Twice a day we check the bell and other equipment for bugs and explosives. And the Austrians are doing a good job—so far. You can see that for yourself, Rick."

West jerked his head, indicating the numerous vehicles parked around the area. Not only did a line of slight armor face the Dead Mountains, but there were armored vehicles parked to the southern and the eastern perimeters. To the south were two Glover Tuareg remote area patrol vehicles. Each vehicle had a 2 × 7.62-mm GPMG, 84-mm anti-tank weapon and was equipped with a 4X electrically-operated grenade discharger. An Austrian *Stats Ordunungs* policeman behind each GPMG. Two more were to the east.

"Sylvester the Cat" Flikkema clapped "Tweetie Bird" Wronkau on the right shoulder with his left hand. "Bruno, good buddy, what say we go have a pow-wow with Doc Messner, then have a conference with Waller and Zarkes?"

Tweetie Bird blinked in confusion. "A 'pow-wow?' "

"American slang. The same as a conference," explained Flikkema pleasantly. "Me, I think we should have the doctor give the divers a last minute checkup before tomorrow morning. Is that agreeable with you."

"Yes. We can't be too careful with the men who will dive. Too many things can occur below the surface." He glanced hesitantly at West and Camellion, then turned with Flikkema and started toward one of the four-sided hut-tents as Franz Ritter came out of the expedition's communication van and began taking brisk, determined strides toward West and the Death Merchant.

"Here comes trouble in sauerkraut," West said, his lips barely moving. "I hate to say it, but Ritter reminds me of yesterday's bat do-do."

"A rule of thumb is to weigh the bad against the good," Camellion said. "There's more good to Ritter than bad, and he's an icicle under fire."

By then Ritter stopped in front of Camellion, his features as fixed as steel. "I talked with headquarters in Bonn, Herr Camellion," he said very proper and businesslike. "You were correct. In regard to any action, the final decision lies within the realm of your prerogative. I shall defer to your decisions."

Ritter executed a slight, stiff bow, turned swiftly on his heel, and began striding toward the operations tent, leaving a frowning West and a stony-faced Camellion behind him.

"I'll swear that kraut's been vaccinated with a phonograph needle," muttered West. "Why couldn't he have just said that you're the boss and be done with it. He reminds me of a joker I know back in the States. Hell, if you said 'Good Morning' to Rupt Rosenberger, he'd end up giving you a national weather report."

"Val, you're looking at the oyster but not seeing the pearl." The Death Merchant let his eyes wander slowly over the huge primitive area. "Ritter had to swallow a lot of pride to come over and say what he did. He has a lot of self-respect."

West gave Camellion a long, speculative look. There was never any way to glean a clue to Camellion's thoughts. His body language was always mute and his expression usually inscrutable. Vallie often sensed that he really didn't know Camellion. He never had. Neither did anyone else. The Death Merchant had always been totally self-contained, a man who needed no one, a man who loved no one, a man who was a stranger to his own species; and maybe that was the way it should be. Maybe that was why there were those times that Camellion *knew*. . . . because he did have that mysterious isolation, because he was an entity wrapped in semi-transparent shadows. Vallie didn't know how Camellion did it, and he didn't care.

"ODESSA—they're coming, aren't they?" Vallie's strong voice was just above a whisper.

"Yes."

"When it's over, how many of us will be alive?"

For five seconds the Death Merchant didn't answer. There were scores of men in the area, absorbed in various tasks. Here and there was an individual whose electromagnetic field glowed like a rainbow, with shades of red, blue, green, orange, yellow and pink. Other men had emanations that were heavily tinged with dark brown—*They will be the seriously wounded.* . . .

In contrast, many men radiated life energy that was mostly the color of India ink—*They are the dead; their time in this continuum is almost over. Shortly, the Great Adventure will begin for them.* . . .

"Not too many will live," Camellion answered West, looking at Marga von Roesch whose life force was a blotch of black.

"And us—you and I?"

"Our luck will be all bad."

Vallie felt an icy wind blow across his spine and scorpions crawl wildly over his brain.

He sighed. "Then we're due to buy the Big One!"

"I said our luck would be all bad. I seriously doubt if you and I will need as much as a bandaid when this mess is over." Camellion turned and peered slyly at West. "Val, wander over to the operations tent and see what Ritter might be up to. It's best to keep an eye on the Germans as well as the Austrians."

"I thought you said that Ritter has a lot of self-respect? To me, that's synonymous with honor." The eerie feeling that still griped Vallie prevented him from making any jokes about Camellion's self-contradiction in regard to Ritter.

"He has, and that's why we can't trust him," Camellion said. "Self-respect and honor are Siamese twins that can't be severed," Camellion said. "Ritter has plenty of both. He'll do anything for his country just as we'll do anything for ours."

"I see what you mean." Vallie turned and hurried toward the Operations Tent.

The Death Merchant turned and stared at the silver and blue Sikorsky S-64 helicopter gunship resting on the middle pad, two order police standing guard beside the chopper, HK 33A2 automatic rifles resting from sling straps on the shoulders of the men. The Austrians had moved in a

130

third whirlybird to take the strain off the other two Sikorskys. The three craft were constantly rotating; one was always in the air.

Camellion moved a dozen feet from the Glover Land Rover, turned and stared at the sinister *Totes Gebirge*. The tallest peaks were snow covered at the top. Farther down, the ugly brown, black and gray rocks were untouched by even the smallest trace of vegetation. No one could explain why. After all, the peaks of the Dead Mountains were not all that high. There should have been trees and vegetation at the lower levels. But there wasn't, and for that reason the mountains were called "dead".

Far to the north, one Sikorsky was reconnoitering the Dead Mountains, the Austrians inside the craft using long-range man detectors of the Plessey type. Developed by Plessy Optoelectronics and Microwave Division, the Long Range Man Detector consisted of a ceramic pyroelectric IR detector and was designed to respond to the IR radiation emitted by a human being, the detection span being in the 8-14 micron region of the electromagnetic spectrum. The device could readily detect an individual and/or individuals against a background of buildings or natural surroundings, night or day, at a range of 100 meters. The field of view was approximately one meter in diameter and the accurate telescopic sight allowed precise alignment of the detection unit.

The third helicopter had flown to Bad Aussee to pick up supplies.

Camellion noted the folds and cracks of the mountains, the ridges and cordilleras . . . all bare, brittle, grim, monotonous. This was the heart of the *Alpenfestung,* of the *Ausserland,* and he could almost hear the laughter of the thousands of ghosts of the SS, hear them laughing insanely, laughing from remembered blood and gore. But they will smile no more. . . .

Again the Death Merchant looked up at the sky. Rain is all we need! The sky was full of webby cirrus clouds and smoke in the distance from Bad Aussee was circling downward, both sure signs that a summer mountain thunderstorm was on its way.

There was more to the clouds than moisture. The Death Merchant could see them galloping in his minds eye: Death, famine, pestilence, and war!

The four horsemen of the Apocalypse!

Chapter Eleven

The thunderstorm broke that night at 23.00 hours. The black sky exploded with thunder. Lightning cracked and stabbed in a thousand directions at once while the wind whipped down with such force that the people in the tents had the feeling that the poled and staked structures might actually collapse. Beaten by the wind, the water of Lake Toplitz became frantic, rising in waves that washed over the pier at the southeast side of the lake. The diving platform, its jib crane moved to the center of the platform, bobbed up and down like a cork; yet it was secure. At the approach of the storm, the men had attached three more anchors to the platform and had moved the West German self-propelled wheeled sea shovels to dry land. The American delivery vehicle was pulled out of the water and secured, as were the three helicopters.

The actual storm only lasted about half an hour, but the rain continued intermittently, the final shower coming shortly before dawn. However, the sun rose in a sky that was rapidly clearing of storm clouds. Among the broken up stratus and blobs of cumulo-nimbus clouds, one could see patches of blue streaked with whisps of cirro-cumuli, a sure sign that drier but cold Polar air had replaced the wet tropical air. Clear weather was ahead. The storm had lowered the temperature. The mercury hung at 64° and the wind was so chilly that many of the Germans and the Americans wore turtle neck sweaters under their German field jackets. The Austrian workers and the order police also wore extra clothing.

In a group that included Ritter, West, Helldorf, Flikkema, Henshaw, and Kausch, Camellion looked around the large encampment. Wet, yet all was in order. During the night the Austrians had not left their posts in the various armored vehicles, although now the men in the Glover Tuareg remote area patrol vehicles were removing the armored coverings over the open half-turrets and replacing them with plastic canopies.

"A nice rain, some wind, and that's all it amounted to," Big Jim Flikkema said, looking around. "I see no reason why we can't start on schedule."

"The vehicles we came in sure got a good washing," Camellion said, turning to the cars of the Cologne expedition. The two motor homes were parked side by side. Behind them, lined up neatly in a row, were the Rabbit, the Datsun, the Audi, and the Subaru. The two small supply trucks and the communications van were behind the four passenger automobiles. However, the large tractor and trailer were parked several hundred feet to the east, not far from the equipment shed.

"Gentlemen, let's have some breakfast and go to work," Camellion said, his hands on his hips.

"I expect good progress," commented Ritter, his voice ringing with satisfaction. He looked toward the equipment shed where Burton Waller and Fredrick Zarkes were giving orders to some of the divers and the tenders. Other technicians were checking the Edis diving bell's lockout chamber. Other men were preparing to drive the bell, still on its six-wheeled platform, to the end of the pier where it would be picked up by the jib crane, on the diving platform.

The search of *Der Abfallkanne des Teufels* was about to begin.

Ten days dragged by, ten days of frustration, work, and disappointment. Progress was very slow. The two sea shovels, starting at the south end of the lake, first had to use sonar to determine the specific depth of the grid they were covering. Once the depth was definitely established, the next step was to lower the magnetometers and to proceed very slowly across the area. The 20-foot-long aluminum boats went first, two preceding each sea shovel. The small boats would first use sonar to pick up the likely lumps at the bottom of the lake. The two sea shovels would then take over with larger sonar sets to determine the precise depth of the positions marked by red buoys dropped by the men in the small aluminum craft. The next step, once the depth had been definitely established, was to lower the magnetometers and determine whether the mass was mud, rock, or metal. The real reason for the slowness was the amount of junk metal that the SS had dumped into the lake. Nevertheless, each time one of the magnetometers "pinged in" on any metal that was large enough to be a foot locker, the target had to be investigated.

In some instances, the TV infrared cameras could do the job, or scuba divers, if the depth was shallow enough. But in the majority of "pings" the bell had to be used, all of which was very time consuming. The two sea shovels would first have a cable onto the diving platform, then move it to a position that would permit the crane to lower the bell to one side of the red buoy marking the area to be investigated. Inspection of scuba gear and numerous other preparations consumed more time. Two divers, one an American, the other a German, would climb into the bell and the ball of high-pressure steel would be lowered into the black waters. On an average inspection, four and a half hours would be spent investigating each discovery. The "treasure" was always the same—rusted, mud-covered junk, parts of rockets or other weapons that, almost 40 years ago, had been the most advanced in the world.

Once a hard-hat diver went down to a depth of 76 meters (250 feet) and spent almost an hour, in mud and slime up to his waist, to check out what every member of the expedition hoped would be a valuable case of documents or jewels. But emphasis was on documents, as far as the Germans and the Americans were concerned. Any jewels would be turned over to the Israeli Fund For Displaced Persons.

The object was a metal case; and because it was wedged too tightly in the muck and mire to be brought up by heavy duty air-lift bags, a cable and winch on the diving platform were used to haul the case to the surface. The mud-covered case was promptly hosed down, then cut open with an electric cutting torch. The contents? Books on the occult. Books on black magic! Books with specific instructions on how to contact *"Die Elterh"*—The Elders . . .

That night the books were inspected in the operations tent—all 211 of them. Each book had that well-read appearance and was in good condition, having been protected over the years in the airtight, waterproof case.

"It all fits together," Ritter said grimly in German, picking up one of the books from the table. "These books belonged to the *Ahnenerbe*, the damned Nazi Occult Bureau."

"Himmler's special unit of lunatics," West said, then took a sip of *Weissbier* from the can in his hand.

"Lunatics—ya, very dangerous madmen," Camellion said seriously. "The rituals of the *Ahnenerbe* included satanic rites involving human sacrifice. Himmler even sent expeditions to Tibet and India to bring back Lamas from the order of Angorthi, a Luciferic order. The Nazis had the crackpot theory that if they combined Western technology with black magic, they couldn't lose."

West spoke in English, "Yeah, they wanted Hell on their side," he said, contemptuously. "Huh! They should have tried to get on the side of the angels."

"*Nein,* Herr West," murmured Alfred Duselbeck. "Evil must, by its very nature, seek its own level. If the Nazis had sought the help of Goodness, they would have not been Nazis."

Michel Tirpitz's melancholy eyes wandered over the books piled on the table. "The demonic nature of the Nazi regime and the fact that the Nazi Party was founded on black magic was one of the best kept secrets of the war," he said in a tight voice. "Even the British and the Americans had good reason to remain silent."

West and several other Americans regarded Tirpitz with Doubting Thomas expressions. Before any of them could speak, the Death Merchant said, "The British and the Americans realized that any serious investigation into the occult might have unveiled spiritual realities which they themselves sought at all costs to keep hidden from the general public."

"By 'they', you mean the British and the American governments?" asked Johan Ebbing, one of the West German tenders. "*Ach!* But why?" He sighed deeply. "But all governments are like that, never revealing the full truths to the people. . . ."

"People, of any nature, can never be for something they can't understand." Artur Laskertitz sank into a camp chair.

"The true answer is more complex," spoke up Ritter. "The truth is that Western technology prefers nice, neat answers that fit completely into materialistic concepts, or else answers in which manipulation of psychic symbols can be used for commercial advertising."

"The great truths are too important to be new!" Camellion said, "too important to be new—except to Western scientists. Conventional physicists in the West are set on following the false thinking that dates back 2,500 years, to the ancient Greeks who thought they could make a clear-cut distinction between spirit and matter. We have been the victims of this dualistic viewpoint ever since. It wasn't until the 1960s that Western science began to consider the possibility that there was an objective reality—independent and apart—that obeyed a fixed set of laws that could be studied and understood. This was inevitable, because as science penetrated deeper into the subatomic world and discovered objects billions of times smaller than the atom, it slowly occurred to physicists that the universe itself appeared to be almost a 'great thought', and that the very act of observation had an organic impact on the object being observed, changing it from what it was."

"Bull! None of that makes any sense," said Gene Slack; yet his tone revealed that he was really voicing a question.

Franz Ritter said, while looking curiously at Camellion, "I think that Herr Camellion is saying that we can never divorce ourselves from nature, or that we can never speak about nature without speaking about ourselves."

"Well put, Ritter," Camellion said, smiling.

"Perhaps, but how can something be one thing one moment, then something else the next?" asked Bruno Wronkau.

"Come off of it, Bruno! Such a question sounds silly coming from you, a man with a degree in engineering!" Big Jim Flikkema said in a quick, almost savage voice. "Look at light. Sometimes it acts like waves! Other times it acts like particles. Light is neither one nor the other. It all depends on how the experiment is designed. You know that as well as I do!"

"What you have just said, Herr Flikkema—and you also, Herr Camellion—supports the teachings of the Zen masters, Hindu holy men and Taoist thinkers," Ritter said studiously. "The Eastern mystics see the universe as one inseparable reality—forever in motion, organic, alive; spiritual and material at the same time."

Richard Camellion laughed. "Try to tell that to a physicist. Most cannot even conceive of a spiritual reality. Part of the trouble lies in language. In any language there are not words to describe the phenomena encountered."

"I'll smoke to that," Flikkema said. "From what I've

136

read of Eastern mysticism, the Oriental mystics maintain that the ultimate reality—whatever it might be—can never be the object of reasoning or of anykind of demonstrable knowledge. Right, Herr Ritter?"

Ritter finished crushing out his cigarette, glancing from Flikkema to the Death Merchant. "Ya, that is correct. They say true reality can never, will never, be adequately described by words; it can't because it lies beyond the realm of the senses and of the intellect. We simply cannot conceive of Ultimate Reality. It doesn't really matter. We're all prisoners of superstitution. Eastern concepts and philosophies would never work in the West."

"Not even with scientists," Camellion said softly. He sounded rather sad. "The biggest product from the East that Westerners have is Christianity. But tell the average person on the street that the Christian 'god' is a product of a Middle Eastern Semitic people and they'll tell you you're crazy."

"That's how superstition works," West said tonelessly. "People are known by the religious company they keep."

"Ditto in spades to Eastern mysticism in the West," Camellion said with a kind of resignation. "And I don't mean the phony brand of Eastern mysticism that's peddled by the cults. I mean the genuine Eastern mysticism that demands a reduction of formlessness and a sort of de-individualization of phenomena. Impossible in the West where people are firmly married to sheer materialism."

Slight, deep chuckles issued from Alfred Duselbeck. "Ya, you are so right, Herr Camellion. It would be especially difficult for people who are spiritual descendants of myth-makers who supposedly had the nerve to ask God what His name was!'

Ritter laughed. Camellion and the others smiled.

"Or for people who believe that their spiritual leader has a 'hotline' to heaven," Bruno Wronkau commented.

The Death Merchant thought of what Vallie had said about people being known by the religious company they keep. Inwardly, he smiled.

In this case the Company is known by the people it keeps!

Chapter Twelve

The exploration of Lake Toplitz continued. By the 15th day (no one took off for Sundays) the find was still zero. Scuba divers and hard-hat boys had brought up a total of nineteen steel cases. All the cases had been filled with documents and records of various kinds which, while they had been considered extremely important to the SS, 37 years earlier, were now worthless. There were no lists of people who had secretly helped the Nazis, no numbered bank accounts listing in Switzerland. In the words of Ritter—"All we have found is waste paper."

The only ones happy about the lack of success was Major Felix Blotz and the other Austrian order police officers, all of whom strutted about with I-told-you-so looks.

In spite of the failure to find anything valuable in the Devil's Trashcan, much of the tension had disappeared, for no one any longer believed that ODESSA would try to interfere with the expedition.

No one except Richard Camellion and Vallie West. . . .

At 14.00 hours on the sixteenth day, the Death Merchant and Vallie West were in the Aristocrat motor home, studying some of the records that had been removed from one of the cases brought up from the bottom of the hellish lake. In this instance, the records were of Treblinka, one of the Polish death camps that the *SS Totenkopf Sturmbanne* had maintained in that slaughtered nation.

Since neither Camellion nor West was taking part in any of the dives, neither man saw any reason to waste time on the diving platform or in one of the West German sea shovels. Half a dozen times both had been on the lake and each time had felt like a fifth wheel.

"By God!" exclaimed West and looked up at Camellion who was sitting on the sofa-bed across from him. "More than 950,000 people were exterminated at Treblinka—

murdered. The motto of the damned place was 'Work, Discipline, Order.' "

For a few seconds, Camellion stared at the PRC handheld transceiver resting upright on a small folding table in front of the sofa, it's 3rd channel open.

"*Arbeit macht frie*—'Work Is Freedom'—was the general motto of all the camps," Camellion said in a clipped tone. "The actual murder camps came into existence as a result of Hitler's decision to arrive at a *Endoesung*, a 'Final Solution', of the so-called 'Jewish problem'. But the SS referred to the Final Solution as *Aktion* 14 F. 13. No one seems to know why."

West, who could read and speak German, read a few more paragraphs.

"Listen to this," he said at length. "At Dachau, Nazi scientists experimented on prisoners in an attempt to endow them with—it says here 'racial memory'. Have you ever heard of anything more ridiculous?"

Noticing that the Death Merchant was staring expectantly at the PRC transceiver, Vallie added, "Hell, don't get your hopes up, Rick. When those cases are hauled up—if they are cases—they'll contain only more worthless papers."

"We won't know until what's down there is on the surface," Camellion said doggedly. "We have no choice but to investigate each find."

At 11.34 hours that morning, the sea shovel, working the east side of the lake, had investigated a lump discovered by one of the small sonar boats. The lump had proved to be a heavy concentration of metal. Depth: 239.5728 meters, or 786 ft. The only thing to do was employ the diving bell. Laboriously, the two sea shovels had towed the diving platform to the designated spot in the lake. Three men had crawled into the bell and it had been lowered into the lake, to the designated spot at 786 feet. Two TV cameras had also been lowered into the black waters.

Camellion looked at his wristwatch—2:18. *It's been half an hour since the bell and cameras were lowered . . .*

He was about to pick up the PRC radio and contact "Big Nick," the name given to the Sea Shovel working the east side of Lake Toplitz, when Franz Ritter's excited voice popped out of the transceiver.

"Achtung, Herr Camellion und Herr West!"

West put down the batch of papers and looked up. Camellion snatched up the transceiver, pressed the talk button, and answered in German.

"Ja, Camellion hier."

"The find is definitely metal. The signals on the close-range magnetometer attached to the bell are identical to the signal patterns that revealed the other cases," Ritter said, his words pouring out of the transceiver. "The searchlights on the bell and the cameras show that whatever the metal might be, it's buried under the three meters of mud, or twelve feet as you *Amerikanerin* would say. Under the mud is a tangled layer of logs. The metal is under the logs. This could be it, *mein Kamerad.* We may have found the pot of gold at the end of the Nazi rainbow."

"You're sure? A diver left the bell to investigate?"

"Ja, der Amerikaner, Gene Slack. He used both a rod probe and a portable magnetometer. Wronkau and Flikkema are positive the metal is cases, similar to the ones we have already brought up."

"How did Slack manage it in twelve feet of mud?"

Bruno Wronkau's deep voice broke in. "At such a depth, we assumed there would be a lot of mud. The bell descended directly over the spot and Slack was lowered on a sling-line from the bell's lockout chamber. He was only in the mud up to his ankles."

"What have you and Big Jim decided? What's your plan of operation from this point? They'll have to use explosives . . ."

"We're going to place enough small charges of nitrozellulose in the area, enough to clear the mud up to an area of forty square meters. Herr Flikkema and Herr Woodside have already gone ashore to get the explosives. We have estimated that——"

The crashing explosion to the southeast of the motor home was so violent that, for a flash of a second, Camellion and West thought the vehicle had been struck by—by what? The motor home rocked on its springs, with such force that Camellion was almost thrown from the sofa and Vallie from the chair. The folding table fell over. Only a microsecond later, a heavy machine gun began roaring, the unintermittedness of the loud chattering punctuated periodically by the rapid and deeper *Bam! Bam! Bam!* of the GPMG 84-mm anti-tank weapon.

"I knew we should have stayed home!" yelled West,

throwing himself to the floor. "It's that Glover Tuareg southeast of us—ODESSA!"

Wronkau's frantic voice jumped out of the transceiver. "*Hurensohn!*[1] What is happening? What is going on there?"

Wronkau and the men with him in the sea shovel could hear the explosions and the machine gun fire not only through the transceiver in Camellion's hand, but also through the ordinary medium of the air; however, since the men on the east side of the lake were 3 kilometers from the firing, distance diminished the volume.

"It's the Austrian order police in the Glover Tuareg to the south of us," shouted Camellion into the PRC transceiver. "We don't know how many of them are ODESSA agents. All you can do out there on the lake is sit tight."

Ritter's tense voice cut in over the radio. "*Donnerwetter!* Those Austrian *Schweinehunde!* But we can't just sit out here. We——"

"Then move farther east on the lake," Camellion yelled into the transceiver. "The farther away you are, the harder it will be for them to hit you if and when you men become targets. No more time to talk. We'll see what we can do on this end—out!"

Camellion switched off the set, jammed it into the right breast pocket of his fatigues and pulled one of the Hi-Power 9-mm Browning autopistols from a shoulder holster.

Another explosion! Again the motor home rocked back and forth, violently, on its springs, and debris, sounding like heavy hail, slammed against the south side of the vehicle. Some of it hit the bulletproof glass of the picture window and filled it with hundreds of zigzagging cracks. Both men knew what had happened! The larger motor home had been hit!

"We've got to get automatic weapons and grenades," Camellion hissed to West as they crawled to the left side door of the Aristocrat.

"It sounds to me like there's more than the one Tuareg at work," Vallie said. Reaching the door first, he stood up, opened it, and he and Camellion stepped out into the afternoon sun already partially obscured by thick drifting smoke.

[1]Son-of-a-bitch!

"Let's take a quick look," Camellion said, starting to edge to the left front corner of the vehicle.

"Damn it! Let's get to the van," growled Vallie. "They'll aim in on this baby next!" The Death Merchant didn't answer. Vallie then recalled what Camellion had said about the outcome of the battle—*"I seriously doubt if you and I will need as much as a bandaid when this mess is over!"* Damn him. He had better be right! I'm crazier than he is—for believing him.

Looking cautiously around the left front end of the Aristocrat, Camellion and West saw that the camp was being systemtically blown apart. Scores of corpses were everywhere, the machine-gunned bodies of Austrian state order police. Four of the tents were blazing, the hungry flames reaching the sky.

From their position, Richard and Vallie couldn't see the Glover Tuareg remote area patrol vehicle to the southeast, but they could hear its anti-tank gun and see the destruction the weapon had done and was doing to the armored vehicles parked to the north. The Glover Thrascian special-support vehicle was a smoking, shattered wreck. So were the Glover land rover escort car and the GKN Sankey AT-105 anti-riot vehicle. Even as Camellion and West watched, the Hotspur armored Land Rover—Major Felix Blotz's command car—took five rounds from the GPMG 84-mm anti-tank gun of the south side Glover Tuareg RAPV and, in a flash of fire and smoke, fell apart into junk.

Only three Gonderfled Troop Carriers and the Shortland MK-3 armored car were left intact. The Austrian traitors in the south Tuareg hadn't wasted shells on the troop carriers because the three vehicles were empty. Why waste ammo? More than half of the order police were already dead. The anti-tank weapon in the south Tuareg vehicle had not fired on the Shortland for a far different reason. The two men in the armored car were helping them by setting up a crossfire.

Captain Fedor Axmann was in the turret of the MK-3 raking the general area with a 7.62-mm NATO MG1 machine gun. Through the drifting smoke, Camellion and West could make out the face of Lieutenant Bernard Webbler behind the windshield opening of the driver's compartment. Webbler was firing an HK 11A1 automatic rifle, the

142

bipod of the weapon resting on the flat cowling over the engine.

Worse, Camellion and West saw that the louder explosions were being caused by mortar shells being lobbed into the camp from the foothills of the Dead Mountains, the shells falling at random, without any specific pattern. The range was too great.

"Axmann and Webbler have got to go," Camellion said in an odd voice.

Vallie West tugged at Camellion's arm. "So do the Judas son of a bitches in the Tuareg. They're all crazy fanatics. One of the mortar shells could just easily drop on them! But we can't do a damned thing here. Damn it, let's get to the van."

Just as West and Camellion turned, another mortar shell dropped down, this one falling among the tents and exploding with a loud roar. At the same instant, Captain Axmann spotted Camellion and West and swung the turret to rake the left front of the Aristocrat. A dozen 7.62-mm steel-cored MGI projectiles zipped into the $75,000 vehicle, but none even came close to West and Camellion. By then, both men had moved from the end of the motor home and were racing to the van that, with the two supply trucks, was parked behind the four passenger cars. Camellion and West saw that Barry Polley, Cyril Purdue, and Ralph Duckworth were standing just outside the van, in front of the open sliding door, to the north, catching HK submachine guns, bags of spare magazines and heavy duty engineers' bags of grenades being tossed to them by others inside the van.

Reaching the van, Camellion and West ignored the three men and their startled looks, and hurried inside. "We thought you two might be dead," Ralph Duckworth called hoarsely after them.

Inside the van, Camellion and West saw that Captain Alois Kalls, Gustav Koerner, Artur Laskertitz and Big Jim Flikkema were pulling quick-kill equipment from lockers, their faces dripping with sweat.

"By God, it's about time you guys got here." Big Jim paused and looked at Camellion and West with slight astonishment.

"*Ach,* you were correct, Camellion!" Laskertitz pulled two bags of 9-mm ammo from a locker. "We should have listened."

"Where's Woodside? He was with you, wasn't he?" Camellion said harshly. He pulled open the door of a locker and took out two belted and holstered 200/International auto mags and the pouches of spare clips attached.

"Dead," Big Jim said flatly. He had just flung an HK submachine gun out the door and was now strapping on a brace of RG .44 Magnum revolvers. "Alan and I were in the shed getting a dozen small nitro charges when those sons of sows in the Tuareg started firing. We figured the only thing we could do was get to the van and arm ourselves. Whoever it is in the armored car spotted us. Alan was gunned down!"

"It's Axmann and Webbler in the armored car," Camellion said, his eyes narrowing to mere slits. "I'm going to cremate those two pieces of trash."

Captain Kalls was thunderstruck. "Axmann? Webbler! I—It's unbelievable! But are you sure, Herr Camellion?"

"Cremate them? With that? They'll gun you down before you can aim the damned thing." The good looking Koerner stared increduously at the Death Merchant who was pulling the Avery AV grenade launcher from its case as West lifted out a canvas bag filled with a dozen 40-mm thermate grenades.

West gave Koerner a look that would have withered a tarantula. The look he stabbed at Captain Kalls would have made a cobra turn and slither away as rapidly as possible.

"Yeah, we saw Axmann and Webbler, stupid!" he growled. "I wonder what the Interior Ministry in Vienna will say when it finds out that four or more of its dressed-in-blue order police were agents of ODESSA?"

Kalls' eyes widened and his face became a battleground of conflicting emotions. It was difficult for one to decide whether he was enraged over the facts or about to cry in total despair.

The grenade launcher in his hands, Camellion turned to go. "We have to get them in the Tuareg before those two jokers get around to us. Axmann and Webbler won't be too much of a problem. We——"

A terrific BLAMMMM, followed by the clanking and crashing of ripped metal, interrupted him. A random mortar shell had zoomed in and turned the Subaru into a thousand pieces of smoking metal.

"Let's get out of here," Camellion said, sounding angry. "You men——"

"Go where and do what?" Laskerwitz retorted, staring at Camellion.

"To the rocks fifty feet west of here." The Death Merchant's eyes glowed with an eerie kind of blue pinpoint light. "The rocks are in direct line with the van. Those two slut-sons in the Tuareg won't be able to see you. But you didn't think that far ahead—none of you! Now move it!"

The men hurried through the side opening of the big van, Camellion and West right behind them. However, once outside, Big Jim Flikkema swung around to face Camellion, one hand hooked on his gunbelt, the other wrapped around an HK 5A3 *Maschinenpistole*, or submachine gun. Kalls, Koerner, and Laskertitz started for the rocks to the west, Koerner motioning for Purdue, Polley, and Duckworth to follow. Unsure of what was happening, Purdue, Polley, and Duckworth just stood there.

Flikkema stared evenly at Camellion. "Listen, I'm not about to hide in any damned rocks," Big Jim said firmly. "No man does my fighting—and the hell with what you say. You got that?"

Camellion barely smiled. *He has moxey. I like that.* "Meaning what, big man?"

"Meaning that I'm the bird that's going to give you and West cover fire!" Flikkema raised the 5A3, muzzle pointed toward the sky, and switched off the safety.

"That goes for me too," Purdue said emphatically. He stepped forward and braced his legs, his jaw set, his face grim.

"Count me in," Koerner said. Kalls and Laskertitz would have also stepped forward, but Camellion's sharp tone stopped them.

"No! Two is more than enough. The rest of you get to the rocks. I'll need your help later, and it would be silly for you to risk your lives now. It's not necessary. Now get to those rocks and stay down."

The men *got*, all except Purdue and Flikkema who rushed to the left front of the van with Camellion and West, all four listening to the *Blam, Blam, Blam* of the Tuareg's GPMG 84-mm anti-tank gun that was stabbing projectiles into the larger of the two motor homes, the large cream and blue vehicle shuddering under the impact of the steel.

"I wonder where the two girls are?" muttered West, conversationally. Carefully he dropped the last of eight 40-mm thermate grenades into the bin-magazine of the launcher. Camellion, while still in the van, had filled the launch compartment with shells.

Down on one knee, Purdue was puzzled. "Damn it, Camellion. You can't aim at the Tuareg from here! The cars are in front of us. And the two motor homes are in front of the cars!"

BLAMM! Another mortar shell, lobbed in from the foothills of the Dead Mountains, exploded to the east, the explosion demolishing the cab of the tractor and trailer rig parked in front of the tin shed. A waste of a shell since the anti-tank gun of the Tuareg had already wrecked the diesel engine.

Camellion laid the launcher on the ground, stretched out on his belly and looked through the spaces underneath the Datsun and the larger of the two motor homes. The motor home was on fire, yet there wasn't any smoke underneath the motor home. The Death Merchant could see only the big wide tires of the Tuareg's left side, the vehicle's being parked so that its front faced the north.

"And underneath shot through the wheels of the Datsun and the motor home!" Purdue exhaled loudly in excitement and tension. "You're not playing with a full deck. A shot like that can't be done!"

"I'm not a percentage player either." Camellion gave a tiny laugh, rolled over, picked up the launcher, went prone again and said to Purdue and Flikkema as he aimed the weapon, "The instant I fire, you two go to this side of the van and sneak around to the rear of the first of the supply trucks in line. From there you can rake the Tuareg with machine-gun fire." He didn't look up at Purdue and Flikkema. "Think you can do it?"

CLANG CLANG CLANG CLANG! The anti-tank gun on the Tuareg began tearing apart the first supply truck.

"Does that answer your question?" Purdue said fiercely. "I don't mind taking a chance, but I'm not going to deliberately commit suicide."

"He has a point," Flikkema sounded equally convinced.

"Neither of you will commit suicide," Camellion said, his eyes glued to the open pinpoint sight of the launcher. "I'll fire when the gunner starts to tear apart the Audi. He can't get to the second truck because the first truck's in the way. The Subaru's already gone, so he'll start on the next car in line. That's the Audi."

"Keep an eye out for the armored car," warned West in a lazy voice.

Twenty seconds more and GPMG 84-mm started to stab into the Audi.

The Death Merchant squeezed the trigger of the launcher, positive that he wouldn't miss. He didn't. After streaking underneath the Datsun and the motor home, the 4 O-mm TH3 grenade struck the back edge of the left front tire of the Tuareg and exploded into a six-foot-in-diameter ball of blue white fire.

Ah . . . welcome to The Kingdom! Camellion moved the sight slightly to his right and again pulled the trigger. Whoosh! Another grenade left the launcher, shot between the wheels of the Datsun and the wheels of the motor home, hit the bottom edge of the left rear tire of the Tuareg, and exploded, its fire mingling with the fire from the first grenade—all to the tune of agonized scream!

Purdue and Flikkema had not seen the two thermate grenades explode. They had been too busy racing around the van, then getting to the shot-apart wreck of the first supply truck. Now they could see the results of the two thermate grenades. Thermate acts like a heat reservoir to prolong the incendiary effect which is white-hot molten iron burning at almost 5,000 degrees Fahrenheit. Only half a dozen drops of the burning thermate had splashed over the front of Hans Krichbaum, the Austrian working the anti-tank gun, and over the legs of Rudert Reit-Winkel, who was acting as lookout.

Hit by a minor kind of SHC[2], the two men were doomed, the white-hot molten iron eating instantly through the blue material of the pants, then their flesh, boring straight down to the bone.

On the verge of madness from the intolerable pain, Krichbaum and Reit-Winkel howled and shrieked at the top of their lungs and grabbed at themselves, their hands clawing desperately to relieve the pain.

All that Purdue and Flikkema could see were two men thrashing about in the open square cockpit of the vehicle and gray-black smoke rising from the intense blue-white

---

[2]Spontaneous Human Combustion. See Death Merchant #38: The Burning Blue Death.

fire covering the left side of the burning vehicle. The thermate was also "eating" the steel and consuming the rubber tires, the entire left side of the Tuareg a shining blue-white.

"We'll fire together. That way we're sure to get both of the jumping beans," suggested Flikkema, a fraction of a second before a mortar shell dropped and exploded 300 feet to the southeast. There was a big BLAMM, a flash of fire and smoke, and a small crater was born 50 feet southwest of one of the three helicopter pads. The pad was empty. But a Sikorsky helicopter rested on each of the other two pads.

Flikkema and Purdue turned their attention back to the two agonized men in the Glover Tuareg. Both fired a few moments later, their submachine gun slugs cutting into Krichbaum and Reit-Winkel and ending the agony of the two screaming men.

It was then that Big Jim spotted a group of men creeping along the south side of one of the tents that had not yet started to burn, 250 feet to the northeast. Two of the men were Michel Tirpitz and Gerhart Kausch. The others were Austrian Order Police, several of whom were wounded and being supported by their comrades.

"At lest we know that they're on our side," muttered Purdue.

"They're in dangerous position," Flikkema said. "They must have heard you and me firing, and maybe even spotted us."

"Yeah, but they know the armored car is sitting out there to the north," responded Purdue, shielding his eyes against the sun, "and Tirpitz and Kausch know it. It's up to Camellion now."

Just then the NATO MGI machine gun on the turret of the Shortland armored car began chattering out 7.62-mm projectiles. Tirpitz, Kausch and the Austrians dropped flat to the ground. Purdue and Flikkema drew back behind the rear of the Wolksie truck. The change in the sound of the firing was the signal that the armored car was moving slowly forward.

"We can't do anybody any good here." Purdue started to move behind Flikkema. "Let's get back to Camellion and West." Deep down, Purdue felt that Camellion wouldn't need either him or Flikkema to destroy the MK-3.

* * *

148

The Death Merchant and Vallie remained in position behind the Datsun. There wasn't anything else they could do. While they too had heard the MGI firing from the Shortland armored car and knew it was on the move, from north to south, they also realized that if they moved to the north of the Datsun and attempted to knock out the vehicle before it was due east of the automobile, there was a 50/50 chance that Captain Axmann would riddle them; and as Camellion had told Purdue—*I'm not a percentage player* . . .

West was down on one knee beside Camellion, his subgun ready to fire. He noticed Purdue and Flikkema slinking around the side of the van and motioned for them to be quiet and cautious. To the west, the other men watched and waited and hoped for the best.

"I take it we're going to take one of the choppers and fly into the foothills to stop the mortar?" he said, turning and glancing down at Camellion who was ready with the grenade launcher. "We could rake them to pieces with an electric mini-gun, with little sweat."

"You got it, but first we have to find a pilot," Camellion said. His eye fixed on the sight, he didn't move a muscle.

"Hell, you fly a chopper!"

The Death Merchant didn't answer, and Vallie didn't press the point. The Death Merchant was the kind of man who, should he be on the middle of a stairway, would not walk to the top to shake hands with God, or turn around and go to the bottom to spit at the Devil. Better not to press him.

Every now and then, Captain Axmann would trigger off long bursts with the MGI machine gun, spraying the tents, to his left, the forward area, and the now useless vehicles of the Cologne expedition, to his right, with sizzling streams of 7.62-mm projectiles. Lieutenant Webbler, driving the vehicle, was not firing.

Within a few minutes, the Death Merchant got what he wanted. The Shortland armored car moved in front of the motor home, and the sight of the launcher captured the right front tire. The Death Merchant pulled the trigger 1-2-3-4 times, knowing that the MK-3's forward momentum would almost certainly permit one of the grenades to strike the right rear tire.

One grenade hit the front tire. One rocketed underneath the vehicle, struck a blazing table in one of the burned out

149

tents and exploded. The last two thermate grenades struck the right rear tire. Within three seconds the tires and the right side of the armored car were dissolving from the molten iron, some of which had splashed upward into the turret and into the open right window of the driver's compartment. Captain Axmann caught several drops on his right fore-arm. Lieutenant Webbler was lucky—for the moment. A dozen drops splashed on the seat next to him, but none had touched him.

With Axmann screaming and jumping about above and in back of Webbler, and the seat next to him smoking and giving off a pungent odor, the terrified Webbler reacted instinctively by breaking the melting vehicle, throwing open the left side door and sliding out. The frightened man didn't suspect that Richard Camellion had put down the grenade launcher, jumped up from behind the Datsun, sprinted forward, then raced widely around the two destroyed motor homes, and now was waiting ten feet to his right of the armored car, a Browning in each hand.

Camellion waited until Webbler was out of the MK-3 and had turned to run to the north. For a shave of a second, a look of shock and horror dropped over Webbler's triangular-shaped face. He saw a smiling Camellion raise the two Brownings, heard the two-auto-loaders crack, and felt both his legs knocked out from under him. His mind askew from fear and shock, Webbler hit the ground and rolled to his back; he heard the blood pumping in his head, the sun and wind and smoke all rolling before him. He became aware that animal-noises were pouring from his own throat.

Once more the Death Merchant fired both Brownings. Again Webbler's body jerked and an inhuman cry jumped out of his mouth. The 9-mm hollow pointed projectile from the right Browning had struck him in the left forearm, the slug from the left auto-loader hitting him in the right bicep muscle. Like a spider with its legs cut off, Webbler quivered and moaned. He could, with effort, roll over on his stomach, then again to his back, but he couldn't crawl.

West, Purdue and Flikkema had followed the Death Merchant. Now, spread out to Camellion's right, they stared at the wriggling, moaning Webbler . . . West with cold detachment, without any pity or mercy, Purdue and Flikkema with disbelief, both wondering how Camellion could be so vicious.

The Death Merchant holstered his Brownings, his expression as calm as the Pope's conscience as he watched the twisting, shot-up body of Webbler and saw that Captain Axmann, no longer jumping around in the turret of the MK-3, must have fainted and fallen to the bottom of the compartment. To the south, Michel Tirpitz, Gerhart Kausch, and six Austrians had come around a tent and were running toward the wrecked armored vehicle.

Big Jim Flikkema raised his 5A3 sub-gun and prepared to put an end to the suffering of Lieutenant Webbler. Vallie West's left hand shot out, wrapped itself around the forestock of the weapon and pushed it to one side.

"No," Vallie said firmly. "If Rick wanted him dead, he would have killed him."

Savagely, Flikkema jerked the machine gun away and loudly addressed himself to Camellion. "Listen, I don't like this sadism. Kill the poor bastard and be done with it, or I will."

The Death Merchant turned, removed his amber sunglasses and gazed directly into Flikkema's angry eyes. "No, you will not finish him off." Camellion's voice was calm, bored, annoyed, and dispassionate, all at the same time. "There's nothing lower on this planet than a Judas. He deserved what I gave him."

"Unless it's a thieving politician," muttered Purdue, as if speaking to himself.

Big Jim did not respond. Staggered by the Death Merchant's gaze, he was suddenly afraid—and felt foolish because he didn't know why. He couldn't put his finger on it, but sensed, in some mysterious way, that he was confronting something incredibly alien, an "it" beyond man's wildest imagination. He flinched when another mortar shell exploded far to the east, almost to the shore of the lake.

"Val, give me two grenades, one at a time," Camellion said. He had turned from Flikkema. He didn't turn to Vallie. He only held out his right hand.

Vallie reached into the bag he carried. "Hell, Purdue. Not all politicians steal. Some are 100 percent honest." He took a 40-mm TH3 grenade from the bag and handed the red sphere-like object to the Death Merchant."

"That's a crock," sneered Purdue. "Why else would anyone want to be a Congressman."

"Because they're fools. They're idiots who see themselves in encyclopedias or enshrined in marble after they're dead." Vallie watched Camellion wave Tirpitz, Kausch and the Austrians—all of whom had reached the armored car—to one side, indicating to them that he was about to toss a grenade.

The 40-mm thermate grenade could either be exploded by hard impact, such as would be supplied by a launcher, or else detonated the conventional way, in which case one had to pull the safety pin.

Seeing that the new arrivals were far enough back from the armored car, now sagging to the right, Camellion pulled the pin and expertly tossed the grenade upward. Right on target! The grenade dropped into the turret. There wasn't any scream of terror from Captain Axmann. He had passed out from pain and shock. So had Lieutenant Webbler.

There was a big whoosh of brilliant blue-white from inside the turret, and the inside of the turret began to burn. Very quickly the strong wind began to blow the stench of burning cloth and flesh toward the knot of men.

The Death Merchant stepped back and took the second grenade from West. "All of you move back. Cartridges will begin exploding in a minute inside the car."

He pulled the pin and tossed the grenade which landed next to the left hip of the unconscious Webbler. Whoosh! A bright blue-white flash, and a ball of molten iron was born, much of it splashing on Webbler. In less than a minute, Webbler would be mostly gray ash.

"Let's get to the van, then to the rocks." The Death Merchant turned and started to run. He and the others were turning by the two motor homes when the MGI's 7.62-mm cartridges began popping off. BLAM! Another mortar shell dissolved the end of the pier and sent giant splinters of wood upward.

Once the group reached the van, Camellion, West, Purdue, and Flikkema hurried inside and began tossing HK submachine guns and bags of spare magazines to the waiting eight men outside.

Vallie West reached into a metal locker and pulled out an aluminum case that resembled a lunchbox, at the same time saying to Camellion, "Rick, it's time for truth. Why can't you take us to the foothills in a chopper?"

The Death Merchant pitched a long canvas bag filled with three spare clips of 9-mm cartridges to Rudolf Loenns, one of the Austrian order police.

"I don't fly a chopper that well," Camellion said. "You can see that the foothills aren't like ordinary mountains. The outer palisades jump straight up, and behind them some of those pinnacles are two hundred feet high and less than seventy-five feet apart. I'd crack us up. What we need is an expert pilot."

"I'm not going to walk those two miles to the foothills!" Vallie tacked on laconically. "And you're not strong enough to carry me piggy-back. That leaves only the undamaged troop carriers, right?"

The Death Merchant grinned like a chipmunk. "That is what I like about you, Val. You're so understanding."

They left the van and, with the other men, hurried to the rocks. While the other men checked their weapons and got their gear in order, Gerhart Kausch gave Camellion a quick report, none of which was good. Camellion took the PRC transceiver from his right breast pocket, flipped the switch, and contacted Franz Ritter. In spite of the gravity of the situation, the West German BND agent's old coolness had returned. In a crisp, businesslike voice, Ritter reported that everyone on the lake was safe, that the two sea shovels had towed the diving platform to the east side of Toplitz as close to the shore as was possible, and that a VHF transmitter on one of the sea shovels had been used to contact the *Staats Ordnungspolizei* station in Bad Aussee. The Bad Aussee post had contacted the station in Bad Ischl. Re-enforcements would be sent from Bad Ischl, but it would take several hours for the soldiers and armor to get to the Devil's Trashcan. Until then, the force would have to survive on its own.

The Death Merchant told Ritter of the on-shore events that had taken place within the last fifteen minutes, including the treachery of Captain Axmann and the three other members of the Austrian police.

Ritter lost his professional composure and a stream of oaths poured out of the PRC, after which he said in a guttural voice, "Damn those *Schweinehunde österreicherin!* What of Major Blotz, that *Hurensohn?*"

"Dead. Machine-gunned. Kausch saw him get it," Camellion said.

Ritter's voice softened. "Captain Kalls is then the only Austrian officer alive. Do you know where he is?"

"With us. He was part of the small group of Austrians

153

alive, who survived in camp. I presume the other order police on the road are still breathing God's air."

"What are your plans, Herr Camellion?"

The Death Merchant told Ritter that the deadly mortar had to be silenced, or there was the possibility that the ODESSA force in the Dead Mountains might come down from the foothills and destroy not only what little remained of the camp, but start lobbing shells at the vessels on the lake.

"There are seventeen of us," Camellion said. "We were going to take one of the choppers, but apparently the two pilots are dead. We're going to take one of the troop carriers, go to the mountains and flush out the ODESSA force."

"It's a crazy plan! You don't even know how many of them are up there!" Ritter said quickly. But you're fortunate you don't have a pilot. A few of the men on the diving platform saw the other helicopter destroyed. They estimated that the craft was 14 to 15 kilometers northwest over the *Totes Gebirge* when it was destroyed, blown up apparently by a ground-to-air missile."

The Death Merchant's eyes widened slightly. "That's a bit over nine miles. Are you sure of the distance?"

"Ya, positive. Why do you ask?"

"Then there are two enemy forces," Camellion said seriously. "Or at least part of the main force is nine miles back in the mountains."

Ritter's quick mind instantly deduced Camellion's reasoning. "You are referring to the mortar."

"Kausch and Tirpitz think it's a German 12 CM GrW42 that fires a 120-mm shell. It they're right, the maximum range is around 6,553 yards. That's 19,658 feet or 5,992 meters. Put another way, the mortar has a range of almost 4 miles, or 6 kilometers. Based on how the shells have been falling, we estimate the mortar to be two miles, three kilometers, inside the foothills of the Dead Mountains."

"Your plan is very dangerous." Ritter's voice sounded sad.

"It's the only one we have."

"Viel Glück, mein Amerikaner Freund."

"We'll need more than 'good luck'. We'll need a miracle—out."

The Death Merchant off the PRC and put in back in his pocket.

Captain Alois Kalls, who was crouched down close by, had heard the two way conversation between Camellion and Ritter; so had several of the other men and Vallie West, the latter of whom was singing the American national anthem in a very low voice—*"Our Father's God to thee . . . We'd really like to see . . . Lot's of prosperity . . . Washington's will be done. . . ."*

Captain Kalls touched Camellion on the arm. "Herr Camellion, I can fly a Sikorsky. I'm an expert helicopter pilot."

Camellion turned to Kalls, his expression acid.

Kalls stared right back. "I was in the Austrian Air Force for four years," he said in a straightforward manner, without any nervousness. "And you . . . and you"—he glanced at a skeptical Vallie West—"are wondering why I am in the order police. For the same reason you Americans change jobs—more money, more benefits."

"Those pinnacles," Camellion said. He turned and glanced at the ugly long fingers of rock poking up at the sky. "One mistake and we'd end up singing hallelujahs."

"Herr Camellion, for a week, before you and your party arrived, I patrolled the mountains in a Sikorsky gun ship," Kalls said curtly. "I have a master's license and a grade A rating, not only with helicopters but with jets."

"Why haven't you been patrolling over the mountains these past few weeks?" Camellion asked. "You haven't gone up once that I know of."

"We cleared out the climbers before you arrived," Kalls calmly explained. "The helicopters that patrolled after your expedition arrived did not have to go close in. If you have watched, you've noticed that they always fly above the peaks. They only drop to large mesas, but give pinnacles a wide distance. The second reason is that Major Blotz thought I could do a better job on the ground. We both know what a fool he was. Believe what you want, but I am positive that I can get us in and down. We can go in low and rake them before the mortar crew can even detect us."

Staring evenly at the Death Merchant, Kalls waited for him to reply.

Vallie West looked at Camellion, singing in a barely audible voice, *"My country tis of thee . . . We're poor but far from free . . . of all our bills! We work from early light . . . Taxes are out of sight . . . There's something not quite right . . . in Washington. . . .*

155

Vallie was actually saying to Camellion, "It's your choice I'll go along with it."

Thirteen minutes later the blue and silver Sikorsky on the middle pad lifted off and swung to the northwest. It was two feet in the air and three hundred feet northwest of the pad when a 120-mm mortar shell exploded the van and sent the twisted metal soaring upward to the wind.

There were times when the Cosmic Lord of Death made the loudest noise and the brightest fire. . . .

Chapter Thirteen

Captain Kalls had not exaggerated his ability to pilot a Sikorsky S-64. A large craft that carried a crew of two and a maximum of 18 troops, it was powered by a 1840 hp Wright Cyclone nine-cylinder radial engine which powered the four-bladed main rotor. Kalls handled the big bird with such expertise that the Death Merchant, in the copilot and gunner's seat, congratulated himself for making the decision to let the young Austrian fly the tiny assault force into the *Totes Gebirge*.

With the exception of Vallie West, the other fourteen men had buckled themselves onto the benches bolted to the walls of the fuselage. West had braced himself in the doorway behind the control compartment which sat high in the top fuselage, both hands wrapped around hold-bars by the sides of the door. West wasn't the kind of man who could sit and wait without seeing what was ahead.

It took only a few minutes for Kalls too take the eggbeater the few miles to the lower reaches of the mountains. To most of the men, the Dead Mountains had their own special kind of life. Early in the morning, they always seemed grim and closer. As the day grew older and the shadows lengthened, the dark, sinister stones took on the terrible features of ferocious beasts or angry gods frowning down on invaders.

By the time Kalls was taking the roaring chopper through the first two chimney-like pinnacles, the Death Merchant had familiarized himself with the controls of the Bernschdardt mini-cannon, an improved version of the U.S. "chain gun;" but instead of a single barrel fed by a revolving chamber and a mechanism driven by an electrically-powered bicycle-like chain, the Bernschdardt had six barrels that revolved like an old-fashioned Gatling gun and was fed from a central bin. Yet, like the chain gun and weapons of similar type, the Bernschdardt was mounted underneath the bottom fuselage and operated via an extremely sophisticated fire-control system, incorporating a gyro-stabilized television telescopic sight, with laser range finding/target designation equipment and infrared for night operations. The mini-canno was positioned below and aft of the sighting system to avoid muzzle flash interference with the night vision system, and could be fired by either the pilot or the copilot.

The Death Merchant switched on the TV sight and pressed the button that controlled the camera that would zoom in on the ground. The tiny TV screen immediately revealed terrain that, due to the low altitude of the chopper, seemed to be rushing by at 500 MPH. But a trained, experienced eye could see that everywhere below was utter desolation. There were boulders of all sizes and shapes, small hills, ridegs, and outcroppings of dirty peneplain rock that contrasted sharply with the highest peaks that, in many ways, were majestic, the bright sunlight reflecting off the snow. Here and there was a twisted not too deep gorge, dangerous slopes of talus and slate that appeared to be defying the forces of gravity. Nowhere was there any vegetation . . . no bush, no scrub, no blade of glass.

"Hang on! I'm going up sharply!" Kalls shouted, the mike on his throat carrying his voice to the speaker in the troop compartment.

Ahead was a dome-like mountain whose top was rough with folds of gray-black lava rock. The east side of the mountain was a sheer wall, 300 feet high.

Kalls pulled up on the collective stick, pulled in pitch and increased the throttle, all in one smooth motion with one hand. Simultaneously his left foot pushed down on the left pedal. Responding, the helicopter rose almost straight up and the tail swung to the right, the sudden movement pushing the men down on their seats. To Vallie, hanging on in the doorway, it seemed that while invisible hands pushed down on his head and shoulders, his Adam's apple dropped to the pit of his stomach. For a few frightful moments, as the roaring of the engine increased, the sheer face of the mountain loomed up gigantically in front of the chopper—so close that Vallie would have sworn that the craft was going to splatter itself against the rock. Suddenly the face of the mountain was gone, and the TV screen briefly flashed the lava rock and other debris on the mountain's top.

Kalls did not lower the Sikorsky. He did press the right pedal and, since it was the foot pedals that controlled the pitch angle of the tail rotor blades, the tail swung back to the left.

Immediately, Kalls, West, and Camellion saw that, now that the chopper was on the west side of the mountain, they were at the east end of a tremendous mesa that had a half mile steep slope on the left, or south, side. The size of the mesa was accentuated by the distance of major mountains, the closest of which were several miles to the north and almost five miles to the west.

But it wasn't the distant peaks that instantly captured the attention of Kalls, West, and the Death Merchant. Several miles ahead and 250 to 450 feet lower than the Sikorsky was an Italian six passenger (two crew) Luconsti helicopter, the red bird only a hundred feet from sitting down on a pebbly clearing on the mesa.

"*Wunderbar!* We have them!" Captain Kalls, unable to contain his excitement, shouted the words. "Do you know what to do, Herr Camellion?"

The Death Merchant did—and he did it. He switched on the forward camera, activated the laser range finding/target designation equipment and wrapped his hand around the firing handle.

"It's either the ODESSA boys with the missile launcher coming in or the sons of bitches with the mortar taking off," Vallie said.

Ahead and below, the enemy helicopter started to rise and swing toward the north, its nose still facing the Sikorsky. Below the Italian Luconsti, groups of men were running frantically to take refuge in small outcroppings of shale that dotted the mesa, each man carrying either a submachine gun or automatic rifle.

West leaned forward on the handholds and stared at the TV screen, his good looking face tense, and there was some anxiety to his voice, "Why there's hundreds of the lice down there. We're outnumbered ten to one! And how the hell did they all get there without being spotted?"

Camellion actually laughed. "Don't give me that Dr. Doom jive, Val," he said happily. "By the time we're finished the odds will be more than even. The explosive slugs will tear that shale apart."

The Sikorsky closed in on the ODESSA whirly bird

which now loomed large in the telescopic laser sight, yet was not centered in the crosshairs on the TV screen.

"Brace yourselves," yelled Captain Kalls. He then proceeded to make sure that the ODESSA craft did not escape by out-maneuvering him. Kalls went to work with both hands and both feet. Pull up on the collective and throttle. Press the left pedal. Swing the tail a bit more to the right. Move the cyclic control stick to the right. A little more to the right, to the north—Now!

"*Feuer! Feuer!*" (Fire! Fire!) Kalls yelled.

At that precise microsecond the crosshairs of the laser sight centered squarely on the forward of the ODESSA craft's starboard side. The Death Merchant's finger barely touched the trigger in the firing handle. The Bernschdardt mini-cannon roared at the rate of 850 30-mm rounds per minute, the six barrels revolving with fantastic speed.

The Luconsti helicopter exploded, less than a thousand feet from the Sikorsky. A giant *WHOOSH!* A brief ball of red and orange tinged with black, and the ODESSA chopper dissolved into blazing fragments. Camellion and Kalls, experts that they were, had timed the kill to the second. At the same instant that Camellion fired, Kalls worked the collective and throttle, pushed down on the right pedal and moved the cyclic control stick to the left; and as the Sikorsky rose and swung to the left, the Death Merchant switched on the bottom TV camera and watched as the flaming wreckage of the Luconsti fell to the bare rocks below.

"Good flying, Captain Kalls," Camellion called over to a pleased Kalls. "I take back all my doubts about you. You're an expert with a chopper."

"*Danke, Herr* Camellion." Kalls grinned boyishly. "I compliment you on your shooting. I know you have done this sort of thing before. What you did takes practice."

Camellion continued to watch the TV monitor. "I've been in a few disagreements in the air," he said mildly.

West pulled a long face. "Stop the damned jawboning and let's get on with it. Rake the lice on the ground."

The big man secured his grip on the handholds as Captain Kalls spoke to the men in the after compartment, "We have just met and destroyed an enemy helicopter. We will now rake the men on the ground with the belly gun."

Vallie West turned and glanced at the men slightly below him in the main compartment. Every man appeared to be calm. Each man seemed to be determined—all except Erhardt Erdmannsdorf, one of the Austrian Order Police. Vallie knew the symptoms: the poor joker was getting air sick.

Big Jim Flikkema's total attention was focused on a tool he held in his hands and was studying. He had picked up the tool in the equipment shed, at the time feeling it might be useful on the lake. Only 11″ long and called the "Red Viking", the gadget was eleven tools in one—hammer, hatchet, tack pry, pipe wrench, etc.

The helicopter dropped sharply, and Vallie's stomach rose up to collide with his Adam's apple. *Damn!*

The Sikorsky had a tactical advantage over the several hundred ODESSA operatives frantically searching for ledges under which they would find safety. The chopper could streak in, sweep the ground at a height of only several hundred feet and still be 95 percent safe. Not only would the terrific downdraft of the four-bladed rotor interfere with the trajectory of projectiles fired from the ground, but the Bernschdardt mini-cannon spit out such an astonishing amount of slugs at such a rate of speed that only a man wanting to commit suicide would dare stand up on the ground and try to fire at the chopper.

Kalls left hand pushed the collective and throttle downward, while his right hand moved the cyclic stick to the left, the latter movement tilting the entire whirling rotor system. Kalls pushed farther down on the collective arm, decreased throttle, worked the tail rotor pedals, and again, moving the cyclic stick, tilting the disc of rotation.

The Sikorsky executed a tight turn and, all the while decreasing altitude, roared back east on the first kill run. Leaning forward, the Death Merchant watched the television screen and automatically flipped the rate-of-fire switch on the panel. The Bernschdardt would now spit out only 500 explosive 30-mm projectiles per minute.

Waiting, Camellion smiled softly. When it came to stepping on trash of the human kind—*which is the worst kind*—he was a firm believer in equal opportunity. The scum on the ground could shoot back, for all the good it would do them.

On the screen, Camellion could see frantic men racing, running, stumbling into each other, all doing their best to find sanctuary from the deadly rain of explosive projectiles they knew would come within seconds. Some of the men threw themselves flat on the ground, desperately hoping that the slugs would miss them. Others ran first in one direction and then another. Then there were those who tried to make themselves tiny behind pathetically small rocks.

The Death Merchant pulled the trigger and pushed the rotation-and-angle switch at the same time. The Bernschdardt roared—one long continuous sound. The firing on the first run lasted only 91 seconds, but the effect was hideously deadly. Not only did the barrel housing of the Bernschdardt move horizontally from side to side, but the ball turret, on which the weapon was mounted, rotated in a 360 degree circle.

ODESSA gunmen fell by the scores, their bodies exploding from the impact and detonation of the 30-mm explosive projectiles, to the extent that it occurred to the Death Merchant that the Bernschdardt was one of the best weapons in existence for professional, big-time exterminators. *Not as good at the H-bomb though. Cost per hit, nuclear weapons are still number one on the hit parade. In 1974 we could kill 10-million people at ten cents a head. Now we can vaporize 40-million at 6.7 cents per head. Efficiency plus by the planet's master murderer—Man. . . .*

Captain Kalls executed a turn so close to the west side of the mountain that again Vallie thought, *this is it!* No, it wasn't. *We're all still alive.*

The helicopter started the return run, Once more the Bernschdardt spit out a flood of explosive projectiles, the barrel house moving steadily back and forth, the chrome turret rotating. This run was a repetition of the first. Doomed men screamed, died instantly, and went down . . . dozens at a time.

A few minutes passed; the chopper turned and made the second run from the west. This time, however, the Death Merchant did not fire. For one thing, there wasn't anything moving on the ground. There were only corpses lying in grotesque positions. The second reason was that the magazine indicator showed that only 1042 cartridges were left, a fact quickly noted by Captain Kalls.

"Why not rake the area again?" Kalls inquired of Camellion.

"I want to use the rest of the rest of the shells to saturate the area when we go down," Camellion said frankly. "Down below it's a mesa; yet there are a lot of slaty structures and erosional forms in which men could hide. We killed most of the dirt bags down there because we caught them with their pants down, because they didn't have time to hide."

"On the other side of that miniature peneplain," declared Kalls. "That's the best place to put down."

"It's the only place where we won't be fired on from all sides," Camellion said. Through the windshield, he studied the small peneplain, a tremendous outcropping of gneissic rock, cut up and twisted like Tufa domes—lava material seen around volcanos.

Kalls swung the helicopter to the left, skimmed over the giant rock, and the Death Merchant watched the TV screen. Not the slightest trace of rock around the peneplain.

"I'll head west to the mountains, then circle back," Kalls said. "We might lure some of the rats out of their holes.

Camellion nodded. "Good. I'll wait until you've made the turn before I notify the men," Camellion said.

The Sikorsky flew toward the west, turned when it was only 600 feet from the closest grim mountain and once more headed east.

The Death Merchant activated his own throat mike. "Men, we're going to land in a few minutes. Unbuckle and be ready to rush through the door the instant we're on the ground."

All too soon, the helicopter was 500 feet above, and 100 feet west of, the peneplain.

Kalls worked the controls expertly. The Death Merchant began firing the Bernschdardt Mini-Cannon. The Sikorsky started to descend.

The Cosmic Lord of Death waited patiently. . . .

Chapter Fourteen

We have failed! The hideous realization of defeat pounded in Hermann Kohne's mind. He wasn't afraid of death. All men died. However, the thought of losing filled him with rage and tortured his violent instincts. Never in his 32 years had he been filled with such bitterness, such pure hatred.

Kohne had been one of the lucky ones. The muscular, round-faced leader of the ODESSA attack group and numerous other men had managed to reach a large overhang of lava rock jutting out from the mesa floor, a hundred and fifty feet northeast of the peneplain. The explosive slugs from the enemy Sikorsky's mini-cannon had shattered much of the lava rock overhead, but the ceiling had held. Kohne, Reinhard Geissler, Fredrich Hohehorst and the others had hugged the ground beneath the long lip of ledge—only five feet above the ground—cursed and hoped for the best. The "best" did not come, not even the "better"! Fortune continued to sneer at the neo-Nazis.

Now the Sikorsky was climbing down from the sky, preparing to land, it's Bernschdardt mini-cannon roaring, the explosive slugs saturating the top of the fifty foot peneplain and the area west of the tiny, jagged mountain.

"*Gott!* What are we going to do?" Hohehorst yelled at Kohne, trying to make himself heard above the racket of the mini-cannon. "They're all dead but us, and that gun is shooting up everything in sight."

Kohne glared at the frightened Hohehorst whose brown hair was gray-white from dust shaken from the overhang. "Idiot! We're still alive. We'll do the only thing we can do. The instant the gun stops firing, we'll charge. It's either them or us. Spread the word and tell the rest of the men to get ready."

Reinhard Geissler spoke up, some hope in his voice, "There can't be more than fifteen or sixteen swine in that chopper."

"They can't know we're here," Hohehorst protested to Kohne. "Maybe after they land, they look around and go away. They might not find us."

Enraged, Kohne grabbed Hohehorst by the front of his jacket.

"You damn fool! Haven't you enough sense to know that we can't take the risk? If we stay here and they do find us, we're bottled up. They could shoot our balls off. Our best defense is an attack!"

With his other hand, Kohne pressed the muzzle of a P-38 Walther against Hohehorst's stomach. "Spread the word, damn you!"

By the time the reinforced skids of the Sikorsky—extra-high skids to accommodate the mini-gun on the belly of the gunship—touched the pebbly ground of the mesa, Camellion and West were at the port side door of the helicopter. All they and the other men had to do was switch off the safety latches of their automatic rifles and go out, and die. . . .

The Death Merchant and big Val were first through the door. They crouched down and covered the area while the rest of the men hurried from the chopper and, once free of the craft, scanned the area for any signs of activity.

The scene was similar to the surface of the planet Mars, except that the sky was not violet. Covering the ground were rocks of all sizes and shapes, some as small as a walnut, others the size of a country store's vinegar barrel.

Captain Alois Kalls was coming down the four rung-steps of the chopper when Camellion turned to West who was snapping the ring, at one end of the mysterious metal case he carried, to a key-snap on his wide gun belt.

"Val, take half the men and go around the north side. I'll take the south side."

"Don't count on prisoners," Vallie said sourly, checking the straps over the butts of the holstered Match Master .45 auto loaders. "On terrain like this——" He grinned. "What the hell am I telling you what you already know?"

Gustav Koerner stared at the Death Merchant who was cradling an HK MP 5A3 submachine gun under one arm and fastening an Armament Systems "Undertaker" to his gun belt.

"We should have brought grenades," the West German said.

"We should have dropped a hundred A-bombs on Nazi Germany but we didn't!" Camellion gave Koerner a *you halfwit* look. "Move out."

The two groups separated, West and his people going to the north side of the peneplain, Camellion and the seven men with him to the south. Because the south side of the peneplain was only half as wide as the north side, Camellion and his people were first to reach the area east of the mesa—just in time for them to see Hermann Kohne and his three dozen men—halfway between the ledge and the peneplain, charging forward.

The Death Merchant and his men instantly threw themselves behind lava rocks and opened fire, every man, except the Death Merchant, convinced that he was about to die.

In contrast, Kohne, Geissler, and the other ODESSA gunmen were elated, convinced that they were facing only a handful of men. With wild shouts that rang out across the gloomy *Totes Gebirge,* the ODESSA killers raced forward. Kohne, Hohehorst, and Geissler, making sure they were in the rear, were more than confident that the Death Merchant and his men would soon be corpses.

Firing short three-round bursts, Camellion worked mechanically, professionally, feeling satisfaction when he saw his 9-mm slugs slam into several men and chop them to the ground. He ducked and blinked rapidly behind his amber colored sunglasses when a burst of enemy slugs ricocheted from a rock in front of him and sent sharp fragments of rock stinging against his face. To his left, Otto Frenzel, one of the order police, uttered a short, agonized cry and relaxed in death, a bloody mess where his face had been. A long moan came from Rudolf Loenns, to Camellion's right, and the Austrian shuddered and lay still. A single truncated cone bullet from a Beretta 12 SMG ahd entered his forehead and killed him.

Just like in the movies! thought Camellion. *Vallie, where in the name of Ma Perkins are you?*

At that moment, another bullet zinged from a rock, streaked sideways very low and cut into one of Camellion's breast pockets, the impact wrecking the PRC radio. Simultaneously, the ODESSA would-be slaughter force was forced to realize that it had been overconfident, that there was not one but two groups.

Chatter-boxes and automatic rifles snarled loudly from the north side of the peneplain, the deadly rain of high velocity, spitzer-shaped slugs slicing savagely into the charging admirers of Adolf Hitler.

Trapped in a gut-cutting crossfire, the ODESSA gunmen didn't know what to do. To retreat meant certain death. At least there was a tiny chance of victory by going forward. There wasn't any uncertainty on the part of big Val and the Death Merchant. Coldly realistic, they realized that the answer was simple: fight and win, or fight and die.

Firing steadily, Vallie and Camellion's groups raced forward, each man ducking from side to side, weaving, zigzagging, at times almost stumbling to the ground, but always following his instincts. ODESSA men screamed, died, fell. And so did the fighters in Camellion and West's groups. Gustav Koerner caught three 7.65-mm Skorpion Vz61 bullets in the stomach and two 9-mm Wz63 Polish machine pistols in the left rib cage. An instant corpse, Koerner sagged to the rocky ground. Sergeant Gotthard Gehroltz and Klement Hagmeister, two of the *Ordnungspolizei*, went down, Hagmeister's skull blown apart by projectiles from a Heckler and Koch 33KA1 automatic rifle, Gehroltz receiving a quarter of a pound of lead in the chest from a German WW II StG44 assault rifle.

Within minutes, both sides—neither of which had time to reload—came together in what would be a battle in which no quarter would be asked, none given, and none expected. Now, the only factor of any relevance was survival. Survival could only be the result of experience, iron nerve, superior hand-to-hand know-how—and fate. For no man can increase, or decrease, his alloted time on the speck of dust called Earth. In the end, each individual must walk through the door of Reality opened by the Cosmic Lord of Death, and he or she must walk through that opening in the same manner in which he or she was born, *alone. . . .*

Death watched and waited while the shouting, gasping men fought and did their best to kill each other.

The Death Merchant had exhausted his supply of ammo in the HK chatterbox and had tossed the machine gun to the ground, knowing from experience that each second made the difference between breathing and lying beneath a tombstone. An Auto Mag in his left hand and a Chris McLoughlin-designed, throat-cutting Undertaker in his right, Camellion blew up a crumb wearing wraparound sunglasses, a cap with flap earmuffs, and trying to swing the barrel of a Schmeisser MP40/11 *Maschinenpistole* in his direction. The .357 mag AMP projectile hit the man high in the left chest, bored a tunnel through his body big enough to stick a rolling pin through, and spun him around before sending him dying to the ground. Just in time, Camellion sensed trouble. He dodged to the left, stepped back, and spun to the right as a stream of slugs heated the air only inches from his own chest, one of the 7.92-mm projectiles tugging at the cloth of his left sleeve as he swung the Auto Mag, muttered, *Take a slow bus to Disneyland, you dip-stick dummy!* and fired at the dark faced man with a short beard who had tried to turn him into a cold cut with a WW II German VGI-5 sub-gun, the big AMP bullet banging into the man several inches above the belly button. Ernst Munden's eyes jumped a quarter of an inch from their sockets and his mouth popped open as though something had just kicked the wind out of him. Something had! The .357 AMP slug had torn out his stomach, ripping arteries and veins in the process. Bleeding to death and dying from shock, Munden's corpse crashed to the ground as Camellion's AMP again thundered. This time the .357 bullet bombed Joachim Pruenin in the belly blasted through his intestines, and blew out part of his backbone. Only a split second from eternity, Pruenin was kicked back from the TNT impact against Fritz Brunning who was so frustrated he had almost forgotten his own identity.

The Death Merchant was about to end Brunning's 27 years of life but Artur Laskertitz, who still had some ammo in his MP 5A2, stitched Brunning across the right hip with the last seven cartridges, then flung aside the *Maschinenpistole* and stormed toward Big Jim Flikkema who was battling with two men. One man had his fingers wrapped around Flikkema's wrist and was trying to force him to drop the .44 RG magnum revolver. The second man had both hands around Big Jim's left wrist, was trying to twist the Red Viking from the master diver's strong grip and knee him in the groin at the same time.

On both sides, it was every man for himself. The Death Merchant found himself surrounded on all sides by ODESSA agents, none of whom appeared to be Rotary Club material. He wasn't unduly concerned or worried in

any way. The cries of battle, of death and dying were music to his ears—"*The sweetest music this side of Hell. This
is the only way to enjoy life, balanced on scales between
the Here and Now and the what?*

The instant Vallie West's sub-gun was empty, he tossed
away the useless weapon, drew a Safari Arms Match Master, switched off the safety, and expertly, with his left hand,
snapped open the metal case hanging from his belt and
wrapped his fingers around *The Butcher*. The weapon fit
over Cal's left hand exactly like a pair of brass knuckles,
the exception being that instead of "knuckles" on the outside, there was a four-inch-long, two-inch-wide steel blade,
the edge as sharp as a surgeon's scalpel.

Val dropped one ODESSA gunmen with a .45 Silvertip
Hollowpoint bullet. The Match Master roared again, and
Val dropped a second man faster than a bad habit, then
spun to his right to avoid an ODESSA dumbbell swinging
an empty 7.92-mm MKb42(H) at his head like a baseball
bat. Vallie ducked and Otto Wesslinbaum struck out. The
kraut was out of the game and out of life. Before Wesslinbaum could make a back swing, Val muttered, "You
should drink buffalo scrotum wine, boob-boy," and
slammed the startled German in the groin with a *Go ju-
Ryu* karate *Sokuto Geri* sword-foot kick. A choked cry of
agony jumped from Wesslinbaum's throat, and he automatically started to fold as he dropped the assault rifle. Vallie
moved in swiftly with the Butcher. With the shiny steel
blade, Val slashed downward across the side of Wesslinbaum's thick neck, then jerked back his left hand to avoid
the flood of blood that spurted from the gaping cavity.
Wesslinbaum wilted to the ground, his head half severed
from his neck.

It was then that Val noticed that Cyril Purdue, just
ahead of him, was in very serious trouble. One ODESSA
gunself was approaching Purdue from the rear, a long
bladed knife in his hand, while a second man, directly in
front of the Company Case Officer, was preparing to put a
bullet in his stomach with a 9-mm Hungarian Tokagypt
auto-pistol.

Vallie was a bit more than surprised when Purdue reacted with instant knowhow and went about disarming
Gevrey Brochon—*And I had Purdue figured as a pomp-
ous, paper-pushing fart-head!*

Vallie put a bullet into the man with the knife as Purdue, keeping his elbows low, twisted his body to the right, struck Brochon's right wrist with his left forearm, and grabbed the Tokagypt with his right hand, making certain his hand was not covering the muzzle. At the very same time, Purdue struck downward as Brochon's wrist with his left fist.

Quick as a striking snake, Purdue applied pressure with his left hand and, in conjunction with his right, bent the pistol toward Brochon's body, forcing the now scared Frenchman to release his grip on the weapon. Brochon had no choice: it was either release the Tokagypt or have his index finger broken.

A high pitched whistling sound coming from his broad nose, Brochon attempted to land a right uppercut on Purdue's jaw, a swing which Purdue blocked with his left forearm as he slammed the man across the side of his left temple with the butt of the pistol. In that moment while the unconscious Frenchman started to sink to the ground, Purdue turned the Tokagypt around in his hand and put a 9-mm bullet into Brochon's head. Purdue then ducked to the left to avoid a knife about to be thrown at him by a stocky man whose florid face was topped by a head of thick black hair.

The knife left Lyonel Feininger's hand at the same time that Purdue ducked and fired. The German WW II trench knife hissed past Purdue and struck Oscar Pillz, another ODESSA piece of low moral trash, between the shoulder blades, the knife burying itself almost to the hilt. As if hit by a ten-ton truck, Pillz jerked upright, did a fast one-two step, twisted around and fell sideways in front of Karl Zuckmeyer who was charging Captain Kalls, a brass knuckle knife in one hand and an empty Schmeisser in the other, his fingers closed tightly around the barrel.

The thickset man with the red face took Purdue's bullet low in the right chest. Purdue fired again and the men took another slug, this one in his stomach as he sagged down. At the same time, the dying and falling Pillz forced a momentary halt to Zuckmeyer's plans and gave Kalls the opportunity to pull a backup auto-loader he carried in a special holster sewn into the bottom left of his uniform coat. With nervous fingers, he pulled down on the zipper, reached in, pulled out a Walther *Polizeipistole Kriminal*, switched off the safety and swung it toward Karl Zuckmeyer, who had stepped over Oscar Pillz and, face frozen in a snarl, was about to lunge at him with the brass knuckle knife.

Kalls pulled the trigger three times, and the Walther PPK cracked, Zuckmeyer taking the 9-mm shorts in the chest. The German staggered and made a final effort to reach Kalls; then his eyes rolled back in his head and he crashed to the ground. However, it just wasn't Kalls' day. So engrossed had he been in killing Zuckmeyer that he hadn't noticed another ODESSA agent coming up behind him. Carrying an empty Schmeisser-designed MP18.1 SMG, Emil Rudluff reached Kalls and swung the empty submachine gun, the blow caving in the right side of Kalls' skull. Dead from the severe concussion, Kalls collapsed to the ground.

Rudluff's feeling of victory quickly turned to caution when he sensed movement to his right. He swung around and saw a tall, angry Big Jim Flikkema coming at him, the giant of a man holding the Red Viking in his left hand and a RG .44 mag revolver in his right. Flikkema had disposed of his previous two attackers by using superior strength and fighting ability. He had stamped on one attacker's instep, kneed the same man in the groin and then had flattened the man's brains with the hammerhead end of the Red Viking. The other attacker had almost been decapitated by the axe-end of the tool.

"Son of a bitch!" Flikkema said and pulled the trigger. Click! the RG revolver was empty.

Brawler that he was, Rudluff knew his only chance against the big man was to land the first blow with the empty Schmeisser. His teeth clenched, he swung the machine gun at Big Jim's left shoulder. Flikkema surprised him by half-turning to his left and reaching up with the Red Viking. Instead of striking Flikkema's shoulder, the wooden stock of the weapon landed between the middle of the Viking's handle and the hammerhead. Big Jim didn't give Rudluff time to recover his balance and attempt another blow. He slammed the ODESSA man across the chin with the short barrel of the revolver, pulled the Red Viking free from underneath the edge of the Schmeisser's stock, raised his right arm and chopped down on the dazed Rudluff's left collar bone, the sharp blade cutting through the man's jacket and shirt, slicing through the bone and sinking four inches into flesh and muscle. Losing consciousness

171

from shock, Rudluff felt his legs melting from underneath him. The last thing he would ever remember was the intense blackness spreading over his dying mind.

Ten feet to Big Jim's left, he spotted a long faced man, with thin, bloodless lip, aiming a P-38 Walther auto-pistol. The pistol cracked once and Ralph Duckworth fell with a bullet in his right rib cage. Reinhard Geissler fired again and Barry Polley fell, a bullet in back, a thin trickle of blood flowing down his unshaven chin.

Flikkema only hoped he could reach Geissler before the son of a bitch could fire again. He didn't. The German heard him coming, turned and pulled the trigger of the P-38. If it hadn't been for the Red Viking, the 9-mm projectile would have stabbed Big Jim in the lower part of the chest. As it came about, just as Geissler fired, Flikkema had the Red Viking out in front of him, the tool held up at an angle, due to Flikkema's movements. The bullet struck the side of the axe at the business end of the Red Viking and ricocheted loudly Geissler again pulled the trigger. Nothing happened. The P-38 had fired its last round.

Flikkema went in for the kill, thinking, *If I tell anyone how this damned device saved my life, they wouldn't believe it!*

Geissler tried to use the P-38 as a club and at the same time draw a bayonet from its metal sheath attached to his belt. He was unsuccessful in both attempts. Big Jim blocked his right arm and, while the German was pulling the bayonet, shattered Geissler's skull with the hammer-end of the Red Viking.

Vallie West made quick work of the slob who had iced Artur Laskertitz with a series of karate blows. Laskertitz went down choking to death, his Adam's apple crushed against the top of his windpipe, hitting the ground as West caught up with Adolf Halder. Vallie had exhausted his ammo in one Match Master and had shoved it back into its holster. Now he didn't bother to pull the second auto-pitsol. He intended to slash Halder to ribbons with the Butcher.

Not exactly thrilled to see the tall, broad, 250-pound West looming before him, Halder tried a left legged short spin-kick to Val's groin, his left hand feigning a *Yon Hon Nukite* four-finger spear thrust at Vallie's throat and his right hand attempting to grab Val's left wrist. Halder was flabbergasted when Vallie didn't fall for the ploy. Vallie blocked the intended kick with a right legged *Kochi* hook block and, anticipating Halder's move, slashed his right wrist to the bone with The Butcher aleady dripping blood and gore.

Halder let out a wail of pain, fear, and frustration. His blood flying in the wind, he jerked back his hand and tried to right thrust kick which Vallie blocked and a Haito ridge-hand to the side of Vallie's neck. Vallie ducked and simultaneously slashed from right to left—downward— across Halder's face, the blade of The Butcher ripping open the man's nose and cutting all the way through his right cheek. Blood pouring from his face, onto the ground and into his mouth, the doomed Halder staggered back and began to make animal sounds. Vallie darted forward, his right hand streaked out and he let Halder have a powerful *Pandae Chirugi* reverse punch straight in the solar plexus. When Halder doubled over, Vallie finished him off with the Butcher—right across the back of the neck, the blade going in so deeply that several of the cervical vertebrae were severed. Vallie didn't bother to watch the corpse do its final fall. Instead he went after the man who had just won a battle of wits and strength with Michel Tripitz. That man was Fredrich Hohehorst.

During the preceding five minutes, the Death Merchnat had killed nine ODESSA gunmen with feet, auto mag, and Undertaker. Now he fought Thornwald Gersdorff with only his free left hand and the Undertaker, having holstered his empty AMP.

Gernsdorff wasn't afraid of one tall man with a short-bladed knife. He hadn't lived this long through the battle by being timid, the proof being in two dead Austrian order policemen and Gerhart Kausch who was unconscious from a bullet wound in his right side. The poor fool simply didn't know whom he was fighting.

The first thing that Gernsdorff did was to execute a two pronged attack, very naturally reaching for Camellion's right wrist to protect himself from the Undertaker and, simultaneously, trying a knee lift to the groin. Camellion arched his body in the middle to avoid the knee lift, let Gernsdorff have a left *Sangdan Chirugi* high punch to the bridge of the nose and moved his right hand away from the German's intended grasp.

In agony from his broken nose, Gernsdorff was vulnerable and staggered back on uncertain legs—more than enough time for the Death Merchant to do what he wanted to do. The situation was grave! Gernsdorff had an appointment with the Undertaker and Camellion intended that the German keep it.

With incredible speed, Camellion plunged the Swedish steel blade into Gernsdorff's stomach. The ODESSA crud emitted a scream of agony. Using the same smooth technique, Camellion pulled out the odd-looking knife all steel: a 4" coffin-shaped handle that tapered to a 2⅛" cutting edge, stepped to Gernsdorff right, tripped the dying man with a *Nidan Kosotogara* reap, and plunged the Undertaker in and out of the German's neck as he fell.

It was survival instinct that warned the Death Merchant. He ducked first, then turned, at the same moment that a thin but long bladed knife with a heavy bone handle left Hermann Kohne's right hand. A few seconds more and Camellion would have been dead. The knife would have buried itself in his back.

Kohne, astonished when the knife shot over Camellion's head, recognized Camellion from photographs ODESSA agents had secretly taken of various members of the Cologne Expedition while the force had been in Ottobrunn. The Death Merchant hadn't the least idea who the muscular, mean-faced man was, but he felt that *he's the leader of the ODESSA attack group up here—or was! And he'll soon join the other dead!*

A man proud to the point of being ridiculous, Kohne stood there, hands on his hips, waiting for the Death Merchant to either throw the Undertaker or else pull one of the auto mags and shoot him.

Camellion didn't do either one. He shoved the Undertaker into its sheath, smiled at Kohne—not over twelve feet away—motioned with both hands, moving them inward, and called out in German, "You're a piece of dirty trash. Your mother was a slut and your father was a growth of slime from a dung heap. What are you going to do about it, you son of a diseased bedbug?"

The Death Merchant could afford to throw out a challenge. He saw that all the ODESSA fighters were dead, their corpses piled like discarded logs. The exceptions were two men struggling with Vallie West, and two other Hitlerloving trash getting the worst of it from Cyril Purdue and Big Jim Flikkema.

With a loud bellow of rage, Herman Kohne charged the Death Merchant, the way he moved, the way he held his arms and hands, a tipoff that he was not a stranger to empty hand fighting. Indeed he wasn't. Kohne was an expert in Okinawan *Te*[1].

Kohne was very fast. He tried a spin kick, a left *Nukite* stab to Camellion's solar plexus and a right *Seiken* punch to the upper lip. The Death Merchant countered with a *Hiju Uke* elbow block, a *Sukui Uke* sweeping black, and a very fast *Ashibarai* foot sweep that blocked the kraut's kick. The Death Merchant then increased his speed and used a simple crosshock takedown on Kohne. Camellion placed his left foot slightly outside the German's right foot; concurrently, he chopped down on the sides of Kohne's neck with double *Shuto* chops, then grabbed the man's jacket at the shoulders. Before the staggered Kohne could put up any kind of defensive action, Camellion shifted his weight, swung his right leg forward in an arc between his own left leg and Kohne's right leg until it reached a point parallel to the ground. The Death Merchant next swung his raised right leg downward, forcefully striking Kohne's right leg and making calf-to-calf contact. As Camellion kicked Kohne's right leg, he exerted pressure and the amazed German fell backward, his shoulders striking the ground.

Instead of following through with a kill-kick—*The damn fool thinks I will*—the Death Merchant toyed with Kohne the way a matador teases a frustrated bull.

"Get up, son of a slut. You couldn't whip a blind two year old midget!"

Swiftly Kohne was on his feet, screaming, *"Du Hurensohn! I'll kill you!"*

Camellion grinned. He didn't mind in the least what trash called him *as long as they're willing to pay the price! And as long as they call me for dinner!*

Kohne, coming in like a runaway windmill, started with double knife-hand chops, one aimed at Camellion's neck, the other at his temple. At the same time, the Hitler half-

---

[1]A combination of the Okinawan *tode* system and Chinese *Kung Fu* techniques. *"Te"* means "hand."

wit tried a *Ka-Soku-Te* bottom heel left kick to Camellion's right knee.

Once more the Death Merchant blocked all the intended blows and the kick, only this time he didn't follow through with a body throw. He faked a left *Yubi Basami* knuckle-fingertip strike, noticing that the German was becoming winded. Kohne wrecked the phony strike with a *Sudo Marki* middle knife hand block. But by using that type of block, he had left himself wide open for what the Death Merchant gave him—a right *Chungdan Sudo Yop Taerigi* middle knife hand side strike to the left of Kohne's stomach. Crying out from the sudden pain, Kohne attempted a *Tettsui Uchi* hammer hand strike, but the torture in his gut slowed him considerably. The Death Merchant sidestepped the strike, moved to the German's right, used his right leg in a *Uchi-Soku-Te* inside edge-of-foot sweep to jerk Kohne's right leg out from under him. Cursing and off balance, Kohne couldn't stop himself from falling forward. Camellion, taking a step forward, used his right arm to deliver a kidney-shaking elbow *Empi* to the German's lower back. Although greatly weakened from pain, Kohne still had a lot of speed. He turned rapidly—and walked right into Camellion's high hatchet kick, the Death Merchant's right heel smashed into Kohne's face, breaking his upper and lower teeth and fracturing his lower jawbone. More pain! More loss of speed and reflexes. Kohne's first mistake had been in charging Camellion. Now he made his second mistake: he began doubting his own ability and let fear erase logic, training and precision.

The Death Merchant made two lightning quick strikes. The first was a *Haito Uchi* sword-ridge hand to the pit of Kohne's stomach. The second, executed in conjunction with the first, was a *Yon Hon Nukite* four-finger spear stab to Kohne's throat. Hermann Kohne was only a few minutes from oblivion. A raspy gurgle rolled from his throat. His eyes became as wide as headlights and his fingers, like talons, began to claw at his throat. The gurgling became lower, deeper, akin to the sound of water struggling down a drain that was partially stopped up. All the while the blood drained from Kohne's face. He sank to his knees, fell over on his back and, for a few moments, stared up at the bright sky with stark eyes. A few more ticks in time and he stopped the frenzied blinking. A final shudder. The body

176

relaxed. The dead eyes kept right on staring at the sky and at eternity.

Vallie West, who had just broken Fredrich Hohehorst's neck and cut the throat of Jose de Canballera, the Spanish neo-Nazi fool who had tried to help Hohehorst, came over to the Death Merchant, holding his left palm tightly against the outer muscle in his upper right arm. Val first look down at the dead Hermann Kohne, then glared at the Death Merchant who was reloading one of the Auto Mags.

" 'Not even a bandaid' you said!" Vallie growled. "Damn it to hell! The last dingbat I sent to his ancestor— he was a rice and beans eater—cut me in the arm."

"Well, deal unto others as they deal unto you, I always say." Camellion cocked the AMP and switched on the safety. "What are you sore about. You're alive, aren't you?" He started to look around the area of bleak rocks and death.

Vallie laughed. "Yeah, but I don't want to lose faith in your 'crystal ball ability. And this little ruckus isn't over. There could be ODESSA stragglers around who might feel they're lucky. There's only four of us left." He pulled the empty Match Master .45 and reached for a full clip, his keen eyes watched Big Jim Flikkema and Cyril Purdue coming toward him and the Death Merchant.

"Kalls is dead," commented Camellion, who was also watching Purdue and Flikkema approach. "We're stuck here in the Dead Mountains until a chopper comes—and my PRC is broken."

"Oh boy!" Vallie made a motion of disgust with the .45 Match Master in his right hand. "This is another fine mess you've gotten me into. I'll be damned if I'm going to walk out of here."

"Not to worry, old buddy. The Austrian Order cops will find us, if they don't get lost on the way."

By then, Purdue and Flikkema reached Camellion and West.

"Either one of you have a walkie talkie?" Camellion asked. "Mine is dead."

"I think Kausch is dead," Purdue said. He was so nervous he almost trembled.

Flikkema reached behind his right side and pulled a 203 UHF transceiver from its belt-case. "I guess we're going to wait for the Austrians?" He handed the radio to Camellion.

"We're not going to walk," grumbled Vallie West.

Camellion said, "The first thing you men do is gather our subguns, and keep a sharp lookout for trouble from any possible ODESSA survivors. I'll contact Ritter and the others on the lake."

"I'm going to check out Gerhart." Purdue hurried off.

Frowning slightly, Flikkema said, "Hell, Camellion! You could fly us out. There's plenty of space."

Camellion shook his head to the negative. "Here, yes. But I'd have difficulty when we came to the Pinnacles. We went through one set in which the space between couldn't have been more than fifty feet."

"Go above the pinnacles," Flikkema suggested. "The danger is over. There's no need for us to fly out low."

"No dice." Camellion again shook his head from side to side. "We can't be positive, not yet, that the ODESSA mortar crew was in the helicopter we destroyed. Why take the chance? No. We wait."

It was 72 minutes before Camellion and the three men with him heard the *thump thump thump thump thump* of chopper rotors in the distance. Standing by the Sikorsky gunship in which they had landed, Camellion and the other three soon saw the four Sikorskys coming in from the east.

"It's too bad about Kausch," Purdue said. "He wasn't a bad sort of person.

Watching the four choppers grow larger, West said, "Rick, did I ever tell you that rhubarb was thought to cause sterility by the now extinct tree people of central India?"

The Death Merchant didn't crack a smile. "Yes, you did, several years ago. About the time I informed you that it was impossible to get laid in Nepal. Because of the mountainous terrain, sex is practiced in an upright position. Having sex in Nepal is called 'getting stood'."

I could tell you two that grape nuts is a common disease among divers and can be cured by soaking the afflicted parts—but I won't,"Flikkema said with pretended seriousness. Then, playtime was over, and when he spoke, he sounded almost angry. "There's still that mass of metal in the east side of the lake. We have a lot of work ahead of us. We did come here to explore the Devil's Trashcan. . . ."

Chapter Fifteen

Time is always neutral; it was neither friends nor enemies and ignores the curses of men. It took three days to clean up the camp and, by helicopters, ferry the dead from the *Totes Gebirge* to a central point in Bad Aussee. The ODESSA dead were buried in a mass grave some distance from Bad Aussee. The corpses of the Austrian dead and of other men who had died with the Death Merchant were flown to various other destinations, this latter group including the remains of Marga von Roesch and Karen Weiss. The two women had been in one of the tents struck by a 120-mm shell.

More Austrian *Staats Ordnungspolizei* were brought in, these troops under the command of Major Rudolf Hinderschatz. Along with Major Hinderschatz came Oltwig Haffner and his assistants. With them were several other tight-lipped men with suspicious eyes—the Austrian Department of State Intelligence. What had gone wrong? Why had gunmen, working for ODESSA, been allowed to sneak into the Dead Mountain. How had they infiltrated the area?

But not a single member of even the Austrian media was permitted to enter the general area.

The nice part about what had happened (as far as Camellion and West were concerned), was that no one out on Lake Toplitz had been harmed. A lucky hit by a 120-mm mortar shell had destroyed the diver delivery vehicle moored at the end of the pier. So what? They hadn't planned to use the DDV anyway.

From a standpoint of engineering, ODESSA had not scored a single point that would interfere with the operation on the lake. Machine-gun slugs had riddled the Shed and destroyed a lot of spare parts, and had struck the explosives chest, but could not pierce the tough steel.

The same problem remained: how to clear away the mud at a depth of 786 feet and get to the boxes beneath the layer of logs. A suction hose was impractical; even if the force had had a length of hose of such fantastic length, the cleared area would fill with silt so quickly that the effort would like trying to sift the entire bottom of the lake.

"There's only one way to do the job," Flikkema said at a general meeting. "Divers can leave the bell and place the nitro charges at the target site. The bell will be centered directly over the target. We'll pull up the bell to a safe distance of 400 feet—121 meters—then detonate the charges electronically."

Bruno Wronkau explained how they would prevent the cleared area from filling with mud.

"We'll ring the entire target area with bags of that new instant plastic concrete. We'll place the bags at the precise distance necessary for the concussion from the explosion to rip them open and disperse the powder. The powder will turn to concrete within ten seconds after its exposed to water. Hopefully, the hardened plastic will cover the area around the target and prevent the mud from seeping in."

"Some mud and silt is bound to get in," pointed out Burton Waller.

Peter Schroetter, one of the German divers, made a noise of disapproval. "It's a crazy scheme. We should wait and bring in hose that is long enough for a water jet."

Flikkema clicked his tongue impatiently. "After the explosions, we'll lower the bell immediately. The boys from the bell can seal off any 'leaks' with more plastic concrete. We can attach the waterproof bags to the bell."

Wronkau wasn't experiencing any doubts. He glanced across the table at Flikkema. "We'll have to do a lot of calculating to deduce where to place the bags around the target. If the bags are too far away, the explosive effect will be nil. Too close and the plastic cement will be dispersed over too wide an area."

It took four days to make all the preparations. Finally, everything was in order, the two sea shovels and the diving platform in position, the bell at the end of the cable on the crane. The bell was lowered.

The plan proceeded on schedule. The instant plastic cement worked exactly as Wronkau and Flikkeman hoped it would.

Gene Slack and Karl Meyer, wearing scuba gear, went through the large hole blasted in the logs and found the mass of metal—six steel cases, each the size of a packing truck. The two divers attached a cable to the first case, gave the signal, and the long-buried case was slowly lifted to the surface. Four hours later, all six cases were safe on the diving platform.

The cases were cleaned of mud and flown to the headquarters of the Austrian Interior Ministry and opened in the presence of intelligence officials from Austria and from West Germany—

And three top Case Officers from the Company. . . .

Chapter Sixteen

Bonn. *Bundesrepublik Deutschland* (Federal Republic of Germany). 14.00 hour. Two weeks after the cases were opened in Vienna.

Dressed immaculately in a light-weight cream-colored suit, Bruce Shawney leaned back in the easy chair, relaxed, and crossed his legs. A trim individual with an affable manner, Shawney, in this instance, was more than a Company street man. He was also a special messenger direct from "Mr. Sanford", the code name Courtland Grojean was currently using with the CI Red Robin network in West Germany.

Shawney looked around the office which was in a building only a third of a kilometer south of the *Bundeshaus* the German equivalent of the Capitol or Houses of Parliament. The executive type swivel chair behind the gray steel desk was empty. Richard Camellion was slumped in an easy chair to the left of the desk. Shawney sat across from him.

"You have checked for spider, cockroaches and other bugs?" Shawney glanced cautiously around the room, noticed that the blinds over the two windows were pulled, and smiled.

"Positive. Give me the report," Camellion said.

"You know, the trouble with duty in Bonn is that everyone is suspect of being on the other side," Shawney said, wrinkling his forehead. "Of course, it's like that in every capital in Europe. We're constantly photographing everyone who goes into the Soviet Embassy and the KGB is doing the same thing across the street at our embassy. Here in Bonn, there are all sorts of visitors from all over the world. A lot of music lovers. Beethoven was born here in Bonn, you know."

The Death Merchant's eyes narrowed. He didn't like

men with baby smooth chins. "I told you that this office is free of transmitters. Get on with the report."

Shawney got on with it. Three of the cases taken from the Devil's Trashcan had contained precious gems . . . diamonds, rubies, emeralds, all the stones cut and polished and removed from settings—"About a hundred and forty million dollars worth at today's prices."

A fourth case had been crammed with papers listing the names of spies/traitors who had helped the Nazis— nativeborn Englishmen, Frenchmen, Austrians, people from South America, Australia, and South Africa."

"How many Americans?" asked Camellion, curiously.

"Five. One was from a very prominent family. Another was a Hollywood actor. They've been dead for years—all five."

The fifth metal case had been filled with detailed mathematical formulae that would have enabled Nazi Germany to explode the atom bomb.

Shawney shrugged and wiped his upper lip with a forefinger.

"The Nazis would have beaten us to the Bomb, if we hadn't destroyed their heavy water plant in Norway. It was all in the report. And without knowing it at the time, we blew up their reactor at a disguised factory in central Germany. It's the contents of the sixth case that threw everyone a curve. It had a lot of top secret reports from the *Reichsishcerheits-Hauptamt,* the Head Department for the Security of the Reich. Among the reports was a file marked 'Plan Ya-4-Flug.' "

"Cut out the deadwood and get to the bottom line."

"Adolf Hitler was never in the bunker off the Reich Chancellery in Berlin." Shawney couldn't understand why Camellion didn't register surprise. "The body the Russians found burned outside the bunker was that of a double, right down to having only one testicle and the proper dental work."

"What about the body of Eva Braun? Another ringer?"

"Who knows? She wasn't mentioned in the Plan. The Plan did name the island of Trischen in the North Sea. Hitler, Bormann, and a few more Nazi big shots were supposed to have boarded one of the new Nazi L-submarines at Trischen. The plan didn't give the final destination. What bothers all the brain boys is why the SS should have

183

dumped such revealing information in Lake Toplitz—assuming the plan is genuine."

A cunning look crept into the Death Merchant's eyes. "I'm inclined to think that it was the cases in general and *Plan Ya-4-Flug* in particular that forced ODESSA to go to such lengths to stop us from exploring the lake. It's only a theory."

"It's as good as any other. There was a lot of confusion and panic at the end of the war. The file could have been put in the case by accident."

"It's no concern of mine," Camellion said amiably. "It's the now that counts. I understand you have an envelope for me from 'Mr. Sanford'."

"The message is oral." Shawney looked around the room and lowered his voice to almost a whisper. "Have you ever heard of the island of Tukoatu?"

"No, but it sounds like it might be in the Hawaiian group."

"Correct. You're to go to London—fly from Paris—to the 'Blue House' on Waterloo Road. You'll be briefed there."

"Can you tell me anything more about the mission."

Shawney slowly shook his head. "All I know is that the home office refers to Tukoatu as *The Island of the Damned.* . . ."